The Gentle Goat

By

Charles Corbett

 New Generation **Publishing**

Chapter One

No problems, just opportunities

Sometimes you believe things are going well: everything sorted; no surprises. You may not want to admit it to anyone, not publicly anyway, but it's what you're really feeling. Well, that's just how I was on the morning we moved house to Crumbly. I had moved many times before and endured all sorts of mishaps but this time it was different. No-one had pulled out of the chain, the mortgage money was through, the new curtains were ordered and even the paper delivery was organised. My boxes were ticked and there was no forecast of rain. But it was when our son Malc came over to help and he saw the case with his coin collection being carried out to the van that things took a turn.

"Bloody Hell," he cried. "You can't take that," and he ran into the van and grabbed it off the removal men. Then he calculated that his stamp collection, which he hadn't even thought about in years, must have been taken too. So he raked around while the men patiently tried to arrange things securely around him.

Then our daughter Lizzie, who was moving into a flat with three others because the family home was no more, decided to throw a crisis of nerve and had to be comforted by her mum. They sat at the kitchen table, hand in hand, both tearful, while toaster, kettle and biscuit tins disappeared from around them.

"S'cuse me, love?" asked one of the men and took their chairs from them. My wife Tess didn't want Lizzie to move out but Lizzie refused to abandon her town mates. "It'll be awful where you're going," she sobbed. "It'll be all sheeps' poo and cockerels going off at four in the morning. You'll smell terrible. You'll sleep terrible."

Then Lizzie saw her sack of teddy bears being hauled off to the dark innards of the van and ran to save them. "You prat," she cried and almost hit the poor fellow. At this rate I began to envisage more stuff coming out of the van than going into it. The tension rose so by the time the van left, with Tess in it, bearing the keys to the new house, we were well spent emotionally. Malc and Lizzie drove off together with their retrieved memories while I set about cleaning the place for our buyers.

That was trying enough. Every corner had memories and I took twice as long while I dithered over every room.

We'd no thoughts of moving, but after an intruder experience and then a health scare from Tess, we agreed it was best to give up living in a central part of town, our home for nineteen years. However, to go 'way out to the country proper was a bridge too far, so we eyed up Crumbly Down, a village only marginally in the country, just two miles away from the grimy acres of urban straggle. A combination of Greenbelt Legislation and a stubborn landowner has left a corridor of undeveloped land between town sprawl and village, so Crumbly stands aloof, leafy and farmed, as it has been for centuries. With only about fifteen hundred inhabitants, it seemed ideal for us and if we pined for the crush of the town, we could walk to the nearest bus terminus in half an hour max.

We didn't know how we'd adjust. We were used to a faster life where everything was on the doorstep; schools, theatre, gym, drug addicts, litter and dog crap. Then we were told Tess should inhale a lot less car exhaust. So she found a job in a garden centre not far from the village and I decided to work from home. I sort of do figures for businesses. So when a property came onto the market, something of a rare event in Crumbly, we pounced. Well, actually we pounced gingerly, because it needed a lot of work doing to it. I deluded myself that I would have plenty of time to do some DIY to keep down the cost of renovation. The truth is I'm a desk person; I can hardly staple two pieces of paper together without finding my finger in between them.

My chest thumps even now when I think of the first hours in our new house. By the time I arrived from cleaning up the old house, things were pretty well advanced. These enormous removal guys, not even remotely of the same species as me, were rapidly stuffing our possessions anywhere they could. I saw one pick up a two-seater sofa, tuck it under his arm, and with a sack of clothes in his other hand, deftly squeeze through the French door. My wife was directing the traffic with some authority so I thought I'd do everyone a favour and stay out of the way. Off I snuck to the local pub and unfolded a newspaper.

Half an hour later my wife ran in, hot and distressed. Where had I been? What did I think I was doing? Why wasn't my mobile on? She had spent ages trying to find me. The removers were finished but my car was blocking the van.

I ran back with her but couldn't find my car keys. I thought I'd put them on one of the packing crates in the kitchen, but couldn't be sure. Those big guys weren't impressed. They were tired and irritable by now but they tried to help. It became chaotic, with people up-ending crates and boxes all over the place. Soon you couldn't wade across the floor, never mind find a small set of car keys. Had I left them in the pub? Where was my jacket? They were probably in the pocket.

Eventually I found them in the ignition.

I shouldn't have owned up to that. I should have lied without qualm or conscience and claimed I'd picked them up off the drive, or wrestled them back off some thief. The removers howled like timber wolves in a cult Russian film and another thirty quid was required to pacify them.

The next week or two saw us wrestle with many things - and I'll come back to the plumbing - but we would be dishonest if we didn't own up to having moments, or whole days, wishing that we had never bothered to come here. Driven by some imaginary ideal of the quiet life, lit up occasionally by peaceful communion with one's neighbours, we had visions of escaping the ceaseless, frantic and health-threatening noise of the town. The reality however was that we knew no one to commune with and the villagers showed no sign of popping round with a few freshly baked pancakes.

Which is why I took to wandering up to the local, The Gentle Goat, to look for company. A lovely old pub, it felt very homely but it still wasn't easy for me to break into the small groups of locals that drank there. Ironically, our problem with the plumbing turned out to be an opportunity to do just that.

It was a curious plumbing problem and as I look back, I am surprised that I wasn't as fascinated with the circumstances as I might have been. At the time I had only one obsession; to get it fixed as soon as possible.

It began a couple of weeks after we arrived. The whole waterworks, central heating included, worked beautifully for fourteen days and then became moody. It was an old place I know, but I expected better. The plumbing didn't actually pack in. That would have been easier to fix. It resorted instead to bad behaviour. You would turn a tap on and nothing would happen. Then you would feel, physically feel, a tension build up before the water would whoosh out with all the power of a fireman's hose, out of the sink, up the window and onto the floor.

I couldn't work it out. Usually you find a knack to these things, something you have to explain to visitors, like you have to give the loo chain a quick flick at the end of the downstroke. It was no good just turning it on a little and waiting. You had to turn the tap on full to get it going, and once you felt the rush coming, there was no time to turn the tap back to a more closed position. Too late. Out it would gush.

So, tired of seeing my wife in wellingtons and a yellow plastic mac, looking like a permanently on-call lifeguard, I trudged out to the Gentle Goat to find local knowledge and a bit of sympathy.

I didn't get much. I stood beside a group of farmers, their pale complexions and soft hands brought on by long hours of riding in their air-con tractor cabins. I told them my problem, expecting them to show interest, at least in the rarity of the symptoms. I was to be disappointed.

"Oh, yes," drawled one particularly large gentleman, his head on top of a neck an Aberdeen Angus would be proud of. "We know all about that one…" and fell into silence. The others grunted and nodded.

No more seemed forthcoming so I prompted him a bit and said, "Do you have the same problem then?"

"Who? Me? No, no problem on that score. But I've heard of it." Again the others grunted and nodded. Their body language hinted that they would consider it a slur on their manhood if they admitted to having this problem themselves, so I tried another tack."

"Know anyone who can fix it?" I asked.

They took their time thinking about it, then one lad with hands as big as a goalie's gloves grunted, "Old Ronald might know a bit."

This was progress, a local expert, experienced in the phenomenon. I began to picture Ronald with all the admiration one might have for a geyser expert or volcano-watcher. He would have a determined, square jaw and clear, Hollywood-blue eyes. Anticipating my next question, one of them, a pipe clenched in his back teeth, said that Ronald came in here quite a lot.

That was good. I had a good chance of seeing him. Mind you, if he was in here a lot, was he capable of doing the job?

I thanked them and took my drink to an empty table to have a think. They looked relieved that the flow of difficult questions had ended. My table was by a window, where I could see both the door and the bar without turning my head. It wasn't long before I wished I had taken another seat. There was a draught from the window, quite a cold one. Yet I didn't want to move. It would have looked odd. Or people would have sniggered because I was new and didn't know all about the draught. I stuck it out, just to show them what I was made of.

I reflected on my problem. How complicated life is when you are out of your familiar environment. The Goat however made up for it. There was nothing special in the décor and in places it needed some renovation, but it was homely and relaxing.

Two people leaning at the bar were talking in low voices, both staring vacantly into the rows of bottled beers on the shelves behind the bar. The softened lights and the occasional ringing of the till were all very comforting. The Gentle Goat was an unusual name, but no one seemed to know where it came from.

As I mused, a man came in, nodding to a few

people. He was obviously a regular but instead of joining them, he brought his pint over to my table.

"Evening," he said in a pleasant baritone voice, enriched by the local accent. He must have been sixty or so, and had put away a few pints in his time, from the size of his middle. I exaggerate a little. He wasn't too tubby, but his short legs lent a roundish look to him.

"Hello," I replied. I'm stuck for words when it comes to the set-pieces of conversation. My small talk is minimal. However, he didn't seem to expect anything more and sat comfortably, opening a small bag of salted peanuts.

I declined when he shook the bag at me but by that time I had come up with some conversation.

"It's a bit draughty at this table, isn't it?" I ventured.

As soon as I said it, I regretted it. You see. That's the trouble when you're not so good at the chat. When you do say something, it seems over-heavy, out of the blue. It doesn't follow from what's been going on before. I hadn't meant to imply any criticism.

He didn't say anything. He looked slightly injured, as if taking it personally.

"It's a nice pub, apart from that," I continued, hoping to sound more positive, more complimentary. I think my work makes me negative. It's an occupational hazard.

"It's nice in summer," he replied eventually. "Not so cold a draught then."

We relapsed into a silence after that. One of the farmers, coming up to buy another drink, noticed us and shouted to Ronald, "Evening, Ronald. That bloke wants a word with you."

"Funny way of showing it," Ronald muttered.

"Are you Ronald then?" I asked, a foolish question by this time.

"Yes." He drew the word out slowly, suspiciously.

"What did you want to speak to me about?"

"My plumbing," I answered.

He was relieved. "You look like a tax man," he explained. "What's up with your plumbing then? I'm not actually a plumber, more an odd job man, really."

"Those chaps over there recommended you. They said you would know about the particular problem I am having." I described the symptoms.

"Oh, yes," he nodded slowly. "We know that one all right. Old Mrs Woolsop up Wood Lane had that for many a year."

"Did you fix it?" I asked.

"Not before she died," he said.

I didn't think Tess could wait that long but he continued.

"I happened to be doing a job in the house before the landlord re-let it. I fixed it then."

"How?" I enquired.

"Well, I traced it to a bend in a vertical pipe, which for some reason known only to history had a joining pipe which was much wider than this downpipe. There was a dead rat in the pipe, so it blocked the water off. Then when there was a lot of water in the bottom of the pipe, it floated the rat up. Some of the water then shot off to the tap. This was her hot water tap, you see."

I nodded, but I couldn't follow this at all. It was too far-fetched. Surely the rat had decomposed, but I didn't want to think about that, so I asked whether blockages had accounted for all the cases.

"Oh, no," he shook his head. "Each one has a different explanation. Up at Gage's farm it took me all day to chase an air bubble down to the tap and let it out. I could hear it, you see. You get to have an ear for such things. Well, it started up in the loft and I beat the pipes and kept turning the water on and off until it escaped. Old Gage, he's the one over there with the big neck by the way, was ever so grateful. He gave me a special ham he said he was keeping for a big occasion. It smelt terrible. Maybe it would have been better in the open air but I had to get rid of it. I didn't like to offend him. He probably knew that when he gave me it."

"How did you get rid of the ham?"

Ronald looked sadly at his empty glass. "I raffled it," he said.

I didn't like to pursue this avenue, although it showed a ruthless native wit at work.

"Would you like another?" I offered.

His face brightened. "That would be very sociable," he replied and handed me his glass. "I doubt that Brown will be coming now."

"Who's Brown?" I asked.

"Oh, you'll like Brown, and the others, I'm sure." He sounded as if he was adopting me into a group of buddies.

"We usually sit here," he said and winked, "despite the draught."

While I waited to be served at the bar, I began irrationally to fear that the friends he was talking about were eccentric in the extreme, or rough and abusive. One moment I'd be supping my pint and minding my own business when a chapter of mid-life Hells Angels would roar up outside and clatter into the pub. A silence would instantly fall and the lame, patch-eyed leader would strut unevenly and painfully up to me to groan, "Out of my seat, Sunshine. No one sits in my seat."

And I'd slip away shamefully, not wanting to be held responsible for making his arthritis worse.

"Yes," Ronald continued when I returned with the drinks, "Brown is a contradiction. He's a company director, but noticeably short on the grey matter. We all wonder how he's done it. You can fool some people some of the time, etcetera. But he *is* a gentleman. You'll like him."

Apart from the gentleman bit, it sounded like the usual profile of a director to me but all I said was, "Are you due to meet tonight?"

"Tomorrow evening is more likely. Anyway," he offered, "when shall I come over to look at your plumbing?"

I was in two minds. I couldn't tell if he was any good, or a tinkerer but I felt he wouldn't do any harm so we agreed to meet at nine the following morning."

As things turned out, I got a call late that night from a troubled client. He needed to see me urgently so we set up a breakfast meeting, which necessitated my getting up and out of the house very early. I don't actually mind breakfast meetings. My meter is running and you usually get a good breakfast.

What to do about Ronald? I decided to leave a written note with my wife to give to Ronald. He however was late in turning up and as she had to rush out to work, she had time only to give him the door key and my note and leave him to it.

My note said, "Problem in the hall, next to the alarm." I have always been proud of my ability to communicate succinctly.

I left Ronald the written clue because, after I returned home the previous night, I decided to put his methodology into practice, put my ear to the pipes and tapped them. Soon I believed that I was beginning to perceive the subtle differences in the sounds that came from them. It wasn't a popular activity. My wife was trying to get to sleep between telephone calls from clients and my clanking, donking noises.

By a stroke of luck, or so I thought at the time, I found a length of pipe in the hallway which sounded suspicious to me. It had a bright sound. The pieces of pipe at either end of this two-foot stretch sounded dull, more normal. I could swear it was because of a bubble and I thought my diagnosis would save Ronald time.

When I returned in the evening, my wife said she didn't think much of my attempts to use local talent. There was a note for me. It was from Ronald. The writing was more what you'd expect from a chimpanzee with a broken wrist. I think it said, "Fixed your alarm," but as I couldn't make any sense of that, I tossed the note away and thought no more about it.

After tea, I made my way along to the Gentle Goat to ask Ronald how he got on. The tap was still temperamental but wasn't as bad as it had been. Maybe it was going to take time to clear properly. In the Goat, two people were sitting in the seat by the draughty window. I deduced they must be Ronald's friends.

I introduced myself and asked if they were expecting Ronald. It turned out I was correct in assuming they were Ronald's friends. It was Brown who spoke first, standing to shake hands. The other, a tall sad-looking gentleman, did the same but only because Brown had done it first. They said it was unlikely that Ronald would be in that evening, but welcomed me to join them.

"So Ronald's working for you," observed the sad one. "That's a pity."

Brown's expression said he agreed it was a pity.

"Ronald might have been good in his younger years," he explained and fell silent.

"Does he get tired now?" I asked.

"No, but you'll tire of him. He'll fix your house until you can't live in it," said the sad man, whose name was Pritchard.

I couldn't get more clarification from them, but I had an interesting hour in their company. They were less directly inquisitive than some of the other locals I had met, which I found refreshing. They seemed to accept me as if I had always been there. I felt so good I bought the next round.

But that night things started to take a turn for the worse. It was one-thirty when the burglar alarm went off.

I don't know if you've had the experience. I'm sure the action men will leap out of bed, glad to be up and doing and proving something to somebody. Without a second thought, they'll bound downstairs to confront whatever they have to. Me? First of all I wanted to believe it wasn't happening. It was a nuisance: at worst, it meant trouble.

Now I know you'll point out to me, and quite logically, that if I don't want trouble I shouldn't have a burglar alarm. Then I'd sleep soundly through whatever was happening and in the morning I could fill out the insurance claim. But who says we're logical?

Once I had forced myself to believe it really was happening, I then worried about what I was going to find. My wife also seemed disinclined to interfere, so I crept downstairs, holding an ineffectual-looking umbrella (I was surprised to find one so conveniently located upstairs until I remembered we had a leaking roof) and a torch with dying batteries.

You don't get too much practice at this sort of thing so when you need to remember how to switch off the alarm, you can't. I got to the box in the hall and after fumbling about, eventually managed to silence the infernal thing.

The silence was worse than the noise. It scared me to death. I could hear my breathing as if it were a thunderstorm on the windows. If someone *was* in the house, listening to my breathing, they would think I was some mad gorilla deliriously searching for a victim. The torch was about to give up the ghost so I tried to find the light switch. Panic was rekindled as I realised I hadn't a clue where the switches were. Eventually my hand felt the wall switch and the hall light came on.

There was no intruder, of course. The sense of anti-climax, relief and guilt, (I should have been more aggressive) all mingled to make me tremble. I took us both a stiff whisky upstairs.

Next morning, I set the security alarm back to its proper setting and thought no more about it. The water problem seemed to have improved too. I was busy that day, so I didn't get to the Goat to thank Ronald.

That night at one thirty, the burglar alarm went off again. This time I was more annoyed than scared and after switching it off, sat in the kitchen, in the dark and tried to think the thing out. That was a mistake. Kitchens are full of strange noises: clicks from the fridge; funny scraping noises from the pipes; creaking and groaning noises from the walls and ceiling; unidentifiable scratching upon the window and little cries and moans from outside in the garden. I looked outside and saw the shadows of the trees moving. I shivered. My imagination fed me the idea that something was about. Well look, I'm a sober accountant type. If I can't take a calculator to the problem, then I usually don't believe it exists, so these sorts of feelings were too complicated for me. I retreated upstairs with more whisky and a resolution to buy a large dog, or a small dog with a large bark.

When it happened again on the third night, we were beginning to worry. In the light of day, we knew there must be a reason for it, especially as it happened at exactly the same time. But lack of sleep, too much whisky and a feeling of being alone with the problem, all conspired to stop us thinking straight. We felt exposed, as if someone was watching us, playing with

15

us even, friendless strangers newly come to the village. The darkness of the countryside can be quite, quite threatening.

Next day at lunchtime I went up to the pub for an hour to give myself a break from the figure-work. It was a pleasant, cold but sunny day, a far cry from the suffocating, threatening, dark nights that my wife and I had been experiencing. The Goat had quite a few people in it, eating sandwiches or ham, mustard and chips. A few groups stood with glasses in their hands and a couple of chaps lounged just outside the front door, putting their mugs down on an outside table, used more in the summer.

I was pleased to see Pritchard. He was sitting with one other at the usual table. Brown wasn't there, nor was Ronald. Pritchard recognised me and almost smiled, without quite pulling it off. I knew he meant to be friendly.

"This is Horace," he said, a thinly disguised tone of apology in his voice. Their glasses were almost empty so I bought three pints and brought them to the table.

The conversation soon turned to my plumbing problem.

"Well, Ronald seems to have cured it, but I have another more serious one now," I told them. "It's my burglar alarm. It goes off at exactly one-thirty every night."

"A thief with obsessive timekeeping," Pritchard commented. "Now that's interesting. I don't remember us having one of them before. But excuse me," he continued, raising his sad eyebrows, "couldn't you make it easy on yourself and arrange for some policeman to turn up at one twenty-five to arrest this predictable fellow?"

I hadn't thought of that course of action but Horace was dismissive anyway.

"Surely you have just set your controls wrongly?"

"So why don't you get it fixed?" Pritchard asked.

"Well, I just haven't got round to it. Besides, why should it begin to go wrong, so precisely, so suddenly, if you see what I mean?"

"Search me," Prichard replied. "Talking of searching, have you any cash, old man?" he asked of Horace. "It's my round and I've come out without a bean."

"Afraid not," Horace shook his head. "I come out with only just enough if I know you are going to be here." They both looked at me to arbitrate.

"It's ok, I'll get them," I said.

The barman gave me a raised-eyebrow look, tinged with disdain. I went back to the table with the beers. The groups of people were beginning to disperse. Horace had gone off to the Gents so Pritchard and I sat in silence until he returned.

When he did, he suggested, as if he had been off to the Gents to have a think about the alarm problem," Why don't you just turn your alarm off? It seems more trouble than it's worth."

"No, no, that would never do," Pritchard countered instantly, as if he had already thought through all the possibilities like a chess player and discounted that move. "I have this one all figured out. It's clear that our friend here is being spied on by an organised and well-equipped crime ring. From a distance, outside your house, they aim a beam at your alarm to set it off. You get so fed up with it that you do exactly as Horace says. They'll know your alarm is off when their beam triggers no response. They'll then know it's time to break in."

"Do you sleepwalk?" Horace asked. "You could be setting the thing off yourself."

"If it goes on for much longer I will be," I

17

responded.

That night it went off again. Our nerves were frayed. Broken sleep made us jumpy. A bloke I met in the pub told me he had heard years ago our house was haunted. That was all I needed. He remembered that a figure used to be seen in the dark emerging from our house. It would make off across the fields. Sometimes, people had seen it coming back, always before dawn, always in the shadows.

Of course once you have heard something like that, you feel that something is well wrong with the house. We both wished again that we had never moved here. Give me the noise of traffic any day, rather than the regular, scary disturbance from an unseen hand. Although I hadn't really believed any of the stories in the pub, I found myself looking out the window into the shadows, trying to detect an electronic beam or a hooded, monk-like figure.

Something had to be done.

The next day, I finished the assignment that had been causing me grief and long hours, and emailed it off by midday. I intended to phone a security firm to have the alarm looked at as a matter of urgency.

Before phoning, I popped into the Goat for a lunchtime sandwich, just in time to buy a round. My timing had become impeccable on that score. Pritchard, Horace and Brown were all there. They seemed pleased to see me. It gave me a nice feeling.

"You'd better get another in," said Horace. "Ronald's just coming round the corner."

"Good," I said. "I'll pay him for fixing the plumbing."

Ronald looked very happy to have a drink waiting for him. He waved aside my attempts to pay him.

"But the tap is working ok now," I protested "I must pay you something."

Ronald looked slightly bemused, but said nothing.

"Tell him about your alarm," Horace suggested.

"Alarm?" Ronald repeated, sounding alarmed himself. "What's wrong with your alarm?"

"Well," I began, "mysteriously, as the plumbing problem was cured, the burglar alarm has begun to go off at precisely one-thirty every night."

Ronald looked distinctly off-colour now.

Something clicked inside Pritchard's head. "When did you do work for this gentleman, Ronald?"

"Monday, that would be," Ronald said, a little huskily, "but it was the alarm that I repaired."

"Why," Pritchard pursued, leaning forward, "did you repair an alarm which was in perfectly good order instead of dealing with the plumbing, which wasn't?"

"Well, that's what the note said," Ronald defended himself. "The note you left me."

I remembered the note. It hadn't said anything about mending the alarm.

Ronald searched in his pockets for the note. "I've probably still got it, but I had terrible trouble reading it because I've lost my glasses. Ah! Look, here it is."

He pulled out a crumpled, grubby note. Stretching it away from himself, he squinted his eyes distressingly and read, "Plumbing all right, but fix the alarm."

Prichard leaned over, removed the note from Ronald and read, "Problem in the hall, next to the alarm."

Horace gave a chuckle. "Could have been worse. He might have dug up your drains, or rewired your hall."

"But why does the alarm go off at precisely one-thirty?" Brown asked.

"Just a long shot," Pritchard suggested, "but my electricity cheap night rate comes on about then. You don't think you've done some creative crossing of wires, Ronald?"

"Well, I did have all the fuse boxes off at the same

time. I might have done something wrong. I'll come round right away."

"I don't think so," I said. "I know what I'm going to do."

When I got home, I disabled the alarm and it's never been on since. Funny thing though. The plumbing problem came back and we decided to live with it. We are now very skilled at tap control. We know just how much to turn it on to coax the water along the pipes and have put the waterproofs away.

My Awful Lawn

Our new home boasts a sizeable front lawn, flanked on one side by a road. On the other side is some rough ground with nothing on it, as you find in old villages. I believe it is common land.

I enjoy cutting the lawn. You wander along behind the mower and soon fall into a dream, and the next thing you know you've cut the whole lawn without changing the grass collector once, so most of the grass is cut, but lying around the lawn in unattractive lumps, as if some deranged barber had carried out a frenzied attack on a customer, leaving tufts of the victim's hair on the shop floor.

Left in this state the lawn looks awful but even when you rake up the loose grass, it still looks mauled. So I try hard to concentrate, get the stripes on the lawn straight and empty the mower's bin when it needs it. Doesn't sound too difficult but the lawn still hasn't improved.

It would be within the first month of arriving at the village that I was mowing the front lawn one peaceful evening. For some reason, a picture burst into my head about when I wrote an essay in school on the subject of humour. I would have been about twelve.

With all the confidence of youth, I wrote that we humans are unique because of our sense of humour, a magical sixth sense that allows us to see the world differently, more appreciatively. We didn't know about DNA then, nor the fact that our DNA is perilously close to that of the fly, but my simple researches traced no other living thing displaying humour. I mean, what else produces sitcoms?

I showed my essay to my grandfather, who always had a willing ear for my ideas, but he took issue with me. He argued that animals have a very strong sense of humour. You only have to look at some dogs to see that they are laughing, mostly at us. Why do penguins do that silly walk? Why, to make each other smile of course. Well, it's a long winter.

And why else would a cat pretend to be stuck up a tree, distressed and mewing, but as soon as you climb up to get it, it calmly runs head first down the tree trunk? Why does a well-trained horse stop dead at a water jump and deftly heave its rider into the trough? Because it knows a large TV audience will laugh like hyenas.

Pritchard called out to me just as I was in the midst of those thoughts. Having a front lawn just next to the road means I get a lot of social interaction while I mow, or strictly speaking, when I am not mowing. Sometimes it can take me all morning.

From the earliest days, people would stand and expect me to cut the motor and go over and talk with them. I get a lot of advice. One elderly gentleman stopped me for at least twenty minutes to tell me at great length and with no small repetition that I needed to get a move on otherwise the rain would prevent me from finishing. Sure enough, after twenty minutes the rain came on. He put his hand out to feel the drips and said, "Told you," and walked off. I am sure his dog was suppressing a laugh and I'll bet that after they turned a corner, they would let themselves go, and howl helplessly at each other.

Anyway, back to Pritchard. He is one of many who look over the chest-high hedge to offer his well-intentioned thoughts on lawn-care. Although people are mostly careful to keep their advice general, I know they really do mean it to be more personal. In short, they think my lawn-care is on a par with the US's care of the environment —incompetent at best, wilfully abusive at worst. I get advice on weed-control and pest-control, on draining and watering, on keeping it short or keeping it long, on light and shade. Collectively this village has the world's most extensive knowledge of lawns; it's just that most of the advice is contradictory.

Which is not to say that they don't have a point. For some reason, I cannot get the damn lawn to perform. It's a desert at one end, and lush at the other, and the stripes I leave behind me suggest that one of my legs is shorter than the other.

Pritchard went on about my grass, while I tried to talk to him about the sense of humour in animals. It would be about nine in the evening, just getting a bit damp, and I wanted to finish it before dark.

"Maybe your lawn has a sense of humour," he said. "It certainly makes me laugh."

He was joined at that point by Ronald, who can be sure to have an opinion when the conversation turns to practical matters.

"Do you know," he yowled – outdoors, Ronald speaks at a higher volume than most – "I was just remembering that the old boy that used to own this place before you had the very same problem as you have, and do you know what we found out?"

Pritchard shook his head dutifully and suspiciously. His large bloodhound features look mournful even if he is smiling. When he does smile, which is not often, his eyes water as if they are crying.

Ronald relieved our waning curiosity. "There's a slope," he exclaimed, raising his eyebrows high as if talking to children. "It goes exactly the opposite way to what you'd expect."

"There's no slope here, Ronald," I said. "Look, it's as flat as a CD."

"That's the thing; it's one of them mysteries. To the naked eye and from a standing position, it looks flat but if you get down on your hands and knees, you'll feel a gradient if you stroke the ground with your palm."

Well, just to humour Ronald, I got down. Pritchard came through the gate with Ronald to lend a hand with the experiment. The three of us were on all fours when Brown happened by and looked smugly at us.

Brown's political nose can tell him when there's fun to be had. He wasn't going to miss this opportunity.

"What are you doing?" he announced, stressing the long vowels to squeeze the maximum ridicule into his question.

"We're conducting a rigorous experiment on the gradient," I explained. Pritchard departed, muttering about getting a golf ball and putter to test the slope.

"There's absolutely no gradient there," Brown said firmly, "but do you know, in this fading light I thought I observed a phenomenon I have been reading about."

"What's that then?" Ronald enquired, stroking the lawn like a fireside rug.

"Well," Brown began, using his breathless, television professor's voice, "there's a theory that your molecules or something – bits of you anyway – actually physically merge with whatever you are touching, so that you become a little bit of it, and vice versa. When I looked at you from here, in this light, it appeared as though your hands and knees were mingling with the grass."

"That's because it needs cutting, which is what I have been trying to do," I whinged, "but I can't because of you lot."

"Just come over here and look," Brown persevered. "Exchange places with me and you'll see what I'm driving at."

I complied, just to get it over with. There was, I admit, a slight, a very slight, impression of what he was talking about.

Next, there appeared out of the encroaching, late-summer gloom, Horace and his over-active dog. Many of us like animals and don't mind someone's dog giving us a friendly slobbering as long as it stops there. Horace's dog is on something; I swear it. Horace just can't control it. It's likable enough, but daft and can't sit still for a moment. Anything excites it. Anyway, more of the dog later but for the moment it's enough to say that it found the sight of people crawling on all fours full of attractive possibilities.

"What's going on here?" Horace chuckled. "Is Browny all right? Why is he down on the grass?"

"Oh, he's lost his senses," I said, exasperated by the fact that I'd never get the lawn cut that night.

"Never mind, we'll find them," said Horace. "Best to do it quick before the dark comes down proper."

I smiled uncomprehendingly at him, having lost all sense of normality. I thought about unplugging my power cable to the mower.

Horace, Brown and Ronald were on their hands and knees, clowning around, with the dog creating havoc, when Pritchard came back with his putter and a couple of white golf balls.

Well, this exceeded the dog's highest expectations. Pritchard put one ball down and stroked it gently to check if indeed there was any slope or borrow. The dog

24

nabbed the ball and promptly choked on it.

"For goodness sake, man," cried Horace, "what are you doing that for? You'll kill the beast and we'll never find his lenses."

Puzzled, I turned to Pritchard, who looked equally intrigued and asked Horace, "Does your dog wear lenses then?"

Even in the dusk, you could see Horace turn red. "When have you ever heard of a dog wearing contact lenses, you prat? He's coughing his lungs up and you stand there asking stupid questions like that."

"I thought you said....." Pritchard replied, trying hard to understand what was going on, but at that moment the dog gave an almighty splutter, firing the golf ball straight at Brown's head. There was a howl, either from Brown or the dog – it was hard to tell which.

Horace was even more incensed now. "Well, that's adding insult to injury, I must say. First Brown loses his contact lenses, then gets a crack on the head for good measure from a golf ball. I can't see why you have to bring out golf balls and clubs at this time of night anyway, Pritchard. It's just asking for trouble."

"What do you mean, Brown's contact lenses," I asked, my patience growing thin, especially as the dog had now got himself tangled up in my power cable.

"Because you said," Horace yelled, "that Brown had lost his contact lenses."

With that, even the dog, wheezing desperately from its ordeal, rolled its lips back in an appreciative if bitter smile.

Chapter Two

Settling In

Throwing in the Trowel

I know I shouldn't have told anyone. I should have got on with it quietly, on my own. But what is it about us, I wonder, that makes us tell the whole world what we swore would be kept a secret? Is it the need to make conversation? Or is it some deep insecurity which denies us privacy, as if we are keeping a secret from God; a rebellion with no possibility of success? We are like children whose mothers know our thoughts before we know them ourselves.

And of course, in the friendly atmosphere and warm fug of the pub, all secrets are squeezed out. We would confess to anything; a liking for Country Music; belief in the integrity of politicians; watching daytime TV; cross-dressing. Making a confession like this got me into trouble one Tuesday evening, when during a lull in the conversation I mentioned to the chaps in the pub that I was of a mind to build a wall in my garden: a low, expensive-looking, decorative stone wall.

I have to hand it to Brown. He has a terrier-like quality behind that polished veneer. I was learning that he can be first off the mark on these occasions. Possibly his mouth doesn't take any time to consult his brain, or he has rehearsed put-downs for all occasions. When I have mentioned this possibility to him, he just adopts what he feels is a pitying and condescending smile, which actually borders on the imbecilic. He hinted that I might be jealous of his lightening mind. Being jealous of a guard dog with a stammer would be higher up my list.

"You wouldn't know where to start," he scorned. "You can't even cut your grass evenly, never mind put up a straight wall."

The grass comment stung. I knew I should have kept that wall ambition to myself, but now I was committed. "I've bought a book on garden projects, and building a wall doesn't seem too taxing. I don't even have to go round corners."

They all laughed, generally looked superior and mocked my plans.

"Books won't help none," Ronald scoffed.

On the contrary, I think Ronald would be helped greatly by books. I have been told that he regards himself as the village handyman on all things, and mends mercilessly. When the village noticeboard was begging to be put into retirement, Ronald shored it up for a little while longer, until one day it leapt from its wall mounting onto an unsuspecting pensioner, almost taking them both to the next world, unannounced.

Oh yes, and it was Ronald who tampered with the village pump, which had stood for centuries without being asked to produce anything. Ronald somehow tapped into an ancient source of water and had the pump gushing. People danced around it in excitement and wonder until they discovered the downside. It wouldn't go off. Ronald didn't know what he had done, so he didn't know how to undo it.

The Water Company sent men but they were mystified.

"There shouldn't be water here anymore," they said.

Soon the pump flooded the street and the fire engines arrived. The television cameras came as close as they dared to film for the evening news but nobody could actually help.

The water gushed, waiting to be capped by some person of authority and the road was blocked for days. Then as mysteriously as it came, it went, leaving only a tide-mark and a community wondering if it could afford Ronald's kindly help.

"Why do you want a wall anyway?" Pritchard asked.

Pritchard's straight-to-the-point questioning always has me reeling because I know he is going to follow up with a heavier punch. He finds your weak point without wasting words.

"I told you. It'll be decorative,"

"Not the way you'll throw it up," Brown chipped in.

"Exactly," agreed Pritchard. "Nothing else is decorative in your garden."

The others sniggered.

"I have to start somewhere," was my feeble defence.

"Yes, well you could start on the flowerbeds, or grow some decent vegetables, or a lawn," Pritchard continued.

"But I've only one gardening book and it's all about building things, not growing things," I said.

"Your garden's going to look like a builder's yard then, isn't it," Pritchard replied, turning the screw ever tighter.

"Look," I cried. "I'm going to build this wall, and that's that."

By the following Saturday I had the materials; nice light grey stone, cement, sand and blocks like square Polo Mints. I had planned this to perfection. The others were going off to support the local rugby team in an away match. They were doing rather well in the Cup and I wouldn't have minded going too. However, I made some excuse about being visited by an old friend, so I had a whole day from when they left at about ten in the morning until they arrived back in the early evening.

Right, no time to waste. I started digging the shallow foundation needed for the low wall. So far, so good. Then I mixed up some cement and slapped it into the ditch, ready for me to place the first course of stones.

So far, so bad. The cement was too runny. I'm sure I had the proportions right, but I found the book was quoting measures in stones and pounds, whereas the bag I bought was in kilos. It was an old book I bought in a sale. I didn't think it would make that much difference. We've been making walls since Hadrian. Obviously I haven't. The proportions of cement and sand were definitely wrong. An appendix at the back of the book showed the proportions in shovels-full, but my size of shovel was obviously wrong.

I didn't know what to do now that all this runny cement was slopping about in the foundation ditch, but I knew I couldn't get it out properly, and I didn't know what more to mix into it. More cement? More sand? I thought about covering all this in and starting again somewhere else in the garden, but a wall isn't built at random. It holds things in, or out. It needs to be, well, exactly where I had put it, so that wasn't a solution. Maybe I could practise elsewhere, round the back out of sight, but that would take time.

I decided to take a chance. After all, the damn stuff had to set sooner or later. So I began laying the stones in the cement, just as the book said.

At first all went well. The weight of the stones made them lie heavily and firmly into the cement. I began to relax and enjoy myself until I remembered something else. I had forgotten, with all this business of proportions, to set a straight line for the course of stones. The trouble was; I had already placed them all now. I got my lengths of string and tied them in parallel straight lines – and groaned. The stones were sitting in a wavy line.

I pulled them out with slushy, sucking noises and began again. It was mid-day by now and I hadn't got anywhere yet. My next effort was a bit better but the stones were now covered in cement and looking about as decorative as waste pipes. I tried to wash them but that added more water to the soggy cement in the ditch. I began to lose hope, but I didn't realise to what depths of despair I could really fall until I tried to put the second layer on top of the first. I cringe even now.

The cement was absolutely useless. I would have been better off using toothpaste to hold the stones together. I couldn't get the hang of the contours of the stones at all, so when I tried to lay the second course down on the ones below, they behaved shockingly, jumping off into the ditch, or swivelling round when I wasn't looking. By one o' clock I knew I was done for. I couldn't bear it. The thought of Brown and Pritchard gloating over my failure and then Ronald offering his dubious but irresistible help was too much.

I prepared excuses. "It was all right when I left it, but a herd of cows must have come along and...." No, nothing was credible. There was no way out. I'd have to become a recluse. The trouble is; a wall would be a really handy thing for a recluse to have.

Eureka! Suddenly it came to me. Thompson Arkwright. Would he be at home?

That was the question, but let me explain. He is a builder, a real builder, and he owes me a favour. Mind you, we don't get on that well. He thinks I'm a handless prat and I think he's a mindless pig. There's a sort of mutual regard in this relationship but well concealed. He is however very well off and lives in a large house not far from me.

I ran along the road to see if he would help.

When I had first met him I had been too clever by half. "Descended from the famous Arkwright?" I asked, "inventor of something or other, ah, was it the Mule?"

"Don't need to invent a mule," Arkwright had replied. "Mules is born."

By good luck, the only luck so far of the day, Arkwright was at home and in a good mood, having put away a nice lunch and a can or two of lager.

He even offered me one. I took it readily and came straight to the point, which I know he likes.

"I need help with a wall," I confessed. "I'm going to look foolish if I don't build one by early this evening. Can you help?"

He's not a bad sort really. I think he was curious to see how bad the wall was, but I also had something to offer. Soon he was in his working kit and ready to come.

"And you'll help me over this small matter of the Inland Revenue and my accounts?" he said as we got into his top of the range Audi.

The rugby supporters returned about seven o'clock, in a jolly mood because their team had done well. I was waiting, peering out from behind the curtains. They stopped in front of the garden as they passed. There were noises of surprise. I came out to stroll around as if nothing was unusual.

"Well, I don't believe it," Horace exclaimed, "but seeing is believing."

"You did this all from a book?" Ronald asked, suspicion barely disguised.

"And a little common sense," I added. I had only just managed to clear up all the materials which I had wasted, and hide them in the undergrowth behind the trees at the far end of the garden. The wall certainly looked very smart and straight. I noticed Pritchard line his eye along its level and raise his droopy eyebrow in appreciation.

Suddenly I noticed a glint of metal at the side of the wall where the evening sun was making long shadows. To my horror I saw it was Arkwright's trowel, a real builder's trowel, not the sandcastle type of thing I would use. Worse still for me, as if summoned by my thoughts, his flash Audi was pulling up alongside. He got out, obviously with the intention of retrieving his trowel. He couldn't have come at a worse time. I was ready to admit everything, pass it off as a joke and take my medicine before he gave the game away, but my voice wouldn't work. I just stood staring.

"Evening, everyone. Must have been a good game to watch," he addressed the spectators, who grunted in agreement and then stood, awaiting developments.

Turning to me, Arkwright then said. "I was just about to do some work, but somehow I lost my trowel. Could I borrow yours? I saw you slaving over the stones this afternoon."

I managed to find my voice, although its octave had risen. "I was just about to clean it."

"Don't bother," he said cheerfully. "It'll do as it is."

I could see Ronald looking very dubiously at the trowel. The others knew that something was amiss, but they couldn't tell exactly what.

"Coming for a drink?" Brown invited me when Arkwright had departed.

"I think I'll have an early night, thanks," I said. After all, it was in the cosy confessional of the pub that I first got myself into this hole.

Local Hero – and a Cat

Tuesday is darts night, so I went up to the Goat to support our pub team. It was a damp, dull sort of evening, the kind that people complain about after being used to the warmth of the summer. I don't. It gives me the ideal excuse to trundle up to the local to fortify myself. I found Brown, Horace and Ronald already there.

"Where's Pritchard?" I asked.

"He's gone to night school," Brown informed me.

"He keeps that quiet," I observed.

"Not really," said Horace. "You've just not known him for long. Mind you, you could listen to people a bit more. You're much too much wrapped up in yourself."

"Ask me what I'd like to drink and I'll listen," I said.

"Don't mind him," said Ronald. "He's just disappointed. His chess class has been cancelled. Not enough people."

"They're all playing at home on their computers," I said. "Can't you do the same and learn that way, Horace?"

"I'm the teacher, you plonker. Not enough people turned up to make a decent sized class. Now I won't get paid. I'll have a pint, if you are ordering. Takes ages tonight to get served. You'd think they'd pull in extra staff."

"I understand your annoyance now," I replied, "but why don't you turn your hand to a more commercial subject, one that will at least allow you to pay for your round. Anyway, what's all this obsession about night classes?"

"Adult education," explained Ronald.

"I didn't ask for another word for it," I complained. "What I mean is: why is everyone so interested all of a sudden?"

"Self-improvement," Brown enlarged. "I believe in it wholeheartedly."

"Must believe in it for others," Horace had a snipe. "Never indulges in it himself."

"You must begin with self-knowledge," Brown continued, as oblivious to the attack as a French waiter is oblivious to a miserable diner, wriggling on the hook of neglect, while his beautiful date for the evening begins to scroll through telephone numbers on her mobile. "I actually took an intelligence test once."

"I hope they gave you your money back," said Ronald.

Brown looked puzzled. "In fact," he said with some smugness, "I got the amazing score of 110%. That's pretty good, no?"

We looked at one another and sipped our newly acquired pints gratefully. I dismissed the idea of telling Brown that he should keep quiet about his score.

I was saved from further action because a bell was struck and the barman called for the darts teams to present themselves to the Referee For The Night. Brown was in our team. They were playing against the Angel Globe pub in Sprighassle, a neighbouring village. Ronald and Horace leapt to life, massaging Brown's throwing arm, cleaning his glasses and generally horsing around in the way they know Brown detests. For all his cultivated insensitivity, Brown hates to be at the centre of silly attention. I think personally, although without real evidence, and Pritchard for one disagrees with me, that Brown is more aware of his shortcomings in the brain department than he appears and so doesn't want the unholy alliance of Ronald and Horace attracting unwelcome attention. I was surprised that he had allowed himself to be selected for the team. We haven't won for years, and Brown didn't seem to be the man who would change that.

Not long ago they even asked me to play. I felt honoured. I felt I had made it in the village. For three days I walked with a jaunty step. I imagined people to be nudging one another as I passed. What no one had told me was that our team was the most incompetent in the County.

My first match told me everything. I was elected to throw first. I went for double tops to open, missed and got a "one". The rest of the team whooped like an American audience watching a golf hero. I accepted it for sarcasm until I saw the others throw. I then realised their cheers had been genuine. If they hit the board they shouted "Bulls-eye!" If by some fluke they actually got a double to start, they walked off to the bar as if honour were satisfied. If the board had been rotated at speed or swung from side to side, they would have done just as well. This was what Brown had let himself in for.

Fortunately he wasn't taking it too seriously. It transpired that for once the opposition were almost as bad. The first game was "Round-the Clock". You have to hit a double one, double two, double three and so on, the first team to score a double twenty being the winner. After twenty minutes, neither team had got past double three, so they relaxed the rule and allowed the teams to hit a single instead of a double. After another exhausting twenty minutes, Brown hit a twenty, then a Bullseye to win the game. Everyone was astonished. He returned, glowing with achievement.

"You got them on sheer staying power," cried Ronald.

Brown flushed with what we thought was emotion but it turned out he just needed to go to the toilet after such a long game. "Get me another pint," he called over his shoulder.

"Get him one with a couple of vodkas in it," Horace whispered to Ronald.

I heard him. "Don't do that," I advised. "You'll kill off the few brain cells he has."

"Nonsense," Ronald said. "It'll relax him. He'll throw all the better. He'll thank you for it."

It was the tradition that normal life in the pub was not to be disturbed overmuch by the darts, so there was a long interval before the second half. The discussion on adult education was resumed.

"I don't know what all the fuss is about," said Ronald. "When I was a lad and had started my apprenticeship, I had to go two nights a week to evening school. We learned all sorts of things, like technical drawing and all about hand tools. It was very good but not all the lads liked it and sometimes a quarrel with the teacher would break out. He was a right grim toad, and no mistake. My theory was his wife was an awful cook because he acted as though he was always suffering from indigestion.

He was very skilful though. I remember one night he was getting lip from one of the awkward lads, so he pulled the lad by the ear to the front bench and said he would show him a piece of nifty woodwork. He grabbed the lad's thumb and before you knew it, he had stuck it in a clamp with just the tip showing. He then said the lad's fingernails were too long and offered to trim them with the plane.

Well you know, not one of us made any move to help the lad. I didn't like him anyway and didn't want to stand up to the teacher in case I was next. Anyway, the lad was shaking by this time and there were nervous giggles from the class when, as fast as you like, the teacher whipped the plane along the edge of the clamp and cut the nail off. It was so quick and so clean that we applauded spontaneously, partly from relief. Then we noticed the blood dripping from under the clamp. The lad fainted, but couldn't fall properly because his finger was still in the clamp."

"That's awful," cried Brown. "The man was a barbarian. Was he sacked?"

"Not at all," Ronald replied. "That was the

difference then. No one complained, you see. It was just a nick. The young lad's family didn't like to cause a fuss, or take on the school and its governors. We got a nice, new clamp though. The teacher said it was loose and a safety hazard."

"When I was young, in my teens, I went to a dress-making class," Horace claimed. We all showed interest, especially as Horace's dress sense is on a par with his dog's.

"I read a magazine article and it said that if you wanted the company of young ladies, then you should turn up to the places they go to. This made good sense to me because I had noticed that young ladies did not hang out at the places I went to, the pubs, the racetrack, the snooker halls and so on. The old bat who took the dress-making class was suspicious and I really didn't want to make dresses, so she got me to do car seats."

"Car seats?" we repeated.

"Yes. Her husband needed them and I had to go and measure the seats as part of the project. I wasn't allowed to measure the girls' seats." Horace went vague for a minute then returned to his theme. "As chance would have it, it worked out quite well for me, because the girls thought I had a car, which was rare in those days. So I had the pick of the bunch, at least for a short while. I went out with this really nice, well-dressed girl and explained to her that the car was being customised at the moment. The relationship didn't last long."

"Because the car never materialised?" Brown suggested.

"No. She just didn't like the places I took her to, the pubs, the race track, the snooker halls."

Peter the barman was calling for the darts teams to come forward for the second half.

This time the game was "501". You have to score as

many points as possible from your three darts, and deduct those points from 501 and so on until you get a low even number, which you dispatch by throwing a double.

This was decided to be too challenging for the teams, especially as you must throw a double, even to begin scoring. It was agreed that 301 was more suitable. There were to be four games, so that each team member could play a member of the opposition. After three gruelling games, our village was behind by two games to one, and it was Brown's turn. If he lost, he would have lost the whole game, but if he won this round he would, by carrying forward the points from the first half, win. Such responsibility had rarely been thrust upon shoulders so sloping.

"Let play commence," said the Referee For The Night grandly, and tottered off to the Gents. Both players managed to get the necessary double to start but found it difficult to score many points, so their scores were slow to come down.

Ronald was getting angry about something. "Watch that fellow score," he whispered to me. "He's cheating. Where's the referee?"

"Absent," said Horace. "But you're right. He totalled only ten with his darts, but deducted thirty."

"He's doing it again," hissed Ronald.

"What can one do?" I asked. "If I remember correctly, it has to be Brown who protests but he's so preoccupied with the game that he doesn't see what the chap's doing."

Brown was playing quite well, building up large scores like twenty-five, and consistently hitting the board with all three darts. The other player was terrible, but with his cheating, they were just about neck and neck. I wondered how long it would be before the vodkas took their toll.

"I can't stand this," said Horace. "I'm going to thump that cheat when the game finishes."

"You'd better not," I warned him. "His team mates are all big lads. All Brown's team have gone off to the bar to drown their sorrows. They don't have any faith in Brown."

However, things took a funny turn and a series of unpredictable events began to unfold which, in the re-telling, even I can hardly believe.

Firstly, news of Brown's above-average throwing filtered through to the bar. His team were returning to watch, their hopes growing. Quite a crowd was now gathering for the end of the game.

Secondly Ronald, in helpless frustration, had dipped a few pork scratchings into the cheat's pint of Guinness, hoping that he'd choke on them.

Thirdly the pub cat appeared, weaving through the legs of the crowd. She came to look for titbits now and again, using her long experience to know that when people are distracted, they leave things lying around. Tail swaying and nose twitching, the hunter stretched up to the table with the Guinness on it. She loved pork scratchings.

The darts match was nearing a climax. Brown needed only a double-two to win but he had to wait before it was his turn. His opponent, needing eleven, prepared his darts.

I glanced at the cat. Its nose was firmly in the pint of Guinness, searching for the pork scratchings. Someone close by shouted encouragement to the players. The cat misunderstood it, thinking it was a personal reprimand for her thieving ways and jerked her frothy nose out of the glass, knocking it off the table. Unnoticed, the drink quickly oozed along the floor to the chalk line where the players stood to throw their darts. Brown's opponent was just stepping up to the mark but instead stood on the Guinness slick and did an impossibly fast version of the splits. As he fell, he propelled all his darts up into the air and the crowd scattered to escape the falling shrapnel.

Fortunately no one was hurt and everyone crowded around again. The cheating player found only two of his darts and threw a one and a double three. Now he also needed only a double-two to win, but without his third dart he was helpless. A debate took place with the referee, who could not grasp the problem and kept asking the player to throw his dart.

Just then, a distressed mewing was heard above the rabble and when a space was cleared, we saw the cat, pinned to the floor by the last dart piercing a hole in her collar. The dart's owner put his hand down to retrieve the dart but the cat, in a bad temper, spat ungratefully and flexed her claws as best she could. He couldn't get his hand close enough to unpin the dart.

Brown was not one hundred percent tuned into events by this time, being too influenced by the powerful mixture of popularity and laced drink. Believing it to be his turn, he walked casually to the line and with his first dart, jammed it between the wires indicating a double-two. The pub was silent for a second in disbelief, then it erupted. We had won our first game in living memory – and Brown was a folk-hero.

"Drinks on the house," he shouted gallantly. I think he's still paying off the debt.

Maybe we can't play darts but we can celebrate with the best. The cat became a folk-hero too and the name of Brown became associated with the cat, like Dick Whittington.

Such is the stuff of legend. When night classes, or evening adult education programmes as they are now called, study mythology in future years, scholars will delve into our village archives to find the truth. Let's hope they never find it. There's nothing like truth to spoil a good story.

The Art of Conversation

I didn't really notice him when we first came to the village but since then I have struck up a friendship with a chap who lives not far along the east road out of the village. We have travelled together by train into London when by co-incidence our work has taken us there on the same day. He's a plain-looking sort, not the one for flashy dress and quite retiring really, but he is very successful at what he does. He writes best-sellers, the kind you grab at the airport and then because you know the author's name, you buy another. Before you know it, you've read the lot.

I always had the impression that such a writer would carry the mark of fame with him, would travel in a large, black car driven by a chauffeur and be seen in the best of restaurants. Alf drives a large car, but it is a nine-year old Landrover, for his two red-setters to ride in and he is frequently to be seen in our company in the Gentle Goat.

Now, I must not mention his surname, because he writes under a pseudonym and values his privacy. I could easily blow his cover by mistake and that would be a shame. I've told him we could let Ronald be his front-man. Ronald could pretend to be him and create a diversion. Ronald would love the attention but he honestly couldn't sound like an author for thirty seconds. Nor has he read any of Alf's books. Come to think of it, I don't think any of us have.

Alf has a bit of a problem however. He has been quite open with me about it but he finds it a drawback in his profession. The fact is, he is not terribly well educated and lacks confidence when the conversation turns to matters of learning and culture. You might think this lack of education would hamper his writing.

"Not a bit of it," he said one day as we supped our pints and shared a packet of cashews. "It's because I'm uncultured, or whatever the word is, that I don't feel the need to include all that clever stuff, so I put things into plain language and get on with the story. I don't spend a page describing a sunset over Heathrow. I know I'm no Shakespeare. There's no use trying to be what you're not, is there?"

He knows however that when he faces tough questions from media chappies, he doesn't handle them well, so he tends to avoid interviews. This puts him under pressure from the publishing house, which wants him to go out and publicise his work. But Alf doesn't and, against all the marketing norms, sells shedloads.

"I do try now and again," he said, reaching for a stuffed olive and signalling for two more pints. "I'll tell you a story about that. You'll like it. Actually," he faltered, fumbling in his pockets, "I've no cash. Do you mind doing the honours?"

I looked at my watch. Alf's stories can take some time but as he was buying me a drink which I was paying for, I felt bound to hear him out. He settled himself comfortably, sometimes looking out into the light of the early evening. Alf can make you feel you have just gone back into Victorian England, where story telling was regarded as the best entertainment you could get. You could almost hear the clatter of a stagecoach coming into the cobbled yard.

"Ever since my books began to sell," he began, "I've taken to popping over to the public library in Humblebridge. I don't borrow anything. I go down to see what other people are reading and to see if they are taking out my books. If they are not on the shelves, great. I go home and bash out another couple of thousand words. It's a motivator. But if they are not out on loan, I try to persuade people that they are a great read. People are suspicious. They don't like you hanging around them when they are choosing what to borrow. It's a very private transaction, you see. Mind you, it's interesting to see who is borrowing my stuff. It might be different at airports and stations, but at the local library I would say it is the very opposite type of person to the jet-setter. It's good for me to know that because I'll never fool myself about who really is reading my books."

He took a pull at his pint and nodded to some acquaintance that had just come in. The pub was more messy than usual, with empty glasses on tables and crisp packets strewn around. Maybe they were short staffed.

"You have to have a good cover design to get people to pick *your* book off the shelf. It can mean more than the story. That puts it in perspective, doesn't it? Anyway what was I going to tell you about?"

I couldn't help him out. He hadn't even begun to tell the actual story. This is why Alf's stories can take so long.

"Oh, yes," he said. "I know. I was going to tell you about one time in the library when my attention was drawn to a book with a bright blue metallic cover. It was called *The Art of Conversation* or something like that. It was in the self-improvement section near the counter. After that little discovery, I took up ironing."

I thought I had misheard, or skipped a few pages. You can do that with Alf's conversation; come in and out of it without any real loss, but this time I was foxed.

"What has ironing got to do with it?" I asked.

"Be patient. Ironing has everything to do with it. Ironing was a recommended topic of conversation. Not that I take everything I read in books seriously. The author of this book probably started off by thinking up the cover, but then needed a subject to go with it. He was probably sitting one night, his TV on the blink and no repairman in sight and his wife would be in a similar state of shock, still making cups of tea when she thought the adverts were on, so he probably thought he'd write a piece on conversation to take his mind off things."

"I still don't see what ironing has got to do with it," I interrupted.

"What the book recommended as a technique," Alf continued undaunted, "was to have a few topics ready in advance of a meeting, or a dinner party or whatever, and you'd never run short of conversation."

"Why would you want to do that," I asked, getting slightly peeved that the ironing business was not yet explained.

"Well, that's the problem I have really. If I get invited to a book launch or a social gathering, I don't know what to say, or worse, I go on about things no one else wants to know about. But if I'm prepared, then I'm more confident. That's where the ironing comes in."

I relaxed on my barstool. I knew Alf would run a steady course now.

"My priority was to improve my table conversation," he explained. "It's easier when you're just standing around clutching a cool glass of bubbly. You can let people make the running and then move off, but at a dinner you are stuck there for a long time. I thought I could kill two birds with one stone because I'm trying to improve my ironing also. I can't seem to get the same quality of wrinkles that my cleaning lady gets. Bless her, she is so unpredictable. Sometimes she leaves just a few lines on the tail of my shirt, and that's ok. At other times, she contrives a deep diagonal across the back. I would wear them regardless, but I got too many comments. People would speculate, either to my face, or indeed with one another as to how they got there. Anyway, we compromised. I do the ironing and she tries to write a few pages for me. She can't do that either, but I need a shirt before all else."

Alf took a moment's rest before resuming. "Where I go wrong in conversation is that unless I am telling a story, I'm not that interesting. I don't catch the news often enough. I'm fairly head-down in my work. People are disappointed. They look past me as I gabble on about something; they drink too much because they can't get a word in; I treat them as an audience. My real problem isn't that I'm tongue-tied. It's that I make *them* tongue-tied.

This book had it figured out. It made me realise that what I'm doing wrong is dominating the talk, freezing them out and hacking them off. So the book said I should assume they had something interesting to say and tease it out of them.

First of all, I had to find a topic, one that wouldn't scare, or disgust people over their meal. Ironing; the perfect subject. The book strongly suggested that your warm-up topic should be completely uncontroversial. What could be less likely to offend than ironing?

The next time I was asked out to dinner, I tried it out. The invitation came from a friend of my publisher to meet some American people in the trade.

I arrived at a solid, dull town house where you ring a bell and speak into a box on the wall. Strange contraptions, I find them. All for the convenience of the occupants, of course, but embarrassing and inconvenient to the visitor. I feel that I am talking to myself in the street and I can't hear the answer above the noise of the traffic. It also explained to me why you see no short salesmen in these neighbourhoods.

The whole entry procedure confused me and I got it terribly wrong the first time. After a faint voice encouraged me to come up, I pushed the door open and bent down to pick up the box of chocolates I had deposited on the pavement while I figured out the speaking box. Before I had the chance to do this, the door closed again, with my tie jammed in it. It was then that I made the connection about short salesmen, because with my tie and therefore my neck stuck at waist height, I could not reach the box. This was embarrassing. I hoped no other guest would come along and find me in this state. They would dine off it for months. I had to take my tie off and repeat the whole operation, pretending to be someone else. In my flustered state, I left the chocolates again on the pavement. The next guest, obviously an opportunist, presented my chocolates to the hostess.

Sadly, the dinner party was flat. It took a long time to warm up. It didn't help that we couldn't identify the starter. We ate suspiciously, making loud, high-pitched noises about how delicious it was and could someone have the recipe? My neighbour suggested sotto voce that it might need translation from some forgotten dialect.

By the time we finished the sweet, I had done all the listening I was going to do and moved to the next stage, as recommended by my book: introduce a harmless topic that everyone can understand – ironing.

I made my first remarks casually but firmly. I leaned over to my hostess and offered a few innocuous remarks about my new interest and how I found that a light steam iron can work wonders with my collars and what it felt like to be free from raucous comments about the lacerations on my back.

I was aware I was attracting some interest because a

couple of the guests near me stopped talking and listened, chuckling now and again. I can tell a story reasonably well but for some reason my hostess was slow to take up the theme for the table in general and tried to freeze me out.

I was disappointed because I felt she had been responsible for the flatness of the dinner all night and so I showed some stubbornness. I did this by trying to tempt her, politely and amusingly, to relate her experiences on the subject, which is what the book said was to be done at this point but my host, who had been, it must be said, rather sullen all night, suddenly broke his silence.

He said in a louder voice than was really necessary and which I attributed to the gritty and anonymous wine we were drinking, that my hostess would be well advised to listen to me because he was obliged more often than he preferred to don items of clothing in the morning with so many creases that you could quite successfully grate cheese on them. His handkerchiefs, he then said, were the joke of his entire firm.

You have never seen a civilised gathering collapse so quickly. Whether it was the enigmatic starter, the heat, the risqué jokes of one of the Americans, or the cheese, which was certainly more alive than the conversation had been, I don't know, but ironing seemed to trigger off more deep-seated grievances than you would care to imagine.

One couple doing role-reversal, she pulling in the bread, he doing the domestic thing, began a squabble about the quality management of his ironing. She expressed the fear that he had resurrected his old skiffle washboard to use as an ironing table, because everything came out pleated.

Would you imagine it? My intentions were good. I didn't treat them as an audience and I tried to get everyone included. But those self-improvement books are useless, you know. They just don't live in the real world. Before I could excuse myself, every couple was arguing the toss about who should or shouldn't do what, and who was going to fire the domestic help, and who was going back out to work again."

"Ah well," Alf sighed, draining the last of his beer. "You can't make omelettes without breaking wind, as they say. I'll have to think of a really harmless topic for the next time. You know, I felt really good for those few minutes when I was guiding the conversation."

I glanced outside. The dark had fallen whilst Alf had been speaking. Time to get off home and do some book-keeping work for the Parish Council. Funny to think that here was a man, who must be worth a small fortune by now, worrying about table conversation and the state of his laundry.

"Before you go," Alf said, "lend me a tenner. I think I'll stay on here for a bit."

Chapter Three

Local Wild Life

A Brush with the Law

I suffer a lot from sleeplessness. I don't call it "insomnia", a dreadful word, but I can cope with "sleeplessness". It is a soporific, lisping, lapping-of-the-waves-on-the-shore sound. But "insomnia" sounds insoluble, insurmountable, and resistant to all attempts to cure it.

I've come to terms with it. I actually sometimes quite like it. It provides a harmless, throwaway party line to elicit a bit of sympathy, but in return I usually get a long account of some other person's sleeping problems. At one dinner party, something like eight out of ten people enthusiastically joined in with varieties of poor sleeping habits. I'll have to find a more unique ailment. At any given time in the middle of the night, it would appear I could telephone my friends and find half of them up and about. I remember too my father insisting he slept badly, was up in the small hours and was a martyr to the disease. However, at no time did anyone actually see him in that state.

Sleeplessness has some advantages. I can get up in the middle of the night, have a fizzy drink and a slab of chocolate, read comics and generally have fun being about when no one else is. It gives you a feeling of being special, even if the fizzy drink is for a headache and the comics are sets of company accounts, which have got to be ready for the following day.

Anyway this is all a longish introduction to explain

why one night I was up at about 2.30 am, groping my way downstairs in the dark so as not to disturb anyone. I was feeling for the hall light switch when something stopped me. It was windy outside and when I heard the rattle of a milk bottle, I put it down to the wind. Then a double rattle, hard to describe but as if the bottle had been propelled rather than blown, raised my suspicions.

I withdrew my hand from the light switch, crept over to the curtain and opened it, ever so slightly. I couldn't see anything at first; it was so dark. I was still getting used to the mean street lighting in the village. Then I saw movement, a furtive movement, down by a hedge across the street. A figure was moving in the shadows. When it came to cross an open driveway, its cover was broken and I recognised the creeping thing. It was Pritchard.

He looked like an amateur in a play, self-conscious, under-rehearsed, miscast, not at all comfortable with the role he was playing. I could not see him clearly, but he made me uncomfortable too. I didn't know that Pritchard had taken to night walks. He certainly doesn't suffer from sleeplessness. That I do know. In fact, we wonder sometimes if he's asleep at his drink in the pub.

"I have no idea why Pritchard joins us," I've heard Brown say. "He's not really there half the time."

"He's just different," was Ronald's tolerant interpretation. "It doesn't mean he's not enjoying himself. He's introspective."

"It's eerie," Brown pressed. "It unsettles me."

And "eerie" is how I would describe the experience of seeing Pritchard steal along the street in the middle of the night. It wasn't as if he had a dog to walk or anything like that.

Soon I couldn't see anything. He was gone.

Early next morning, I went up to the shop for a few, fresh morning rolls and some odds and ends. Sigmund was having his ear bent about inflation by a young lady. According to her, Sigmund was responsible for rising prices. If he weren't such a profiteering capitalist, then more people would have jobs. I think that was the gist of it. I felt it was rather personal to attribute all this to Sigmund who, good shopkeeper though he may be, doesn't seem to me to be a self-seeking oppressor of the poor. I said so after she left.

"Oh, don't mind her," he said. "She's doing a course in economics and was just practising an argument."

"Oh, I see," I said. "Now, do you have any fresh fruit in today?"

"Not much to talk of," he mourned. "Deliveries have been poor of late. Lots of things are out of season and the supermarkets always get first pick.

"OK, I'll have a few of those bananas and pears."

He named a price. I came round to the young lady's way of thinking. "Who is she anyway," I asked.

"Alf's niece," he said over his shoulder. "She's come over for a week's vacation. Poor Alf is not used to the noise, and his housekeeper's off with a bad back, and he's got to finish something or other for his publisher by the weekend. He was in quite a two and eight this morning when he came in. The usual sherry, or something else?"

"Know how he feels," I said. "I have to get something finished for today, and another job by Monday."

"That means you'll be working over the weekend again," Sigmund said sympathetically. "You chaps are all the same. The stress will eventually get you, you know. Our bodies weren't built for it. I bet you've got your insomnia again."

"Sleeplessness," I corrected him.

"I bet you did not get a full night's sleep last night," he persisted. Sigmund is uncanny. You go in for a can of beans and come out with a complex, no extra cost. However, I wasn't in the mood for that today and I didn't want to be drawn on seeing Pritchard. I felt that if Pritchard needed privacy, then he should have it.

"Alf was up last night," Sigmund lowered his voice confidentially. "Thought he heard burglars, strange noises down at the end of his garden. He took a powerful torch and shone it round the garden. He says the noise stopped, or so he imagined. He was sure that someone was out there but the noise didn't start up again."

"And do you know," he went on, "I've had one or two other people telling me that their sleep has been disturbed?"

I went back to my house, and to the room I use as an office, and gave no more thought to what Sigmund had been telling me. My work pressures were enough to drive anything else out of my mind and it was Monday before I was presented with any more unusual information.

I like to give myself a little reward for finishing work which has caused me overtime, so on Monday night I dawdled up to the pub, hoping to find someone to talk to. Peter was serving that night so I didn't expect or get conversation from that quarter. You wonder why some people do certain jobs, don't you? I mean, you expect a barman to be just a little on the extrovert side, a little louder than most, especially during the early evening when the pub is half empty. A bit of lively banter and hearty greetings helps the place warm up.

Peter is not of that school. Sometimes that's ok. He compensates for it with his very expressive face, which gives a silent, running commentary on life. I read somewhere that deep down we are all trying to confess something about ourselves: who we really are, what we are like. Even our handwriting could be a disguised confession. Peter's face cannot help but express his feelings about what is going on around him. He employs face muscles that haven't been invented yet for other people.

So when I ordered up my drink, I had to make do with a monosyllable and a handful of beery change because he was trying to put on a new lager barrel. But within ten minutes Ronald, followed by Alf and his niece, joined me.

"Evening," said Alf loudly. I could tell he'd just finished a spell of writing because he always shouts. I don't know if he is still living in his storyline or just glad to be out but it is very noticeable. Well, it was noticeable after Sigmund pointed it out to me.

"Had a spell at the desk then?" I enquired.

"Yes. Got pressure on a deadline at the moment. I can't see why it matters whether I produce something by next week or next month. The reader doesn't care, but my agent is insistent. It's like a factory, you know. I'm sure James Joyce didn't have to bash out the stuff like that."

"So would you like to be given time to produce a great novel?" I asked.

"I would like to write one for myself one day. It may not be a great or even a good book, but it *would* be a change," said Alf.

"But you'll just make another million first, to be on the safe side," said Ronald. Alf laughed. He never mentions his money, but he doesn't mind when others allude to his rich pickings.

"This is Alison, my niece." He turned to the young lady, who until now had said nothing.

"I saw you in Sigmund's shop this morning. What would you like to drink?" I offered.

"Thanks, a sweet sherry please. I didn't notice you," she replied candidly. "I went in for a few things to stock up Uncle Alf's larder and before I knew it, I was accusing the shopkeeper of all sorts of capitalist crimes. He didn't seem to mind. It was quite strange." Her eyes lit up extraordinarily well when she spoke.

I ordered the drinks. I always do when I'm feeling good, having finished a piece of work and in the knowledge that the cheque's on its way. Funny though, at a dinner party last weekend, one chap said he felt he paid for far more drinks than he got back. Everyone piped up, saying much the same. So who's getting all the beers, I want to know?

"I heard you had a mystery night visitor," I said to Alf.

"Yes, don't remind me. I *write* about adventure but I don't want to be in it. I was actually a little frightened. I knew someone was there and I knew I was being watched. You can tell, you know. It's intuition."

Ronald asked Alf who he thought it might be but Alf wasn't to be drawn.

"I can't tell," he said. "I don't have valuables in the house. I never have time to buy any."

"That's true," his niece agreed. "The place is like no one lives there. It's so bare."

Ronald finished his drink with a noisy slurp. "The very fact that it's a big house, tucked away down that track, will make people expect that there's something worth nicking. Want another?"

He was the only one ready, so he bought himself one.

"I was doing a spot of work up by the old shepherd's cottage," Ronald said, "where that new family with the yellow Mercedes have moved in. They were telling me the old man next to them had his telly pinched. It was a portable and he kept it down in his garden shed so that he could watch the racing in the afternoon. Just a few days ago it was taken. The padlock was forced. They took a few power tools too."

"I suppose it's easy to steal that sort of thing," Alison said. "The thief doesn't need to risk going into a house. Lots of people keep quite good things in their garden sheds and the locks are never that strong."

Alf and Alison stayed only for the one. I was left with Ronald. He is an open book: I could tell something was bothering him.

"It's Pritchard," he blurted out, unable to contain himself any longer. "I seriously think he's going off the rails. I'm very worried about him."

I didn't say anything about seeing Pritchard the other night. It's too easy to get these things out of proportion.

"He's been acting strangely, even more strangely than usual," Ronald expanded. "I saw him the other night – and I mean in the middle of the night - it must have been about one o'clock. It was raining slightly but he didn't seem to notice. He had no coat. He was just wandering about, and looking very guilty indeed. I had just answered a call of nature. I didn't put the light on and then I heard footsteps. There he was, shuffling around, carrying a haversack type of thing and looking back over his shoulder like a criminal."

It was Ronald's use of the word "criminal" which startled me and I was shocked into sharing what I had witnessed. Although I hadn't seen Pritchard carry anything in the shadows, we of course jumped to conclusions. Was he responsible for the break-ins? It seemed unthinkable but people do lead double lives, if we are to believe what we read in the newspapers.

I felt bad about it afterwards but for a time our imaginations stretched themselves to breaking point, fancying all the things Pritchard might be up to.

Next thing he was at our shoulder. Ronald almost squealed with surprise.

"What's up with you two? Guilty secrets?" he asked glumly.

"Us?" Ronald squeaked. "Absolutely not. We've nothing to feel guilty about."

He emphasised "we've" too much for my liking, but Pritchard seemed not to notice. Conversation was uneasy. If Pritchard isn't in the mood he can be hard work and tonight he seemed more distracted than usual. He looked awful, in fact. At best, he looks like an under-slept bloodhound, but his baggy eyes and heavy jowls were even more pronounced. He looked like he would be as an old man. A wave of sympathy came over me.

"Haven't seen you much of late." I tried to massage the conversation like a stalled heart. "You been busy?"

He looked me over for a while before answering. He does this frequently but this time it made him look shifty – no other word for it.

"No more than usual."

Ronald and I looked at each other and slumped over our pints in an awkward silence. Peter's mouth turned down at the ends like a circus clown.

I telephoned Ronald the next day.

"Did you know that a couple of expensive mountain bikes were stolen last night?" I shouted. I always shout over the phone to Ronald. He himself bawls down the phone like he's giving instructions to the ship's engine room. If you don't shout back you sound like a man on his deathbed. Very therapeutic to have a good shout.

"No, I had not," he hollered back. "I think we ought to take some action."

"Like what?" I asked. "Set up a village militia and a night watch?"

"In a way," Ronald replied. "You and I should tail Pritchard."

"What, all night? How?"

"We don't need to watch him all night. We know we've seen him between one and three. We'll park one of our cars near his house and stake him out."

"Sounds dramatic. What if he goes out the back and through his garden?" I countered.

Ronald was resourceful. "He's sure to put a light on somewhere in the house when he's getting ready, so we'll see that. I'll go round the back. You watch from the car, and we'll have all the exits covered."

"How will I let you know if he comes out the front? Sound the horn?" I said. I know I'm frustrating to work with sometimes.

Ronald just said. "I'll think of something." The man has patience.

"And won't he recognise my car? I suggested.

"Don't flatter yourself," said Ronald, by now quite exasperated by my objections. "Your car wouldn't stand out on an empty football pitch."

Maybe it wouldn't, but while we sat in it, near to Pritchard's house, late that night, trying to keep our heads down like they do in the gangster movies, *we* felt very conspicuous. It was dark and chilly. Ronald was feeling more discomfort because we had drunk a few beers to pass the time before our assignment. He's getting on a bit and his bladder can't take it like it used to, but he couldn't get out of the car because I couldn't find the interior light switch to cancel it in case it came on when he opened the door.

"You'll have to get out at some time, so it may as well be now," I said.

"I'll think of something," was his irritating reply. I had heard this argument frequently. It meant, "I haven't a clue what to do."

"Can I put the radio on," I asked. "I'm bored."

"No you can't. You might be heard. Anyway, you'll get distracted. You don't get Hercule Poirot sitting listening to Radio Luxemburg, do you?"

I couldn't argue. It was just as well. We only just saw Pritchard's tell-tale light in his house go on and then quickly off again before he emerged, shutting his door gently. He moved deliberately but quickly, and with much more confidence. He was obviously growing accustomed to this life.

We let him go off along the street before we dared to get out and follow. A car door sounds loudly when there are no other night sounds. There was a slight wind, which assisted us inasmuch as it was more difficult to hear when you were heading into the wind. To hear clearly you had to hold your head to the side, so Pritchard was unlikely to be alerted by any sound we made behind him.

We expected him to make for the lanes to the rear of the houses, if it was indeed Pritchard who was stealing from garden sheds or outbuildings. However, his route was not leading to anywhere that *we* were expecting. As we followed, my thoughts wandered about Pritchard. Perhaps he was afflicted with a disease, like a shoplifter with a compulsive tendency to steal. Or maybe he just did it for the kicks.

Distracted by those thoughts, I almost lost him. Far from keeping within the village, he was very deliberately taking a path away from the village.

Puzzled, I looked at Ronald. He shrugged and indicated that we should press on. It was getting harder. We couldn't see Pritchard very well because of the dark, and the rising wind made it harder for us to listen for his footstep. We were as likely to bump into him as lose him.

Deeper along a lane and into a wood we went. It occurred to me he might be trekking to another village and my heart sank at the thought of a long walk. Ronald held open his hands in a "don't know" gesture, but we were by now too committed to turn back. Whatever Pritchard was up to, it was certainly not obvious and we needed to find out. There was no normal explanation for this behaviour.

The lane was turning roughly in the direction of Alf's house. I couldn't imagine that Pritchard was going to rob Alf, but you never know. Maybe Pritchard was Alf's intruder. I have certainly heard Pritchard say rich people have more than is good for them. Maybe he was determined to do Alf a favour by relieving him of some of his burden.

Ronald was certainly feeling the burden of his bladder. The poor man was wriggling as he walked and pleaded with me to stop for a minute, but I refused on the grounds that we had come this far at Ronald's insistence and we didn't want to lose our quarry now. Ronald said that by now he didn't care. He was going to pass out if he didn't relieve himself, so that was that. He dodged behind a bush and seemed to take at least five minutes. I had it in mind to turn back when I saw, not twenty yards away from us, and down a slight incline, a light. I guessed that it must be one of those will-o'-the-wisp things and drew Ronald's reviving attention to it. We saw a movement by the light. I was uneasy.

Curiosity is overpowering. We found ourselves, without conscious decision, moving towards the light. Employing all we learned from our Boy Scout days, we slunk cautiously and expertly forward. Davy Crockett could have done no better. There was definitely someone next to the light. In the dark and the whispering wind, I even thought of the supernatural. Past a few more trees we slithered like snakes on our bellies, then drew ourselves up on our knees behind a wide chestnut trunk and looked out.

Pritchard too was on his knees, intent on something.

We moved forward more until we were within yards of him, when he turned round and gently motioned us to stay quiet.

"You took your time," he said calmly.

"How did you know we were here?" we asked.

He gave us a look that indicated our tracking techniques needed to be brushed up. Then he waved to us to come forward. We did so and looked down, feeling like the shepherds in the manger. On the ground were fox cubs with the vixen, a magnificent-looking animal, more like a large dog than the foxes you see in cartoons, and much fiercer too. And here was Pritchard, kneeling amongst them like an honoured guest.

"Pritchard," I said, "this is like something out of David Attenborough. Why are they not running off?"

From the look of the place, they had just eaten supper. There were bones and feathers everywhere. The smell was pretty strong: I was glad of the wind.

"Look at this little fellow," Pritchard spoke gently, putting a hand on one of the cubs. "He has an injured leg. I don't know how it happened, but I found him in the woods a few nights ago, dragging himself around. And then, by amazing luck I found the den. I've always been able to get animals to trust me, so I took him home in my haversack to clean up the leg. I think he had suffered from an attack, maybe a dog, I don't know. Then I brought him back and the mother didn't mind me. So then I brought stuff here to change the dressing. I think I can take it off now."

Pritchard's presence seemed to make it all right for us to be there. It was magical; these beautiful animals, wild and proud, seen only by the light of a small torch. It was all very natural and we felt privileged.

"Oh, oh," Pritchard whispered. "The leg's not fully clean yet. I need to take him home to do this properly. That's all right. I'll pop him in the sack and bring him back again when it's done."

There was merely a token growl from the vixen when Pritchard put the cub into his sack. The cub seemed very calm about it all.

"I know where we are," said Ronald. "There's a shortcut down that path. It's a bit overgrown so I'll go first."

"Overgrown" turned out to be "impenetrable". Ronald's optimism might have turned out to be ok by day, but in the dark of the night it was impossible to get along this path without a great deal of effort and the tearing of clothes.

"Not far now," cried Ronald, oblivious to his unpopularity. "Alf's place is just over there. We can get onto his driveway soon."

But the last few yards were the worst. Branches sprang back into our faces. Brambles captured our legs. Hollows awaited our tired feet and made us trip. It must have been one such hollow that accounted for Pritchard stumbling as he emerged from the thicket. I was already out of the worst and stood on the driveway, picking bits of thorn off my jacket. Pritchard however seemed to lose concentration and faltered and as the fall brought him to his knees, the little fox tumbled out of the haversack. It scurried across the driveway and out into an area of open grass.

Pritchard failed to see where the fox had gone and ran off the wrong way. Ronald was sharper and followed the cub. Pritchard ran towards a large garden shed. He had almost reached the near corner of it when two men burst out of the shed's side door and almost collided with him. Thirty feet away was a pick-up truck, which they made for.

They didn't reach it.

For suddenly, this quiet lane became crowded. Powerful car headlights picked out the two men and

Pritchard in their beam. A voice from behind the headlights ordered them to freeze and from a clump of tall bushes next to the pick-up, four policemen ran out. They gathered up the two men and Pritchard with admirable efficiency, and two police cars glided up to the group.

I ran towards the scene. I had worked out by now that the two men must have been responsible for the break-ins. The police had obviously followed and trapped them.

"He's not one of them," I shouted, pointing to Pritchard.

"What's he doing here then, and you for that matter?" demanded one of the policemen.

This would take some explaining, but Pritchard went straight for the truth. It sounded none too good.

"I was chasing a fox cub," he said simply.

"Not legal any more, Sir. They used to do that on horseback," said the policeman dryly. "Lots of 'em, with a pack of dogs in case the horses aren't sufficient, and trumpets going all the time. Always seemed one-sided to me. You on the other hand must be very courageous, Sir, taking on a fox cub all by yourself – and at night too."

"You don't understand," said Pritchard, exasperated by the heavy humour. "It has a bad leg."

"Ah," the policeman pounced. He hadn't had a straight man as good as Pritchard to feed him such lines for years. "That evens it up, I suppose. Frankly, Sir, you'll have to do better than that. Are you associated with these men?"

For mischief's sake, one of them grinned and called out, "Yea, too right, Chief. He's our getaway driver but once he smells a fox, there's no holding him back." They laughed.

Ronald came up. "Now then, Tommy Barr, what

have you caught in your net?"

"Evening, Ronald," the officer said. "Well, I think I've got a couple of thieves and someone who's escaped from the asylum. He's a big-game foxhunter, you know, but these blokes say he's one of them."

"Yea, too true, squire. He's an ex-Indy driver. You should see him go. It's just that he has this weakness for foxes," the two men teased.

"He's not a hunter," said Ronald. "He has a gift with wild animals." And he unzipped the top of his jacket to reveal the long snout of the cub. Pritchard gasped with relief and, taking the cub, popped him back into his satchel. Everyone was amazed.

"He's taken it to fix its leg." Ronald explained.

The police lost interest and concentrated on taking away the real felons. Alf strolled up and chatted with Tommy Barr."

"Thank you for your help, Sir," he called out as he left.

"What's the thanks for?" I asked Alf.

Alf looked up at the night sky. "Well, the story I put about wasn't quite correct," he said. "I actually do possess valuables in the house, some of which includes special night camera equipment. The first night I heard the intruders, I shimmied out and photographed them while they were spying out the land. Then I ran back and scared them off with the light, but I knew they'd return. I gave the photographs to a friend of mine in the Force and he set the thing up once they had identified them. It was a sting, I'm afraid."

"You're afraid?" said Pritchard. "That's what you told us the last time, but you seemed to be able to carry off all that action rather well."

"Oh, I just imagined I was one of my own characters and did what he would do," Alf said modestly. "Why is there a fox looking out from your

63

sack?"

"It's a long story," we said. "Let's get home and back into our coffins before dawn."

At least three versions of the story had reached Sigmund by the time I went up for the morning rolls, none of them remotely accurate. And Pritchard? He had already given some newspapers the brush-off.

Enigma Variations

It was a Monday evening. I don't normally trot off to the pub then, but I had just finished another weekend piece of work and justified it to myself on the grounds that I was due a treat. I've described myself as a sort of accountant. If not quite accurate, it's the best I can do. I have to make it simple for people like Brown to grasp. Anyway, the point is that it has little in the way of glamour or excitement, or indeed company, so after a heavy programme of work, I need to get out.

I was peeved to discover no one there. Peter the barman was in uncommunicative mood. Perhaps he couldn't be bothered putting on the friendly patter for just one customer – not very cost-efficient after all.

So there I was, standing at the bar, my glass my only companion, and wondering what was on television, when Horace stomped in. Body language is a wonderful thing: it communicates so easily. Horace was livid. He's an irascible old sod at the best of times but you should see him livid. He goes a strange, bloodless colour, his lips tight as if refusing food from his mother's spoon. I didn't dare speak. I bought a pint, put it in front of him and waited.

"I get more sense out of Hardy," he said angrily and sucked down at least three quarters of the pint.

Hardy is his dog, by the way, an affectionate animal. He appeals to Horace's softer side, which is admittedly like the dark side of the Moon – you assume it to be there, but rarely get to see it. Given the dog's tendency to slobber all over you, we all assumed its name was short for "Kiss me, Hardy."

I was trawling through a file in my mind to see if I could come up with anything less sensible than Hardy when the next eruption took place.

"They think they always know best. Never let anyone else have an opinion. It's what democracy's for, you know, to let the little man have his say alongside the big guns. Well, it's the last time I'm going to be made a fool of." And with that, he slammed down his empty pint pot on the counter and was gone.

It's difficult to remain entirely calm after standing next to a volcano, so I thought I'd have another beer before going home. I was just paying for it when Callum stormed in.

"Excuse me," he said. He is never impolite. He then grabbed the end of the counter, raised his head to the ceiling and went "OOOoooohhhgggggww".

Peter and I looked at each other, Peter twisting his nose to suggest maybe it was a full moon. Not knowing what the best remedy for werewolfery is, I asked Callum, "Would you like a drink?"

Peter pulled another pint and placed it warily in front of the trembling Callum.

"Sorry about that, old man," said Callum in a low breathless voice and drank his pint in one, without really noticing it. "I think I should go home before I say something improper."

"You don't have it in you to do that, Callum," I said.

Callum is in every way a gentleman; tall, distinguished-looking, with a moustache like a nineteen-twenties aristocrat who has seen active service in the Great War. He is everyone's picture of a soft-spoken, caring young man, forever cool in the face of danger and warm towards his friends. In fact, he is a farm labourer up at Bert Green's farm; there he needs every bit of his calm disposition because Bert is a genuinely evil piece of work.

"There's just no need to be so rude," Callum uttered, more to himself than to me. I looked around, searching for what had given offence. Peter squared off his mouth to say he didn't know either. Peter's expressions are priceless. He can tell you a barrel of beer is off, he is sorry and what would you like instead, all with a downward tug of the mouth, an inclination of the head and a widening of the eye. It's a useful art in a noisy bar. Visitors, watching his performance with a local who could be twenty paces away, have compared it to tic-tac men at Newmarket.

"It was your friend, Horace, who brought it all down to the level of the jungle, you know," Callum continued.

I sympathised. It was all too probable. If only I could have worked out what he was talking about but I didn't get the chance, because he turned to go. "Thanks for the drink, old man, but I must go home."

So what had Horace done, and where?

I didn't have long to wait for further information. Pritchard rolled in, looking almost happy, if you could ever imagine his drooping jaws to express happiness. The ends of Pritchard's mouth are weighed down with heavy, fleshy jowls. It must take a real effort to smile. However, by this time in the evening, I was learning my lesson. I waited to see what mood he was in.

"Evening, young sir," he said breezily. "I'll have a pint with you, thank you very much."

I was pleased to get a drink for anyone who wasn't going to shout at me.

"Why are you of all people so jovial tonight?" I asked.

"I have had a very entertaining evening," he replied, looking very comfortable with the world, "at a meeting of the Parish Council. I haven't been to one for some time, but from now on, it's in my diary, a fixture. All else will be de-prioritised."

"So what happened," I pressed him. "There's been a succession of very upset people in here. Are local taxes rising?"

Pritchard was silent, then said, "Well, I hadn't thought about that, but there may have to be a one-off tax to meet expenses. That wasn't discussed tonight, but you're well informed obviously."

By now I was getting annoyed. "I don't feel informed at all. Everyone's speaking in riddles."

"Right again," said Pritchard. "It's what I feel happens on these occasions. No one speaks the plain truth. They want to hide the implications of their proposals until they have support, and only then the downsides appear. How wise you are. Then there are others who cannot take part without blowing their tops. That never helps, you know. Take Horace."

"Yes?" I eagerly waited.

"Oh, yes, the trouble with Horace is that he has good ideas but can't express them."

"But how do you know he has good ideas if he doesn't express them?" I objected.

Pritchard looked bemused for a moment. "Good point," he conceded. "You're on the ball tonight. Have you had a day off, or something? Maybe Horace has fooled us into thinking he is smart, but in fact is not so. No, I believe he has a lot to contribute, but he gets flustered and raises his voice. That just rubs people up the wrong way. Even when he's saying something constructive, it comes out sounding like an insult or a challenge."

"What was it all about then?" I felt I was getting

closer.

"It was Digby's proposal that started it all off," Pritchard began. "He described his scheme to the Council and then the fireworks began."

"Oh," Pritchard suddenly said, looking past me at the door. "Must disappear." Finishing his drink, he quickly left.

I was astonished. I sniffed at his glass to see if something had been amiss, caught Peter looking at me curiously and was just putting the glass back on the counter when Digby himself came in. Looking at the empty glass in my hand, he said, "If you're buying, I'll have one. I sure need it." And went off to the toilet. "I've got a bone to pick with your mate, Pritchard." He called over his shoulder. "He can be very sarcastic."

I calculated how much cheaper the television would have been, even if I had drunk a bottle of champagne with it, when he came back. I've done business with Digby. He knows his mind.

"I heard you put the cat amongst the pigeons tonight," I said.

"You've got your ear to the ground, haven't you," he picked up his glass and went to join a party of six or seven people who had just come in.

A few more people, mostly young, were coming in for the last hour but I knew very few of them. I was still relatively new to the village myself. They grouped around Digby, who seemed to be terribly popular. Loud bursts of laughter and confident poses gave the solid impression that they were pretty pleased with themselves. Digby himself is convivial, full of bonhomie and loud laughter, but you get the impression that people are most at ease when he has just departed. Tonight, his popularity was strengthened by his performance and his proposal, whatever it had been.

An unexpected source of information arrived, Paula

Parkinson, whom I knew even before I came to live here and who is on the Council. Paula is level-headed and without malice of any sort and I looked to her to rid me of my ignorance.

"Yes, I'm well, thank you," she said to me. "Look, I'll have a gin and tonic and have what you like yourself." Things were looking up.

No they weren't. By the time Peter brought the drinks, we had been joined by two of Paula's lady friends, gins and tonics all round, and Peter, being a traditionalist, looked to me to pay.

"I think it will be good for the village," said one of the friends, tweed coat and soft leather gloves. "It'll put us on the map."

"I have my suspicions," said the other, heavy cloth trousers and scraped-back hair. "These things can get out of hand. Look at Woodstock."

"Woodstock," I thought. "A stately home is to be opened to the public?"

"It'll mean a great deal of organising, and advertising. I mean, one has to attract people from all over the country," said Paula, glowing with anticipation.

"Absolutely," said the gloves. "It could bring in a substantial one-off income, you know."

"I agree in principle," said the trousers, "but music is so deja vu these days."

"Nonsense," Paula argued. "Look at Glyndebourne."

"Glyndebourne is hardly a proper comparison," said the gloves in a sniffy sort of way. "Although I quite see your point. There is an audience if you can attract it."

"Glyndebourne," I mused, impressed. "Obviously Digby has something big – he has found a stately home nearby where an up-market musical evening can be held."

"I think three days will be a bit much," the trousers said. "Where will we put them all?"

"Well, in the fields, I suppose," said the gloves. "but many will, I'm sure, want something more comfortable. We're not all hippies now. More like hip replacements."

"What do you think?" Paula turned to me. "Would you be prepared to help out, with accommodation, perhaps?"

"Well." I hovered. I'm no good at thinking fast, and it was far too late to say to them I didn't know what they were talking about. "I suppose so," I stammered.

"Very good," cried Paula. "There, you see? The village always comes up trumps. It's that get-up-and-go quality which makes you proud to be part of a dynamic community."

I began to feel a warm glow myself. After all, it might be quite fun having guests coming to see the concert. I began to picture it. An internationally renowned orchestra, conducted by a big name, would put on a superb show of a warm summer evening, with the men strolling around in formal garb, the ladies charming in long dresses. The men would look bored and languid, passing cigars around with instruction books and setting fire to their spectacles. Why it needed three days I couldn't work out, but the trousers said they would probably have to be realistic the first year and be happy with one day.

Yes, it would be quite exciting, having the village known for an internationally recognised, cultural event. You might meet all sorts of interesting people; artists, politicians, men and women of the Church, writers, criminals, television personalities, all coming to be seen at our festival.

I was thinking that we could accommodate a few but I wouldn't know where to stock their picnic hampers. They would feel as if they were getting away from it all and letting their hair down a little, but not of course too much.

Paula was badgering me again. It's her greatest quality, apart from being level-headed. "How many could you take, a dozen?"

"A dozen," I replied, astonished. "I only have one spare room."

"Keep that for storing things. They'll camp on your lawn. It won't look any worse than usual."

"I don't understand," I said. "Why do need to have a dozen people camping on my lawn?" I let the insult to my lawn pass. I'm used to it.

"Have you never seen these rock concerts on TV?" said the trousers." They're happy to camp anywhere as long as it's near the music and a toilet. You might have to heat up a few baked beans as well. It'll be fun."

"A rock concert? Here? For three days?" Peter sculpted his features into a face which said. "I know. Can you imagine it? Still, you have to live with the times and it'll be good for business; it's only three days." He had known all along.

"Now don't be a fuddy-duddy," ordered Paula in her head-girl, sensible way. "You accountants are all the same. The world's not totally about figures, you know. You have to get out and enjoy yourself sometimes. Live a little. Too much work makes Jack a dull boy and all that sort of thing. I'll put you down for a dozen and oh, I'll include you in the waste recycling group too."

"Rubbish collectors," the gloves translated for me.

I rolled down the road back home. All was plain now. Horace is a jazz fan and hates rock music. He would have wanted a jazz festival, but would have got little support. Callum will get landed with lots of work and doesn't like disorder at all. Pritchard just loves to stir things up. Digby will make money out of it.

71

My wife Tess was just going to bed as I got in.

"I hope you relaxed," she said kindly. "I sometimes think you don't get out enough, take more part in things. You can't spend your whole life at a desk. You should offer your services more."

She trundled off, personal stereo in her right hand, cup of tea in the left, a book under one arm and hot water bottle under the other; all senses catered for.

Coward that I am, I didn't find the strength to tell her what I'd let us in for. She looked so content that I didn't want to disturb her.

Chapter Four

Power Games

A Poet or a Pirate

I was invited to play cards with the others at Pritchard's house. Over the winter they meet every Tuesday. His wife, Jenny, doesn't mind. She drives off to visit her mother over at Touselhead, another village a few miles up the road. I don't often see Jenny. I can go several weeks without seeing her. Pritchard gives that impression too. If I ask him how she is, he will stare vacantly for a time and reply, to his own surprise, that he doesn't really know.

Maybe he is more honest than the rest of us. I mean, if someone asks me how my wife is, I always say she is fine. I'm not absolutely certain but she hasn't mentioned anything being wrong with her and I don't want to give any impression whatsoever that she is anything other than first class, or else I'd have to name her malady. Rumour spreads so fast around here that by the time I arrived home, she would be suffering from some appalling new virus fresh out of Asia.

I can understand why Jenny might want to get a break once a week. It must be wearing living with Pritchard and his moods. He can be hopelessly uncommunicative, or utterly unstoppable, depending upon how he's feeling. You just have to accept it.

One Tuesday evening I strode over to his place, some beer comfortably under my arm. On that particular evening he was absolutely the genial host. It was Ronald who was irritable. Someone had made reference to his roundish shape. It wasn't just anyone. It was the attractive widow who lived just outside the village and whom Ronald had taken a shine to. To be told in no uncertain terms that he weighed in too heavily for her liking had dampened his spirits.

"You're looking at it the wrong way," said Horace, spreading the green cloth on the table. "If she didn't think anything of you she wouldn't even bother to comment, would she? Maybe she wants you to shape up. I mean, it proves she notices."

"Notice?" Pritchard interrupted. "She didn't have to go out of her way to "notice". Our little friend's roundness blocks out the light."

Brown was kindly. "Maybe a diet would impress her."

"Do you think that's the answer?" Ronald perked up. "I hear a lot of people go on diets these days."

"The trouble with diets," I commented, "is that when you stop, the weight just goes on again. You'll have to stop drinking, you know."

"And pies," Pritchard added.

By now we were seated. As there are five of us, one person has to sit out each round. Usually the game is peaceful, predictable and companionable. We have our stock of beer and nuts. Everyone gets good and relaxed.

Then the lights went out.

You are caught by surprise, wondering if your sight has suddenly failed; then you feel relief and annoyance that it is only a power cut. Someone stood up and knocked the drinks. Ronald looked for a cigarette that he had just lit and then dropped with fright.

"I can't see it," he grumbled from somewhere under the table.

"You'll see it fast enough if it gets onto that sofa," Horace warned. "Come on Pritchard. Where are the candles? We'll be locked in here and burned to cinders."

There was a lot of bumping around, because Pritchard was vague and sent us off on wild goose chases. The trouble was he couldn't remember which room he was in and gave a stream of entirely spurious directions.

Ronald, ever the practical one, sparked a match and took himself off to the kitchen to find some candles. Like a water-diviner, his twitching match soon found them. In a trice he was back and the room became a cave of flickering light and shadows.

"Let's get going again," he said.

"We can't play like this," Horace objected. "I can't see you cheating."

"I do not cheat," Ronald protested. "Bend the rules to accommodate my genius perhaps, but no cheating."

"What can we do then? There's all this beer. I don't want to go home yet," I said.

"Let's watch TV," Brown suggested.

"Power cut!" everyone else shouted.

"All right," Pritchard piped up, still acting the genial host, "let's play a game, an unusual game. Each one of us must say who or what he would have liked to have been in history, and why. My grandmother used to play it with us. She called it *A Poet or a Pirate*."

For some reason this captured our imaginations. Normally on principle we would carp at any suggestion but the flickering lights created an unusual ambience and we stirred with curiosity.

"You go first, Ronald," Pritchard urged. "You don't usually need time to think."

Ronald grunted. "You are so right. I'm a man of action. No dreamy poet stuff for me. I'll tell you what though. I have had one particular dream for years. It comes on when I've had too much Brown Ale."

He took a mouthful from his can of bitter. "I fancy

being a wealthy Mississippi gambler, you know, on one of those big riverboats. I'd wear a broad-brimmed hat and a small firearm. I'd have to learn how to play Mississippi though. It's probably no more difficult than the games we play."

I glanced at Brown's knitted brow. "The Mississippi," he said slowly and with devastating tone of voice, "is a river, not a card game, you ass. How can you want to be a Mississippi gambler and not know the meaning of "Mississippi?"

"I didn't know that," Ronald admitted humbly. "It takes the shine of it. I wonder what else I've got wrong. It's a shame. I've had that dream for years."

"No matter," said Pritchard, sensing that his game was in danger of being ditched. "What was it that appealed to you about being a Riverboat gambler? The women, I bet."

"Oh, yes," Ronald's eyes crinkled. "They'd be crowding round the table where I was playing, winking at me and egging me on. I'm dealt a fairly poor hand but a smile plays around my lips and then my whole face goes expressionless. That drives the women mad. My opponents don't know what to expect. They try to bluff their way through but one by one they drop out, leaving only one mean-looking guy who needs a shave and a lesson in manners."

"What happens?" asked Brown. "Do you have the same dream all the time?"

"Always," Ronald said. "When you have a good dream, why change it? Anyway, eventually there's a pile of coin and paper on the table, big enough to sink the boat, and my opponent calls me. I lay down three aces."

"You said you had a poor hand," Horace objected.

"Everything's relative," said Ronald. "My opponent goes wild. He slams down three aces too and accuses me of cheating. Well, I can't allow that, so I narrow my eyes and pretend to reach for my handkerchief to blow my nose."

"Is that why you narrow your eyes?" asked Brown.

"Germ warfare," Pritchard explained. "He'll aim a sneeze at him."

"But instead of my handkerchief," Ronald persisted, "I go for my small pistol and shoot straight through my pocket below the table, intending to hit his knee."

"Shoot first. Blow noses later. A good tactic," I said.

"Handkerchiefs at twenty paces," shouted Horace. "I'm gonna blow your head off."

Ronald ignored the noises off. "Instead of hitting his knee, I shoot the table leg. It breaks, dropping the table on my opponent's foot. The women cheer and beat him about the head with their parasols or whatever, and I scoop the lot and go."

"But how come you both had three aces?" asked Pritchard.

"I don't know," Ronald shrugged. "I guess one of us was cheating."

Pritchard was enthusiastic. "That was good, Ronald, very good. Now, who's next?"

"I'll go," said Brown. "It's a co-incidence that you should call the game, "Poet or Pirate" because I could well see myself as a poet or a painter in Italy at the time of the Medici."

"Why then? Why that particular period,"' I enquired. "I thought they had more than enough poets and artists. You couldn't move in the supermarket for them."

"Because it was dangerous," Brown replied with vigour. "You had to wear a sword to protect your honour."

"I was protecting my honour, Your Honour," Horace interjected. "That's all right then. Take one hundred lines –I must not pierce my patron for persistently poking puns at my opus."

"That's it, exactly, Horace. It was an age of intensity, of light, of discovery." Brown was unusually animated. In the candlelight he became quite different.

"What would you have done?" asked Pritchard. "Would you have added to the civilising process of man?"

"I would have painted portraits - and gone to the wars," Brown claimed.

"That's not very civilising," Ronald observed. "What's the point of being a poet or an artist if you still had to fight in the army? Couldn't you have claimed exemption, or poetic license?"

"Oh, no. I would have wanted to go to the wars, to be able to come back and paint passionately and credibly about life and love," Brown declared, looking around at us in the darkened room, his face aglow with the romanticism of it all.

"What if you got killed?" Horace asked. "If Rembrandt had been killed, the museums would have been short by a few paintings."

"And if Shakespeare had been killed, who would have been the father of English drama, keeping the theatres full of people listening to plays where they understood hardly a word?" I added. "You have a responsibility to stay alive."

Brown hadn't thought of that. You could see his expression change to one of bewilderment, then the spark of creativity set him alight again.

"I'd paint all the pictures," he said, "before I went off to the wars."

Howls of protest came from the listeners, sending the candles into a spin dive. You have to understand that, given the right atmosphere, a group of people can really get into someone else's dream. Horace was incensed that Brown should take such a calculated approach to his art. Ronald, on the other hand, was taken with the commercial aspect.

"If you were killed, so much the better," he said. "A dead painter is worth a dozen live ones."

Pritchard intervened. "That, by the way, is the origin of the phrase, a baker's dozen; wrongly attributed to the habit bakers had of slipping in an extra loaf to the customers most likely to complain. A Baker's Dozen actually refers to the first character to use the phrase, one Bassanio Baker in a play by Hamlet, who stated that one dead painter was worth a dozen live ones."

I entered the debate. "I am more of the view that it's from the play by Macbeth, The Builders' Merchant of Venice, where the main character complained bitterly about the day rates of painters and decorators."

"No," Horace contradicted me with confidence. "I feel we would find the true origin in that brilliant historian, Stanley Gibbons, whose most famous work featured stamp painting before printing entitled, "As You Lick It".

"That's not fair," Brown said. "You didn't make a fool of Ronald when he told you his dream."

"It didn't grab them as much, old boy," Ronald said. "You obviously have the true artist's temperament to inspire and be inspired."

Ronald's honeyed words did the trick. Brown grinned and asked, "Who's next?"

Horace didn't wait to be asked again. Anyway, I had no clue yet about what I was going to say. The wind outside was howling through chinks in Pritchard's doors and windows but there was nothing we could do except sit it out. I broke open another six-pack of beer and handed them around. Pritchard opened his can carelessly and extinguished the second last candle with a blast of beer-spray. That left only one candle in the middle of the table, throwing a pale light over our faces, but not beyond, like one of those dark Dutch paintings of people wearing black, Quaker-like suits, and staring vacantly at the painter as if he were the ten o' clock newsreader.

"I would have been a complete character: I would have been a Poet and a Pirate," Horace began.

"Sounds schizophrenic to me," Brown commented.

"I don't know of any pirates who were poets. I thought you had to be one thing or the other," Ronald complained.

"Well, Brown's story took us half way there," Horace explained. "He said he would have liked to have been a man of action and a painter. You have to be able to experience life to be able to create art. But you're wrong about pirates not being poets. Dick Turpin wrote The Highwayman, in York gaol as an anti-militarist poem," and he quoted,

"The road was a beam of torchlight, cutting the frosty air.
The moon an unlikely galleon, making the troopers go spare.
They wanted to catch Dick Turpin and throw him into gaol
for evading his Road Fund License and for robbing the Royal Mail."

"You have a point," I said. "There was that other famous pirate, Captain Hook, who wrote Peter Pan just to give himself the best part. And the instructions on where to find the gold are always in verse."

"Seventeen paces south of the tree,
one foot in the grave you there will be.
Eighteen steps taken due north,

you'll be up to your waist in the old pigs' trough."

"Thank you," Horace said, "and now that the precedent has been established without a doubt, I can tell you of an adventure I wrote myself into. Being a pirate gives one every opportunity to steal the glamour and to plunder without justification. If you can't, you're not a pirate. Being a pirate means you are obliged to do those things, otherwise you are struck off the list."

"Would that be like solicitors?" Pritchard offered. "You know, where a self-regulating body takes it upon itself to uphold the integrity of the profession and to debar misfits and backsliders?"

"Precisely," cried Horace. "You pay your subs once a year, you prove you have kept the bad name of piracy on the tabloids, and you are allowed to pass go and pick up two hundred."

"Now," he continued, "the bit I like is where we have sighted a Man o' War, a King's ship, and we bear down upon it like a wolf on the fold, crying havoc."

"A wolf wouldn't cry havoc," I objected.

"True," Horace admitted, "but it would howl a bit, just like that wind. Anyway, we would pursue the Royal Navy ship until nightfall when, amidst a storm, we would engage in battle. The cannon would pound, and there would be a dreadful noise, and in the midst of it all, I would scribble a few dramatic verses on the fo'c's'le."

"Wouldn't that be like fiddling while Rome burned?" Brown said. "I mean, it's not very responsible. What would your crew think?"

"They might not like the dramatic verse. They'd probably prefer me to do a few sea shanties so that they could sing them on Radio Three, wearing striped Breton jerseys bought from a mail order company. Now! Imagine the scene. There's water coming into our ship and the Man o' War's on fire. You can hardly breathe for the acrid smell of gunpowder."

"This is very good," Pritchard said, excited that the game had gone so well. "I can almost smell the smoke."

"So can I," Brown agreed. "It is very real. Is it the smoke from the candle?"

"No," shouted Ronald. "It's smoke from the settee. It must be my cigarette burning. Quick. Get some water."

"No," I said. "That's no good. You need a proper extinguisher to smother the fire. Pritchard, do you have a fire blanket? And open a window."

"Don't," Brown yelled. "That will just fan the flames. I can't see any fire."

"It'll be smouldering," Horace screamed. "When you see it, it'll be too late. For God's sake, this isn't a debating society. We need some light."

He got up. At least I think he got up, and stumbled into someone else who had also got up. Between them they rocked the table and the only remaining candle, which was almost finished anyway, went out. Panic reigned. In the dark, none of us could remember where the door was. We were all shouting by this time.

The lights went on.

In the doorway, her hand on the light switch, stood Jenny, Pritchard's wife. The room was a disaster area, beer cans spilling their contents, crisps trodden into the carpet. Jenny's face said everything.

Pritchard attempted explanations. "We were just killing time during the powercut by telling stories. And the settee's on fire."

There was no sign whatsoever of smouldering. We looked sheepishly at one another.

"The powercut ended ages ago," Jenny informed us. "You should have kept the switch on, then you'd know.

Honestly, have you lot got no imagination?"

The Domino Effect

I was in the local shop the other day. The local shop is the only shop. It serves as a Post-Office, news nerve centre, book and DVD library, off-license and informal crèche.

It was looking more like the latter when I went in to get some sherry. There must have been six or seven kids, either through the back or in the yard, or in front beside the telephone kiosk.

"You have to keep up with the times," said Sigmund. "Mothers need to do a bit of extra work for their own satisfaction and to earn that little bit extra."

"Which they spend in here," I cracked.

"Well, there is that," Sigmund had the honesty to admit, "but the kids are no bother. When there are a few of them, they look after themselves."

"It could get a little out of hand. It's supposed to be a shop you know," I said, a little more testily than was called for.

"What's bothering you then?" Sigmund asked kindly.

I wasn't going to be lured into one of Sigmund's counselling sessions. For one thing, he conducts them while still running the shop, so there's always too much of an audience for my taste. It works for some people however. They say a visit to the shop's as good as a session on the psychiatrist's couch.

"You look a bit worried, that's all," Sigmund persisted.

He's very good actually. There is something about his thin features, with a comfortable grandfather's beard, that gives you enough confidence to let it all out. He says that most people don't mind other customers hearing. We're all supposed to look after each other anyway, so why make everything a secret. Our little problems are not wicked or sinful, they're just some of the normal problems in life that need someone to listen. That's all.

"And I don't want you coming for more sherry before the week's out," he scolded gently, returning my change with the bottle.

I smiled without looking at him. I wasn't used to a shop-keeper telling me not to buy something and was at the same time comforted by his concern. It seemed, like Sigmund altogether, of another age.

As the bell tinkled its little "see you again", I was reminded of an incident last weekend, when I had heard Ronald pour his heart out to Sigmund about his longing for the lady who lives on the outskirts of the village. She's a widow, probably just turned fifty, who was hiring Ronald to do some repairs to her cottage. Ronald is completely gone on her. He prolonged the work interminably and actually did a fair job, for Ronald that is. He took several days to repair a fence and a few more to decorate the kitchen. The lady in question didn't mind how long the fence took but preferred him out of the kitchen, so she asked him to work next on the old greenhouse, which allowed Ronald miraculously to be out of the kitchen within the hour.

"I don't know what it is," he told Sigmund, "but I've never really found anyone I could share my life with. I suppose I have become selfish and rough, not someone a woman would warm to. And now, when I'm getting on in life – I am sixty-one after all – I'm smitten, I tell you, with this woman. I don't know what to do."

"Didn't you see her around the village before? She's been here for years," Sigmund asked.

"That's the strange thing. There can't be more than

fifteen hundred people around here and yet I don't recall hearing about her before now." Ronald shook his head.

"What do you mean, you're smitten?" I asked Ronald.

"Love, Dear," said a woman, picking a tin of sweet corn off the shelf. "It's very romantic. I never thought Ronald had it in him. Batchelor for life, us women all thought. Mind you," she said, whispering so that Ronald could not hear, "not that any of us were complaining. I mean, he's not much to look at."

No one would deny it. Ronald has a battered, punch-drunk face, rough-red and full of character, and his shape is round in the middle, where he has processed too many pints and pastries. Being an odd-job man brings with it the occupational hazard of excessive cups of tea and scones from grateful householders.

But Ronald is lovable and kind, with a quick sense of humour and I would have thought that people would see through his rough exterior to the equally rough man within.

I happened to know of the lady he was talking of. She's well-off and quite beautiful. Her husband died about two years ago and she has always kept herself to herself, except to attend fetes or school events to raise money. She asked me to do a piece of work and so I know her, but only a little. She is always very polite to me, if a little formal.

Her house is large, too large for her, although she keeps her extensive garden in impeccable order, measured to the inch, the cabbages growing to supermarket standards. Her husband travelled extensively on business and eventually it killed him off with a heart attack in his mid-fifties. What bad luck, with all that to look forward to in retirement.

In short, she's the kind of woman who would hardly

notice Ronald, never mind seek his company.

"She played chess with me the other day," Ronald told Sigmund.

I was astonished. "You don't play chess."

"I know," Ronald said ruefully. "I didn't like to refuse, but of course she could see within a few moves that I was useless. She just put the board away and told me to get on with my work."

"So she asked you?" Sigmund clarified.

"Oh yes. We were getting on famously."

I could just imagine the scene; poor Ronald, out of his depth and feeling rotten. "You should play on your home ground," I said.

Ronald gave me a look. "What? Invite her round to tea?"

"No, no," I cried. Ronald may mend other people's houses, but his own is beyond repair. He wouldn't have been able to find the table under all the magazines, junk, "antiques" and tools. "What I meant was, play her at Backgammon. You're good at that."

"I never thought of that. I don't seem to think straight when she looks at me."

"Isn't he an old softie?" the woman said, putting an arm round Ronald. "You'll get over it."

"I could learn chess from Horace," Ronald tried.

"No," Sigmund said, tidying up his counter. "That would take too long and if Horace finds out about this lady, he'll be round there like a shot. Then you'd have competition."

"That I doubted. I thought Sigmund was just joking with Ronald. Anyway, Horace can sometimes be cool towards his wife, Belinda, but he knows which side his bread is buttered. Belinda is a warm, welcoming woman and very much keeps their act together, despite Horace's irritable moods. She balances his miserly ways with open-handed generosity, which accounts for why lots of kids play in the lane near her house. When they are hungry, they look in for a treat.

I was coming around the corner of the shop to go home, when Brown rolled up in his rather large, gleaming car. I can never remember all the models of cars he has told me he has had, but this one was a sizable BMW. The passenger window descended silently.

"You're not on your way home, are you?" he called from within.

"I was. Why?"

"I have a problem. Let's have lunch in the pub."

I had the drinks set up by the time he parked his car.

"Thanks, old man," he said. "Much obliged that you had the time."

"What's the problem?" I asked.

"Let's sit over here," he said furtively. "I don't want a soul to know."

"Don't go near Sigmund's then. Too much publicity."

"Publicity is what I have been instructed to get," he said gloomily. "My boss wants me to do a talk to the staff."

"Well that's all right then. You're ok. You know what to say presumably."

"You don't understand," he interrupted. "The company is going through a rough patch and the workers have become downhearted. Because of that, the goods and service are not up to quality and sales are down. My colleagues want me to do one of those up-and-at-'em speeches, fire and brimstone, to enthuse them for the fight, so to speak. I've to go on video and it'll be seen round the whole company."

I saw the problem now. Brown is mostly quite dim, bless him, but his impressive chairman's voice and the odd intelligent thing he says has somehow allowed him to rise in his career. None of us can understand it, but obviously he has got something. What he has most definitely not got is star quality. He abhors too much attention, so the thought of a widely circulated video would appal him.

Ronald came in as Brown was telling his tale. "We should rehearse you," he said simply.

I was less optimistic. Asking Brown to be inspiring on video was about as realistic as getting Obama to tone down a rally. It was just too much a stretch of the imagination. Ronald was much more supportive. Ever since Brown's divorce some years back, I am told that Ronald has been an encouragement to Brown, much more indeed than Horace or Pritchard, who assumed Brown would carry on unchanged, without his wife and three children. Somehow, it was Ronald who grasped what Brown was going through. Brown told me his marriage came apart not long after coming to the village from a very beautiful suburb. His wife didn't take to the new life.

Horace and his dog now arrived, so we had to repeat the problem for his benefit. He was instantly helpful.

"They do evening classes in public speaking at the place I teach chess," he announced.

"Yes, but I can do that. I've done lots of sales pitches. This is different," Brown said.

"No, I understand," said Horace. "I sat in the class once. They teach you how to speak to different audiences."

"But I've got to be inspiring and act the part, you see," Brown whined.

"I think Ronald had the right idea. We'll rehearse you," I said, more firmly than I was wont.

"Now," Ronald addressed Brown, "On another matter, I need you to do something."

Horace and I broke off to talk with someone who

wanted us to take part in some money-raising event for the Church, a guess-the-weight-of-the-vicar competition being the highlight. The Vicar was, like Ronald, a little portly or to be more accurate, a little, portly man whose littleness exaggerated his roundness and vice-versa. His lack of inches brought about another problem. He couldn't easily be seen when he stood in the pulpit. He scorned to use a box or something to stand on. Some of the smaller primary schoolchildren thought they had actually experienced God talking to them because they couldn't see the man behind the voice. It probably had them converted for life, an impressionable moment in their little lives. Shortly after, he gave up the pulpit and spoke from the floor.

The Vicar had set himself a target to lose weight. The question was: what would his weight be on the day of the event?

We agreed to meet in the Village Hall kitchen in the evening to put Brown through his paces. It was reasonably private, apart from the indoor bowls going on next to us in the main hall. The kitchen was warm, if rather cluttered. We put the table to one side, where Brown was to sit as if for the video camera and we stood around, ready to give advice.

"Did you manage to do my little errand?" Ronald asked Brown.

"Ah yes, in a manner of speaking," Brown replied, a little defensively. "I did go over to see her."

Brown had to explain for the rest of us. Ronald had asked him to visit the widowed lady, object of Ronald's devotion, using the fact that Brown had known her husband slightly, as he had now and again been involved with Brown's company. It was a trivial excuse to permit Brown to call upon her but once he got in, he was to turn the conversation to Ronald, saying what a good chap he was, a true and loyal friend, and how useful too. The exercise was cooked up to persuade her to look more favourably upon Ronald.

"Come on then," Ronald chivvied. "Did it work, do you think?"

"Oh, I'm sure it did, sort of… well, it ended rather unexpectedly, actually," Brown faltered.

"What do you mean?" asked Ronald. "You've a guilty look about you."

"That's because I feel guilty. You see, she did listen and then we talked more and she invited me to stay for supper and then she asked me to drive her on Friday evening over to the Women's Institute Dinner in Sprighassle."

"Just drive?" I enquired innocently.

"Not precisely. She invited me to be her dinner guest, actually."

"Oh, actually," Ronald mimicked. "So you went in there to soften her up for me and you end up walking off with her. Some mate you are."

"I couldn't help it," Brown insisted but not convincingly. "She gave me a very good supper."

"Well I wouldn't know about that, would I?" Ronald retorted.

"Look, there's a very easy way out," said Horace. "Friday is tomorrow. Brown, you telephone her to say you are not very well. Your torture wounds are opening up again, the ones you got whilst spying in dangerous Iron Curtain countries before Glasnost, where you wouldn't even reveal what you wanted for breakfast, or whether you were a card-carrying David Bowie fan in your twenties. And even when they forced you to watch endless Dixon of Dock Green programmes with only a bare electric light for company, you kept quiet about the camera in your mouth so that every time you opened your mouth to scream, you took an incriminating photograph of your torturers."

"Get on with it. I want a drink soon," I said.

"Ok," said Horace, "Sorry about the deviation, hesitation, repetition and the use of words in the title…."

"GET ON WITH IT," we shouted.

"You then say that your good friend Ronald can drive your car and she shall go to the Ball after all."

"Not bad," I conceded. Ronald cheered up. Brown looked as if he really wanted to go, but I knitted my brows at him and he relented.

"Let's get on with coaching Brown now that Ronald's problem is settled. Have you prepared a script?" I asked Brown.

"Yes," he said. "Shall I run through it?"

He began, "Ladies and Gentlemen,"

"Wait a minute," Horace interrupted. "You're talking to a video. You never hear news presenters or chat show hosts saying, *Ladies and Gentlemen*. It's too formal. Just say hi."

"Hi?" said Brown. "I'm not an American sports commentator."

"No," Ronald gave support to Horace's point, "but you have to try to let them warm to you. The beginning is very important, and smile."

"All right," Brown sighed, and he worked his way painfully through his five minutes of why the company wasn't going well and what they had to do to pull together or they might fail. He wasn't talking about a burning platform, not at all as bad as that, but complacency is the enemy of keeping focused, etc. etc.

"Phew," said Horace. "Pritchard would like that sort of stuff: miserable, with a touch of self-pity thrown in as a concession to the age we live in."

"The message has to be given. It's a tough one but people have got to hear it. I'm not congratulating them. These are the facts of life for us at the moment," Brown explained.

"I've got it," said Ronald, a twinkle in his eye. I should have been suspicious. When he gets that twinkle it usually means he is going to do something daft soon.

"I watched a programme about politicians and the way they present themselves to the public. It was all about the words they used, "power words" they called them, and the way they use their facial gestures and body language to emphasise what they say."

"Give us an example," I asked.

"Well," Ronald explained. "When you first look at the camera, you incline your head a little, like this. It's supposed to show friendliness and reduces the hostile stare into the camera."

"Ok," said Brown. "I can handle that. How's this?" And he angled his head.

Ronald cried, "Good. Now use your hands more. You'll have them clasped on the desk, probably. Well, open them out, like this. Do it now and again to show openness and reasonableness."

Brown again did as he was bid and I have to admit, it all looked much better.

"What else have you got?" Horace asked Ronald.

Ronald was terribly excited now that he had lifted Brown's performance. He got to his feet.

"I'm not sure you'll be able to use this, Brown, but they showed how great public speakers emphasise their words by using their hands to make grand gestures. When you're sitting, there's no space, but they showed speakers jabbing the air with their fingers to punch home the points."

"Yes, I can do that," Brown cried, experimenting more violently than probably was necessary, and becoming quite excited too.

"Look," Ronald shouted, working himself up to a fever pitch. "Great speakers use all the space around them to make grand gestures and use their fully outstretched arms to punctuate their messages. Then they finish with a triumphant salute."

With that, he shot his clenched fist up into the air, shouted "Up the workers," and punched his way through the kitchen fluorescent strip light.

Not only did the lights go out in the kitchen, where we were situated, but also a groan from the bowls game in the hall suggested that Ronald had put the whole place in darkness.

"It's all right," he shouted. "I know where the fuse box is. I'll have the lights back on in a second."

He dashed out into the hall, howled immediately in surprise and pain and toppled onto the floor. I couldn't see him but I could hear him. We groped our way to where he was.

As we got to him, the lights came on again.

"A bowl hit me," He explained between gasps of pain. "Right on the ankle. Brought me down like a racehorse."

"Warhorse," Brown suggested. "Brought down by a cannonball in the thick of battle."

"Let's get him out of the line of fire and have a look at the damage," I said.

Just then the thrower of the bowl appeared. It was, of all people, the beautiful widow, apologising for only just realising what had happened. The lights had gone off just as she bowled, so the bowl must have been travelling when Ronald charged into its path. We assured her Ronald was ok and sent her back to her game. She looked doubtful, especially as Ronald was bleeding from cuts sustained from the light but eventually she left us.

Ronald was however in some discomfort, having twisted something in his ankle in the fall. We decided to get him to A&E. Brown's car was sitting conveniently at the side entrance so we covered Ronald's cuts and hoisted him into the car. Brown got in and turned the ignition. Nothing happened. He tried again but the only sound was of Ronald groaning.

We lifted the bonnet and looked into the engine compartment but none of us knew what to do. Ironically, the only one with some knowledge was sitting helpless in the car. "You're not getting power from the battery to turn over the engine," he shouted. "It's probably just a loose connection on the battery terminals."

"What do they look like?" we asked.

"My God," he groaned. "You lot wouldn't know a battery terminal from a battery hen."

"I have sympathy with battery hens," said a softer voice out of the dark. "What's the problem?" It was the widow. "I thought you were worse than you were making out," she said to Ronald. "I'll give you a lift in my car."

With that she disappeared, to return in a moment, driving a rather sporty, small hatchback.

"Lift him in," she commanded. "And don't bleed on the upholstery. It gives other passengers a bad impression."

Ronald was helped in. He put on his safety belt. We suggested we should come and help at the other end.

"There won't be any need for that," she said. "What do you think is the matter with this car, Ronald?"

Ronald repeated his diagnosis. She got a small leather bag from her glove compartment which, instead of having make-up in it as we expected, actually had a set of spanners. Ducking under the bonnet, she took a small torch and looked at the battery.

"When did you last clean in here?" she demanded and fiddled about for a couple of minutes. "I think you were right, Ronald. That should do it."

Brown tried the ignition again and the car purred into life.

"Right," she said briskly. "We're off. We'll soon have you patched up, Ronald." And then, as she climbed into her hatch, she called out to Brown, "I hope the inside of your car is cleaner than under the bonnet. I'd like to get to the dinner in pristine condition if it's all the same to you."

She drove off without further delay.

"I see why you couldn't refuse her invitation," said Horace. "If you're ill call me, not Ronald."

"Games night at the Village Hall," I reflected as I wandered home. "One bowled out, and the other two feeling the domino effect."

Chapter Five

Reality and Illusion

A Bike for Brown

Wednesday evening, and we were gathered at Brown's place to watch football on television. I'd much rather go round to Horace and Belinda because it's more homely. It's much more like in that film, "The Odd Couple", where all the guys fetch up at Walter Matthau's place and they can make a mess and drink beer out of their cans and spill cashews on the floor. We wouldn't actually do that of course, but Belinda does somehow make the place comfortable and nice without making you feel you have to be on your best behaviour.

Brown's house is lovely, all thick carpets swept by some invisible hand while he is out at work and curtains so heavy you feel you could swing on them. But it's, it's, well, not – it's – hard to explain really, but it's for having dinner guests and formal occasions, not for watching football with your mates.

The television is one of these flat things, sits into the wall and is as large as a cinema screen. No complaints on that score. And sofas? You could have one each to sprawl on. Yes, all creature comforts are there, but it's too much like a furniture showroom for you to be relaxed.

However, I think it gives Brown some pleasure to have us all round. At least that's what I tell myself as I sup his expensive German beer.

So there we were, sitting expectantly, Pritchard,

Horace, Ronald, Brown and myself – all grasping our beers, the peanuts reposing in pretty dishes on the nest of tables and all sounds muffled by the soft furnishings. It's always a problem for everyone to get here on time but here we all were. The television wasn't switched on yet.

"How do we organise a picture then, Browny?" Horace asked. "Wind it up?"

Brown looked puzzled. "Oh, yes," he exclaimed. "The control, the remote control."

We all looked round for the object.

"I keep it on top of the television," Brown remembered.

"I can see why it's called *remote,*" said Ronald, getting out of his couch, with not a little difficulty as the couch showed reluctance to give him up. He returned with the control and pressed it but nothing happened.

"Your battery's run out," he said.

"Oh," Brown was downcast. "I hardly use it. Does it need a battery?"

"No matter," said Horace, losing his calm a little. "Let's be really old-fashioned and switch it on at the set. The previews will be on. We're missing them."

"You can't," said Brown. "There are no switches on the set. You have to use the remote."

This news was met with cries of dismay, Pritchard especially baying his disappointment. Ronald however, beer in hand, just went up to the set, pressed some invisible panel, and a small flap came down, exposing a set of controls. The television came on. Cheers from the gang. Ronald bowed and spilled his beer on the carpet: groans from the same gang.

But it wasn't long before the evening was seriously threatened. After five minutes or so, a transmission fault stopped the programme altogether.

"Is it just Browny's set?" Pritchard asked. "Let's go to your place, Horace."

"No," Ronald said. "It's general. Let's hope they fix it quickly."

"So how come you never watch this beautiful TV?" Horace asked Brown.

"I guess I'm not here that much these days. Since Yvonne left me, I find I've been kept busy at work, or I'm out at business dinners, that sort of thing."

"I don't like to mention it," Ronald looked with concern at Brown. "But I believe you're putting on some weight. Am I right?" He appealed to the rest of us.

Brown chuckled. "I believe I am."

"Then why are you so pleased with yourself?" Ronald demanded. "It seems to me you want serious exercise."

"I'm smiling," Brown admitted, "because when I was much younger, there was a spell when I was quite tubby and it led to an interesting little episode. Shall I entertain you with it while we wait for the programme to restart?"

Well, there was nothing for it but to settle down to listen. Pritchard fetched more German froth from the kitchen and turned the lights down so that if anyone wanted to doze, they could. We hoped the programme would return soon.

"I must have been in my twenties," Brown began, "a long time before I came to this part of the world. I wasn't married, but it was when I gave up regular sport and started regular pub-going. I put on weight but because I'm quite tall I got away with it for a time. I could carry it; in fact I quite liked it. It gave me a feeling of prosperity and importance. That's always turned me on. But before long, friends ribbed me about it, and you know I'm sensitive to that sort of thing."

We said not a word. Our genuine impression was that Brown is impervious to any form of ridicule, kindly or otherwise. Funny how people see themselves.

"As you also know, I don't like being talked about," he recommenced, causing us to raise our eyebrows again. Horace actually checked with Brown who he was talking about.

"But in the pub they would start on me, only because they didn't have much else to talk about. Must have been the silly season. They speculated about what was causing it. Not just overeating of course. They produced outlandish reasons or diseases, malfunctions of the body, and then they imagined what I'd be like in a few years. It was frightening. They had me up to twenty-five stones with my eyelids so fat I would hardly see through the slits in my eyes.

"Not so good for pulling the women," Ronald observed.

"I didn't mind that so much, but you can imagine the expense of new clothes all the time," Brown continued. "Then someone came up with a suggestion."

"Stop eating?" I tried, just to prove I was listening.

"Stop drinking," said the puritanical Pritchard.

"Stop worrying about it?" Ronald offered.

"No," said Brown. "Exercise. But we couldn't think what form of exercise was best. I couldn't start rugby again and I didn't know how to play any other energetic game. Then one lad suggested cycling. It's convenient, you do in when you can and you don't need a team. Another bloke said he knew where there might be a bike for sale. He'd noticed a woman who lived out in the country arrive at the village shop in a car. She had always cycled before, so maybe the bike was available.

"I was motivated by the appalling future I might face if I didn't solve the weight problem, so I decided to try this course of action. I found out where the lady lived. Jack at the village store knew. He was very different to our Sigmund. You only went to Jack's store because you had to. He seemed to take offence just because you entered his store. He would abuse people, especially those who asked for something he didn't stock. He did everything he could to have a quiet life, but as his was the only trading post around, he still did good business.

So I drove the little banger I owned in those days, certainly something pre-upholstery, out into the country, about three miles from the village, to a smallholding. I knew nothing of the lady except that she might have a bike for sale and even that was a flimsy piece of evidence. I suppose by the time I got there, I was feeling a chump for even having started out, but I couldn't go back and admit that I had chickened out, so on I went with the mission.

Her place was quite neat, the yard was tidy and deserted. I could hear animals out the back but no sign of human life.

I knocked at the door. I could hear some form of noise from within but nothing I could identify. I knocked again and again. This time the music stopped and after a time, a woman's voice shouted, "You'll have to open the door," with the emphasis on *You*. I didn't know at first if this was a challenge to a suspected robber, a stubborn and plucky defence along the lines of the three little pigs and the wolf but I did as bidden. Behind the door, in the half- light of a small hallway, stood a woman with mud up to her elbows, and indeed anywhere else you cared to look."

"Pottery," she explained, noticing my problem with the mud. "Just throwing a few pots."

I was about to say that I hadn't heard any breakage when it dawned on my slow wit what she was meaning.

"You make pots and things?" I said to her.

"You don't miss a trick," she replied with a wink. "Although you may have thought I had been playing with the pigs. What can I do for you? A few nice, hand-painted bowls perhaps?"

"Not at the moment," I answered. "I know it may be an unusual question but do you have a bike for sale?"

"No," she pondered. "A bike is quite difficult, with all the spokes and all. I couldn't do a bike in clay. I have seen carriages and old stagecoaches but with those, you are trying to give the impression of wooden wheels, not the close, steel spokes of a bike. What about a nice pair of plates instead? I do a lovely bit of painting around the edge and you can choose from four patterns."

I stopped the sales pitch. "A real bike," I said, "not a pottery bike. Someone in the village saw you driving a car the other day and thought you might not be using your old bike any more. Maybe we've made two and two equal five."

She changed demeanour. "I see. One doesn't realise one is being observed so closely. No, I wouldn't want to sell it. We may have petrol rationing again. Besides it's not very safe."

"What's wrong with it?"

"Well, it only has two wheels and you could fall off. Anyway, you have a car."

"I need exercise," I pleaded.

"I can see that!" she laughed. "You are just like my dead husband. He was too fat."

"Is that what killed him?"

"In a way. He went into hospital for a hearing test, misheard them at the desk, got mixed up with another fat person, was sent for an operation intended for the other person, and died from an anaesthetic mishap."

"That's terrible," I cried. "What happened to the

other fat person?"

"I suspect he passed the hearing test. So I don't think you want the bike."

"Look," I said to her, at last getting onto her zany wavelength, "from what you yourself have told me, I need the bike more than most. I wouldn't want to be in an identity mix-up. You wouldn't want that on your conscience, would you?"

She relented. "It would be a dreadful responsibility, and all for the lack of a couple of wheels. All right. Five pounds and it's yours. That's what it cost me, twenty-three years ago. I'll show you."

We went through the hall and out into the back. She washed her hands at an outside tap and then unlocked an out-house to reveal a stack of old machinery, including the bike. It was old and filthy and looked past its best, but I had tried so hard to convince her to sell it to me that I had to have it.

"Is it mechanically sound?" I checked.

"Caveat emptor," she quoted. "What you see is what you get. I make no promises, but I'm pretty good with mechanical things. I've kept it working all on me own."

I believed her. She was unusual, independent, and a character. I took the bike.

"To cut a long story short...." Brown proceeded.

"Good idea," Horace muttered.

"Can we try the football again?" Ronald sighed.

"To cut a long story short," Brown persevered, "the bike rode smoothly for a couple of days, then broke down. To my utter discomfort, it broke down right in front of the pub."

"Seems ok to me," I said.

"Seems symbolic, I would have thought," said Pritchard.

"No! No!" Brown cried. "It was awful, because they all came to the window and laughed and then I had to look as if I knew what I was doing to fix the bike. Some of them implied I hadn't a clue, which was entirely the truth, but you know how things are, you don't want people to know it. So I just said something about not having my toolbag with me, shouldered the bike and staggered home."

"But you still don't know anything about bikes. How did you get away with that one?" Ronald interrupted.

"Not easily," Brown admitted. "I couldn't think of anyone who could fix it for me, anyone, that is, that I could trust to keep it to themselves. So I had a go myself. Everyone says at some time, *it's as easy as riding a bike*, but I now know why no one ever says, *it's as easy as mending a bike.* The fault seemed to be somewhere around the rear hub, where there are all those sprockets and things. I would manage to get the chain round the sprocket at the back, but when that happened the chain wouldn't go round the other wheel, you know in between the pedals."

"How you can run a business I'll never know," Pritchard sighed.

"Well, this bike was obstinate. It was not co-operating," Brown enlarged, "because even when I did get the chain on the front sprockets, it wouldn't stay on the back ones. There seemed to be a superfluous link in the chain. The more I tried, the more trouble I got myself into. It was Saturday and I was getting desperate. The folks down at the pub would expect results by tomorrow. Then I got the idea. Take the bike back to the lady. See if she'll help.

I had to do it when it was darker, so it was after nine o' clock when I lashed this bike onto the back of the car and made off for her smallholding. When I got there, I ran out of courage. I knew it was possible that she might not take kindly to my turning up in the dark.

Young man arrives at the door of an old widow and demands his bike be fixed. It wouldn't look good.

However, there are many forms of cowardice, and the sort which makes you afraid of looking foolish in front of your mates is infinitely stronger than the one which makes you preposterous to a stranger. I knocked at the door.

The kind of welcome she gave me was totally surprising. As soon as she opened the door and had seen who it was, she clasped her hands, looked to heaven and said that her prayers had been answered. Certainly she had not yet seen the bike, so maybe in the dark she was confusing me with someone else. I had even more second thoughts about going through with this.

Then she insisted I come in and when she saw the bike, I thought she was going to suffer a stroke."

"I knew you'd come back," she exclaimed.

"I almost said that if she went about selling bikes that were obsolete in two days, she'd be damn right I'd be back.

"I knew I shouldn't have taken advantage of an innocent young man," she cried. "It was too bad of me."

"I was confused by now. Was she freely admitting that the bike was faulty?"

"I'd better take the bike back – it was far too expensive. I'll get your five pounds."

"Oh, no," I protested. "I was hoping that you would repair it for me."

"I'll take the bike and you can find a much better one," she said, nodding solicitously.

"It was a swizz. It's on my conscience. The bike was not worth five pounds."

"Look," I said, trying to stem the flow of this cross-talk. "You don't understand." I then explained how I needed exactly the same bike tomorrow. She listened better than I expected.

"Well, young man," she looked across at me with a thoughtful expression. "I'll tell you my side of the story. When I sold you the bike, I didn't know what I was doing. I didn't want to sell it and I'll show you why. I think you'll be more than mildly interested. Follow me."

"She led me through the back of the house. Taking a large torch, she stepped out into the yard and along to a well-maintained building. She unlocked the door and shone the torch inside. My bike was standing in there. I got a shock, I can tell you, alone in the dark with a woman who could remove my bike by some form of magic."

"Exactly," she whispered. "A double. My husband and I bought two bikes, exactly the same, on exactly the same day, just for the thrill of it, years ago. I put it in here when he died, but I kept it in working order. The fact is, though, that I am not really sure which is which and I'd hate to have sold you my husband's bike. Sentimental reasons and all that."

"I get the picture."

"Tell you what we could do," she went on. "I'll do a deal with you. If you let me have your bike back, for keeps, and if I give you your money back, I'll let you borrow this one to show your friends that you're a sound engineer. Then you can bring it back here and afterwards, go and buy another bike. Meanwhile, I will repair the one you have brought back and I'll have my matching pair again. How's that?"

"I had to give it to her. That lady was eccentric, but sharp. We shook hands on it, then I took the good bike home with me. Fortunately, I got the bike into my house unobserved, or so I thought at the time.

The next day, I will remind you, was a Sunday. I

positively looked forward to lunchtime when I could cycle round to the pub and do some serious gloating. One-upmanship is something to be savoured. That's the whole point of it.

One o'clock came. I knew the crowd would be there by now so I went to the shed to collect the bike. When I saw it I nearly collapsed. Of course I did not see it properly in the dark on the previous evening. Firstly, it was not quite the same colour. This bike was more of a green than a blue. Maybe I'd get away with that, but the major problem was that this was a woman's bike. I must have been so keen to make off with it that I hadn't noticed, and how could she not tell the difference between the two bikes?

There was nothing to be done but to brazen it out, but suddenly the prospect was filled with risk and anxiety. Most people down the pub hadn't seen my bike properly anyway, so maybe I'd get away with it.

As I rode up, they were all outside. It was quite a warm day.

"Ay, ay," cried one. "Browny's back with his boneshaker. I'll bet it's held together with string. Let's have a look."

They crowded round.

"Fix it yourself?" said one. "Never would have thought it. Good for you. I've got one wants sorting out."

I sensibly kept quiet and didn't let myself in for any more trouble. They began to drift away. The chap who originally gave me the idea spotted it was a ladies bike and asked what I was doing with one of those. I reminded him it was a lady I bought it from.

"That's not just an ordinary ladies' bike," an older member of the group said, looking very curiously at the bike. "It's an early type of folding bike, before they became popular in cities. "I have heard they made matching pairs for couples. Could be worth a bit of money if you had the other in the set."

"Hallo, Browny," called a bloke from another group of people standing across the path. "Saw you out last night unloading your bike from the back of the car. Take it out for a drive, do you? Better than riding it I suppose, but you won't get rid of the spare tyre."

They all laughed. I didn't mind: I was getting off lightly.

I took it back. I didn't say anything about it not being the same but I mentioned the difference in colour.

"Are they?" she said. "Well, I wouldn't know. My eyes are none too good on colours. I suspect that's why I sell so few of my pottery pieces."

She took me to her pottery room. Sure enough, it was filled with grotesquely coloured vases, bowls, plates and mugs. The colours were primitive, thick-looking, frightening even. You couldn't live with them in your home.

"TV's back on!" Horace shouted. The others immediately assumed the vegetable position and began to utter disparaging remarks at the undeserving box.

"Did you ever see her again?" I asked, always keen to have a tidy ending to a story.

"No," said Brown wistfully. "She was injured in an accident in the car she just bought. Went through a red light, I believe. Another lager?"

Divide and Conquer

I could never spell "diary" when I was at school. Was it "dairy" or "diary", and when the ancient ink pen was also giving me trouble, such that one blot in the middle of "diary" made the word impossible to read anyway, life was tough. I got to the point where I could expertly blot any word I could not spell. It seemed more acceptable to be punished for blotting than spelling. One morning however, my teacher called my bluff, brought me to the front of the class and asked me to prove that I really could spell "diary". "Darie" I spelled up on the board, and to increasingly hysterical laughter from my classmates, "dayrie" or "dyry". After writing it out fifty times at the back of the class, I still couldn't remember on my own, so we put it down to a mental block.

But what is a mental block? I see the phrase used all the time. I think it's the equivalent of my inkblot, an excuse, but I have to admit that sometimes we really do have a mental block. For me, it's when I have something in my mind that I want to get out. I know it's there. I can see it lurking indistinctly behind something else, a shade that won't come out into the light to be identified. But do I know how to entice it out? No way. I promise it rewards, sweets, money, a good time, but it's stubborn. Then at a time when I have my head stuck in a basin, washing my hair, or I'm in the bath, up to my ears in soap, it dances out, smirking. And I say: of course, that's what it was all the time, but at that point I can't write it down, not having got that box of underwater writing paper for Christmas. So I commit it to memory, and I don't have to tell you what happens after that.

So what I want to know is; whose side is my mind on, because it sure doesn't feel like it's on mine?

When I was small, probably about the time I was trying to learn to spell "diary" and to face up to the other quirks and conundrums of the English language, my Grandmother used to tell me that the mind likes to fool around and play jokes on us. That was her explanation, her big insight into life, and to this day nothing I have read has bettered it. To me, all the theories about conditioning or heredity, or anything else that pulls our wires, still have a flavour of mythology about them. They tell us a lot. They are complex. They satisfy the intellectual lust of those who devise them, but leave the core problems unsolved. So I still have to hear something that satisfactorily replaces her theory; that the mind is a joker, plugged into a great, cosmic comedian, who has us all running around, trying to make sense of a very elaborate, obscure, but meaningless comedy.

I tried to get this across to the guys in the Gentle Goat the other week, and caused quite a commotion. Not only did I cut across the track of an argumentative churchgoer, but also someone who was doing a long thesis for a PhD in psychology or something, maybe it was psychiatry. Brown, Pritchard and the others were still at the bar being served and had got caught up in the conversation there. Indeed, the conversation roamed around the whole pub that night. The argument as usual generated more heat than light.

But this episode began really with a disagreement later that same evening; I think it might have been over something critical such as when Andy and Zelda took over the Gentle Goat. Someone said eight, someone said ten, another thought it might have been twelve years ago. No matter; it was responsible for bringing to the fore the interesting fact that Horace has always kept a diary.

"You've never told us that before," Brown said, slightly injured. "Am I in it?"

"Oh, yes," said Horace, and left it at that.

"What do you write in it?" asked Ronald.

"What do you think?" Horace answered, wishing he had kept his mouth shut.

Ronald took a sip of his beer. "Well, I don't know," he replied. "I mean, I don't keep one so I don't know anything about it. You're the first person I have known who keeps a diary."

"Maybe others have and you've not known," said Brown.

We were intrigued, but the feeling was complicated, a mixture of devouring curiosity, especially to know what Horace thought of everyone, and a sense of having a spy in our midst. It's not like in politics, where everyone keeps diaries to ensure a pension when they are thrown out of office, and where everyone expects to be commented on, and feels neglected when they are not. This is real life. What could Horace possibly record?

"Well, you can record whatever you want," Horace said, a little defensively. "It's your diary. You can make up your own history, you know, things that interest you, local things, usually. Pritchard knows. He is interested in local history. He makes notes about the past. I record the present."

"So do you put down other things too?" I asked. "Your thoughts?"

"Slim volume," muttered Pritchard.

"Oh, absolutely," Horace confirmed. "I have a cupboard full of notebooks. I began when I was about eleven or twelve. I sometimes look back through them. I used to cut out cricket and football scores and paste them in. I think I noted when the pub changed hands, so I'll look it up. Who's taking bets? I'll put a tenner on Pritchard's date."

"This is probably a scam between the two of you," Brown said smiling, "but I'll take you on."

"Bring one of your diaries one evening," Ronald suggested. "It'll liven up a dull winter night."

"Absolutely not," Horace said, quite hot at the thought. "They are very private."

"But why do you keep them?" I asked. "There's

surely not much point in keeping them to yourself."

Horace refused to budge. "There's every point. I won't write honestly if I know someone else is going to read them."

Brown shifted his weight in his chair and looked puzzled. "I still can't see the point. If you're just going to keep it to yourself, why write down something you already know?"

"That's the mystery of diaries," Pritchard tried to help. "The writer strangely gets satisfaction from communicating with something, in this case a diary, only if it is going to be locked up. Diaries come with keys."

"Got any good jokes in there?" Ronald nudged Horace. Ronald doesn't like heavy conversation for long and was bored by this talk.

"I don't care for jokes," Horace replied, "but if you kept a diary, you would probably record all the jokes you heard, because that typifies you. Your diary will say what you are."

"Look, I know what," Ronald came to life. "Let's all keep a diary for a week and then we'll compare notes next Wednesday."

"Good idea," I agreed. "I've never kept a diary up for more than two days running so I might be encouraged to keep it going if I know I'm going to have to report back."

"You probably won't if that's the only thing driving you," Horace said.

Brown and the others thought that it was a good idea too so we all solemnly contracted to return with our week's diaries next Wednesday.

As it happened, I had an intensely busy week. It was all work and no play so I never did get down to writing my thoughts in a diary. I guess I'm not wired up that way. Anyway, the life I lead is hardly sufficient to base an adventure story upon but it suits me. Although I looked forward to hearing everyone else's story, I did feel guilty about not having anything to contribute.

"It's ok," said Horace, when we all met on Wednesday night at the Goat. "I knew you'd never do it. You're not obsessed enough with what's going on around you."

I felt that was rather unfair but when I thought about it later, I saw that Horace had a point. I tend to get on with my paid work and when there's a deadline, I don't think of much else.

"I'm glad you haven't done your homework," said Brown with relief. "I haven't either. I never even thought about it again until last night."

"I knew that too," Horace said. "You're not a person who finds it satisfying to communicate with yourself but I would suspect that Pritchard has written every day and Ronald has had a go, but not every night."

"Correct as far as I am concerned," said Pritchard. "I quite enjoyed it."

"Right about me too," said Ronald. "I didn't like doing it. I couldn't get started easily."

"Well, what did you write?" Brown asked Pritchard.

"I'll only read out the bits that'll interest you," said Pritchard. "I wrote too much and with time I'd learn to prune it down."

"Day one –Thursday," Pritchard began. "A visit to the dentist for a check-up. Nothing felt wrong with my teeth and I was given the all-clear. I felt she prodded around more than was good for me but assumed she knew what she was doing.

Friday. Had lunch at the Gentle Goat with Brown and Ronald. Ronald was aggressive after only one pint and I left early. I took the car for its MOT. It looked ok to me but the garage man attacked the wheel arches with his spanner and knocked a hole through what he called rust. Car failed MOT but I thought the garage was just creating work for itself. The car was absolutely safe and I told him so. I took the car to another garage but they refused to pass it because of the hole. It's a racket! I asked the first garage to fix it but the garage man said he preferred not to be sworn at so much. I finally told him what I thought of him. I've been meaning to for years.

Saturday. Felt a twinge, more than a twinge actually, of toothache. Strange. My teeth were feeling fine until I took them to the dentist. Just like the car in fact. I decided to patch up the car myself so I got a bodywork kit and spent all afternoon on it. Not as easy as you think. After three hours the car looked dreadful. I decided to sell it and put an advert in the shop but then realised I'd still have to have it MOT'd, so I took the advert out again. Sometimes I wish Sigmund would look less understanding. It makes me feel even more stupid.

Sunday. Mouth in real pain, so I telephoned the emergency dentist, who does only private work. It would cost an arm and a leg to do a filling so I took aspirin instead. Wait till I get my dentist tomorrow. People asked solicitously about the vandalism done to my car. I didn't have the neck to explain. Even the police stopped to ask if I wanted to report it. Too embarrassed to admit the truth. They took details and said they'd keep an eye open.

Monday. Why can't life be simpler? My own dentist couldn't treat me because she had to have emergency work done on her neck, which went into some sort of spasm. More aspirins. Began to get heartburn from too many aspirins. How many do you need to take to become addicted? I took the car to another garage, which only charged me twice the normal rate for doing the repairs right away. The car failed on its handbrake this time but as it was only a bodyshop they couldn't help with the repair. Took it to the recommended garage which by amazing co-incidence is owned by the same proprietor. They fixed the brakes and granted the MOT. The car then stalled on the way home and had to be rescued by the AA, who took me back to the same garage that had given me the MOT, certified only an hour previously! Going to tear my hair out.

Tuesday. Things are going from bad to worse. I've decided to use public transport instead of a car. I got to see the dentist at last but it didn't do much good. She was walking around like a Zombie. She could move her head only by moving her whole body from the waist up. When I sat in the chair, she clambered onto a stool and knelt stiffly and precariously over me, bending at the waist like a crane at the dockside. She couldn't angle her head to see into my mouth otherwise. But like this, she had to peer into my mouth from a great distance. I tried to complain that the chompers were all right until she had smitten them with her cold steel, but I couldn't say it properly with my mouth fully open and filled with more cold steel. Anyway, she was in pain herself and at her least sympathetic. When she grabbed the drill and asked me to press the foot control because she couldn't reach it, I almost passed out. I couldn't think of her drilling in my mouth, stiffly and at long distance, so I made lame excuses and left. Miraculously the pain has gone.

Police phoned to say they have caught the vandals and could I come to give evidence. I seem to have a choice; to give false evidence or admit to wasting police time.

"Wednesday. You see," said Pritchard, "I've even kept it up tonight before coming to the pub."

"Best day of the week so far. A chap called Windsor telephoned to say he wanted to see me about an investment opportunity. Apparently we knew each other some time ago, although I can't remember. Never mind. Says he has a sure winner. He knows for a fact that the price of gold is going to double in the next few weeks because of something political which is about to take place. I couldn't follow it totally but he seems very genuine, especially as it is only me that he wants to let in on this. He said I'd done him a big favour in the past and he wanted to repay me. I hadn't to let a soul know but I know you lot will keep quiet. I had to keep this diary exercise intact otherwise it doesn't work. I'll get out my life savings and put my shirt on this gold thing tomorrow. Maybe I do remember this bloke after all. I believe he may have had a moustache in the old days."

We congratulated Pritchard. There was something he said which triggered something in my mind but I kept it to myself for the moment. Pritchard's diary had been very entertaining.

Ronald came next. Brown got some drinks in and we settled to Ronald's diary but quite honestly not expecting much.

"I only managed it for a couple of days," Ronald apologised, "and I'm not much of a writer so I just made notes."

"Ok, Thursday, Anvil Cottage, Harris Lane."

"Wait a minute," Brown interrupted, bringing drinks to the table. "Have I missed something? Why did you write your address? It's not a letter."

"I thought that's what you did," Ronald said.

"Never mind him, Ronald," I put in. "Did your cottage used to belong to a blacksmith?"

"I dunno," Ronald answered truthfully. "Never given it a thought."

Pritchard growled, "The enquiring mind, that which differentiates us from the animals."

"I'll differentiate you from your problem teeth,"

Ronald replied hotly. "You were just like that on Friday lunchtime. I made a note of it. All smart little digs at me. I can get fed up with it, you know. Anyway, you've all known me for years but you've never known the name of my cottage. That's not very enquiring. It's the familiar which is least understood." He finished on this enigmatic note.

"Thursday, Anvil Cottage, Harris lane. Waited around for the postman but nothing came. Read the paper. Story about some dancing shark in a circus in China – ate one of the audience. Should have been bad for business but the audience doubled just to see what the shark would do next. Front two rows got in free. Alf telephoned to ask if I'd do a couple of jobs over his place so I said yes. Got there by midday to find him going out. Said he needed his gate fixed, the one at the top of his drive. Had a look at it. He wasn't kidding. The wood was rotten. Had a lovely afternoon putting on new crossbeams and a lock so that the gate wouldn't swing open. Had just finished and was washing up when heard almighty crash. Ran out to find Landrover and gate as one. Landrover 1: Gate 0. Alf forgot he had asked me to fix gate.

Friday. Waited around for postman but nothing happened."

"Why are you waiting for the postman?" Horace asked.

"Well," Ronald was reluctant, but kept to the spirit of the game. "I've sent away for chess lessons so that I can hold my own against Mrs Webster. She said she might invite me over sometime."

We remained silent. What could we do, or say?

"Paper arrived. Follow up to the shark story. Shark builds up a large cult following. Seems to be off his food. Leaves the audience alone but nabs a passing clown. Other clowns go on strike in protest. Circus improves immeasurably."

"You're making this up," Brown accused him.

"Not at all," Ronald was adamant. "It's there in black and white."

"Saturday. This was the last day I took notes. Re-did Alf's gate and put large reflectors on the spars to make sure he saw them as he came up the drive. Post arrived with chess lessons. Couldn't make head nor tale of them. Instructions clear as mud. As it happened, Mrs Webster phoned to ask me to replace some loose tiles on her garage and I blurted out the story of the instructions. I was so disappointed. She was very nice and said that if I came over in the afternoon to do the tiles, I could stay to tea and she'd help me out with the chess lessons. I don't think she tumbled to the idea that I'm just learning chess to impress her. All to the good. Just as was leaving, got another call from Alf. He'd forgotten again. Smashed through gate as he was leaving. Didn't think to put reflectors on that side of the gate too. Opinion of Alf's common sense declines."

"Very entertaining, Ronald," I said. He had done better that we thought he would.

"I had a nice time having tea with Mrs Webster and forgot about the diary. By the way, I had to leave because she had an appointment with a man who was calling on her about investments, just like you Pritchard. I saw him get out of his flash car."

Now it was Horace's turn.

"I'll start at the week-end," he said. "There wasn't much to interest you before then."

"Saturday. I've always had trouble between my wife Belinda and the dog, Hardy. I have a lot of sympathy with Belinda because I know he's hard to like, but I'm stuck with him. I've tried to train him but he's so active that I can't get him to settle down and listen. The vet has given up and says Hardy will calm down when he's older. Too late by then, though.

Anyway, today Belinda put spare ribs out to defrost on the kitchen worktop. The postman came in and distracted her and when she returned, the ribs had gone. She blamed Hardy. No eye witnesses, but she's probably right. What the stupid dog wants with frozen meat I have no idea. Belinda is a kind soul but at that point I got the "Either that dog goes, or I do," speech. Well, that's all very well but who's to have him? I can't just turn him loose on the motorway.

So I went looking for a new home for him. I didn't tell Hardy, mind. He'd have taken it very badly. As it was, he looked reproachfully at me but I think that was just my conscience. Save some money, considering all the food he puts away every week, and that's not counting his theft. Paid Alf a visit. Thought he might want a guard dog but was in a dreadful mood about Ronald building a gate across his road. Terrible language for a man who's usually so suave. Told him to keep it for some violent novel he might want to write.

Then I had a brainwave. Take Hardy to Sigmund for a session. He's good with humans. Bound to be good with dogs. But Sigmund had the wrong attitude from the start. Hardy took the interview seriously and tore round the shop just to show what a good runner he is. After ten minutes, I eventually caught him and tethered him to the door while I helped Sigmund to calm down and put things back on the shelves. When I went to get Hardy, found a queue of people outside waiting to get in, while Hardy proved his guard dog credentials. Asked queue if anyone wanted a dog. No immediate takers.

As a last resort, I took him to the Police Station in Sprighassle to see if they could do anything with him. He failed the height qualification. Back home, Belinda had calmed down again but fed us with scrambled eggs instead of spare ribs. I took the point.

Sunday. I don't know what's got into Belinda this week. She's usually so unobtrusive. She wanted a new dress. Goodness knows what for. She must have at least two or three hanging around in the wardrobe doing nothing. She said I was a skinflint. I suggested we get her some material and she could make something but she claimed that before she had it made, the dog would have savaged it. She's just in one of those moods. Besides, I might need the money, because a chap called Windsor phoned, primarily about the dog, but mentioned that if I did him a favour in giving him the dog for nothing then he might let me in on something.

Monday. Saw this Windsor chap. Said he knew me from way back. Didn't like to be impolite and admit I didn't recognise him from Adam. I suggested it might have been sometime on holiday somewhere, and he agreed. Anyway, I can't go wrong. He's going to take the dog and in return he'll let me in on a few sure bets on the dog-tracks. He says he's made a fortune and you can tell by the car he drives. His face is certainly familiar. I might get Belinda two dresses with the winnings."

At this point, we didn't wait to hear the rest of the diary.

Brown interrupted first. "Look," he cried. "Pritchard, Mrs Webster, Horace and me – we've all been tricked by this bloke Windsor. He must be a fraudster. I've been offered the chance of some shares that he knows will go up suddenly, because of some movement on the Stock Market – and I'm to give him ten thousand pounds tomorrow."

"I'm going to give him three thousand pounds tomorrow," said Pritchard.

"He's going to get a few thousand out of me too," I added.

Someone at the bar happened to hear our raised voices. "Did you say you are going to hand over money to a bloke called Windsor? I am too, and he said I'd be the only one."

It transpired that about a dozen people in the bar were involved, each thinking he was the only one. If it hadn't been for the stunt with the diaries, we would never have known about it. Each would have suffered his loss and humiliation in private and this chap would have gone off with well over fifty thousand pounds.

"But he was going to take Hardy," Horace whined.

"That was just a way of disarming you," Brown suggested. "He'd have dumped the dog."

A look came over Horace's face. "Right," he said firmly. "What are we going to do?"

The rest of the story is probably recorded in Horace's diary. I never asked him. I've often wondered how his diary compares to my account of these tales. It's all a matter of the angle you're looking from, the inside information you have and the signals you pick up.

What happened was that we primed the police to be at Pritchard's house the next day. We worked out that he was to be the first on Windsor's schedule of pick-ups. Pritchard had the money waiting. The room was equipped to record the conversation. Pritchard handed over the money and acted very well. He's good at that sort of thing. Windsor was caught in possession of the cash. The police had statements from everyone else he was going to turn over.

I'm not sure what the charges were. He certainly was out to steal our money, but none of us was entirely innocent. He obviously knew how to prey on our greed or inner desires for something more. Anyway, we all agreed it was a rum thing to do to diddle people out of their hard-earned cash.

Pritchard's troubles with the police and his car also found a solution. Someone hinted, and I honestly can't trace who it was, that Windsor doubtless had something to do with it, so the police happily added that to the charge sheet. Talk about giving a dog a bad name.

And while we're on the subject of dogs, just to complete the record, Horace's dog came out of it all right. When Belinda heard what Windsor would have done to the dog, she had a complete change of heart and wouldn't hear of the dog going. She took it under her wing and actually did have a calming effect over it, except when he's out with Horace, that is. Funny thing, chemistry.

Chapter Six

Human Frailty

A Homing Instinct

I suppose it must have been half past two when we left the pub that afternoon. A warm July day it was, when you didn't want to be too energetic. Yet here we were, setting out to walk up the hill, all of us wondering why we were doing it, but no one prepared to call a halt.

It had been lovely in the pub; cool, relaxed, not a care in the world. But no one had wanted to go home. There was nothing on the box, and a hot July afternoon with nothing to do can seem quite interminable. So we debated what we would do, and that's when things went downhill. Actually, they started to go uphill. Let me explain.

We became over-polite, an unusual, possibly quite unique situation for us. No one wanted to be the wet blanket. No one wanted to be negative. Yet we still could not agree what to do.

"Look," said Horace, "we seem to have about eight or nine suggestions here and no one will object to any of them. Browny, what would you prefer to do?"

"Oh, I'm easy," Brown replied with unbecoming nonchalance. "You just say the word and I'll fall in, right in step, absolutely."

We had two more rounds of drinks before we came to the decision that we would walk up the hill behind the village. Even then, it was decided only because someone showed a faint preference, tipping the scales so delicately that the naked eye could hardly perceive movement. Once the choice was made, it gathered momentum.

Mind you, it was the kind of decision that you make in the cool of indoors without realising that your familiar world outside was doing a convincing impression of the Kalahari Desert. Nothing stirred, not even a louse, or whatever the creature was in the poem. When we spilled out of the bar, two extra drinks for the worse, into the bright heat without a dark lens between us, our collective deference converted into open bloody-mindedness.

Off we trudged, up the public footpath and across the fields. I tried to be reasonable, but only annoyed everyone all the more.

"What this is," I said, trying to make myself heard above the rumpus, "is an example of the Abilene Principle."

"Chuck Berry sang that, or was it Elvis Presley?" Pritchard mused, and caused a diversion for at least five minutes.

"The Abilene Principle says that people in a group would rather conform to the wishes of the group rather than express discontent, even though others in the group might also be feeling unhappy."

By the time I finished that mouthful, and I thought I expressed it rather well, pretty clearly in fact for one so burdened by lunchtime beer, I had completely lost my audience. I tried repeating it, but didn't bring it off half so well the second time.

Horace grasped some of what I was saying, but he was still stinging from one of Ronald's cutting remarks. It could have been about his thinning hair; that is sure to set Horace alight.

"You are talking through a hole which is clearly not in your hat," he yelled. "I've never heard of anything so stupid. Why would I do what you lot wanted to do, just because all of you lot wanted to do it and I didn't, but I wasn't going to want to be different because you would all think I didn't want to…." He petered out, confused, but unconvinced.

Ronald had a go. "I think most people with common sense would speak their mind."

"Wouldn't take you long then," Brown commented.

"And wouldn't," Ronald continued, "let themselves be sucked into doing what they didn't want. Anyway, what's it got to do with anything Chuck Berry sang?"

"It hasn't," I raised my voice. "I'm told someone from Abilene invented it. Or was it Abe Lincoln?" I began to lose faith in what I had introduced.

"Not invented," Pritchard corrected. "Discovered. Columbus did not invent America. He discovered it."

I gave up. What with the heat and a steep climb up the fields, we were all feeling cross. Brown and Ronald were bickering. Brown I must say, can be extremely irritating, well to the right of pretentious and just upward of condescending. This brings out entirely the worst in Ronald, who then acts out the vandal-about-the-village to the extreme.

Brown happened to mention that before meeting us at the signpost, he had been browsing through the works of Shakespeare. I didn't put too much store in what he said. He could have been dusting them or moving them to another room when one fell open, allowing him to glance at a page, or he could have been looking for a telephone number and had confused the rows of addresses and telephone numbers for some of the Bard's more densely packed pieces. But I guess what got up Ronald's easily aroused nose was the language Brown used.

"Oh, you browsed, did you?" Ronald whined in an awful attempt to mimic an actor with asthma. "You didn't just read, you browsed. How do you do that? Do you stick your snout in the book and snuffle? And why for God's sake are Shakespeare's books always called *works*?"

"They just are," Brown replied, not yet rising to the bait, "and if you had received some education, and goodness knows what you wasted your time on between the ages of nine and sixteen but it certainly didn't trouble your eyesight, you would have worked out that there are more important questions to consider than the trivial word used for his collected writings. Anyway, he wrote plays, not books."

"What sort of important questions then?" Ronald pressed. "Go on, you educate me."

"Well, even a backward peasant like you has heard of Hamlet. The question is: was he mad, or merely weak and indecisive?"

"Seems like you intellectuals are all weak and indecisive if you can't work out the answer between you after all this time," Ronald said.

"Point to Ronald, I think," Horace came in. "It seems to me that Hamlet mirrors whoever is watching the play."

"Anyway," Ronald pursued his quarry, "if it's only a play what does it matter? I watched a film last night. Some bloke murdered a woman, but it's only a film, so it went out of my head in minutes."

"Typical of your retention," Brown jibed. "The point is, if he was mad he wasn't responsible."

"I knew a woman once who wasn't responsible," Horace interrupted again. "She was an absolute stunner and she lived next door. I could smell her perfume as she went out in the morning. It hung about in the air after she had gone. I used to wonder, if you put colour in scent, so that you could actually see where it was, would it spread very far? You could smell this stuff at twenty paces."

"Go on, get to the good bit," Ronald egged him on.

"That's it. That's all there is. I just thought you'd want to know about her being irresistible, as you were talking about Hamlet being irresistible." Horace reddened as he explained.

"I sometimes think I associate with morons and then I remember it's just human frailty," said Pritchard, breaking his silence. Actually he had broken his silence by breaking wind as we came up the hill, but that didn't count.

"Shakespeare also said something like, *Frailty, thy name is woman,*" Horace tried to quote.

"Little did he know about it," said Ronald. "When I was nine I knew well enough not to believe that one. I don't know if any of you knew a girl called Betty Trow. Well, I was swapping stamps with her. She claimed I was cheating so she bashed me on the head with her album and chased me all over the school playground. It was embarrassing."

"They are the weaker sex. They need protecting," insisted Pritchard.

"I think you want protecting if you think like that," Brown growled. "For once I'm with my tubby and prejudiced friend here. Protection is superfluous."

I could see that a few more minutes of this conversation would lead to even more squabbles, so I suggested that we stop for a rest and drink the cans of beer we had brought with us. They had come from the cooler in the pub so they were still quite cold. We sat on the hillside at the edge of the path and looked back down on the village.

"It's quiet up here," Brown spoke, relaxing a little. It was a little cooler too.

"We should do this more often," Pritchard sighed, quickly forgetting the irritations of the last hour.

"There go Paddy McGraw's pigeons," Horace

126

observed. "I wonder if you ever get a rogue pigeon, you know, one that doesn't want to come home?"

"Where else could it go?" Pritchard enquired.

"Well that shows a lack of spark and imagination," Horace replied. "It could go anywhere. It could migrate."

"I don't see the point. It's got a perfectly good home. It doesn't need to wander off thousands of miles just to find the same thing when it gets there. Pigeons are smarter than that."

"It might be different there. It might be better." Horace persisted with the notion.

"Chances are it'll be worse," Pritchard replied. "Why not be content with what you've got? You see, humans have got too much of an anti-homing instinct. They want to go off, wandering about, hoping something better will turn up. If it's not covered wagons, it's spacecraft, always running away from putting things right on their own doorstep, always thinking that they can get a fresh start. We have put more effort into understanding transport than into how to make things better at home, and do you know why? It's less effort, more excitement, and you can make money out of it." Pritchard reclined again, content in his moroseness.

"I had a problem with a pigeon once," said Horace. "I'll tell you about it."

Usually when one of us tries to tell a story it's quite difficult to gain attention. It seems like everyone wants to join in, but what with the hill and the cans of beer in our hands, we lay on the grass like lambs, half-listening, half-dozing while Horace got up a head of steam.

"I had a job in London for a time," he began. "The usual thing, I suppose, in an office, commuting in every day. It had its moments, but eventually I quit. Had to, but that's another story. Well, you know in the summer, London is packed with tourists. You can't get on the Underground, the shops are packed, the streets are full of people going slowly around in circles and you can't get past them. Despite all that, I used to try to get out of the office at lunchtime. You need a break.

One day, I had to run round to the ironmonger, only a few streets away, to get birdseed. We were looking after someone's budgie, staying with us for a week, (we were trying to keep it for a week, but the cat wanted to trim a bit off that target) and we had run out of birdseed. This ironmonger had simply everything, so soon I was walking off with my brown bag of birdseed.

I was threading my way through a busy section of pavement, close to an exit from one of the main Underground stations, when I found my way blocked by people coming off a bus. Maybe some were trying to get on the bus: it's hard to say. All I knew at the time was I had to pass through or around a dense crowd of people, all mingling around the bus stop.

I was almost through and the crowd began to clear. I must have speeded up and taken a longer stride than usual, when I felt as if I had stepped on something.

I looked down. To my horror I saw a pigeon. It was a scraggy-looking thing, mottled grey with dark blue blotches and wearing white on the tips of its wings like a sign of old age. I seemed to have stood on it, for it hobbled around in a bent line, dragging its wing and falling on one side as it scrabbled to keep going. It was hurt. No doubt about it. A mixture of feelings ran inside me. Maybe it hadn't been me. I knew I'd stood on something, but then you're always bumping into something in the street.

No one else seemed to be involved – at all. Everyone, and there was quite a long queue at the bus-stop, all looked at me and the pigeon as if we were associated, so in a way even if it wasn't my fault, I felt I had to take responsibility for this stupid bird.

What did that mean? Well firstly, I couldn't leave it to be run over or walked on. It looked pitiful, struggling to keep going, quite a brave bird in fact: horribly ugly though. What was I to do? I mean, was I supposed to put it out of its misery? The trouble was I didn't know how badly hurt it was. Maybe I should leave it to nature's way. That would let me off the hook. And then I looked at the bus queue. Of course, I had to have it happen right in front of a bus stop and a ready-made audience with nothing to do but watch me and this bird.

How do you put a pigeon out of its misery? Maybe I wouldn't have to if it were just winged. I could take it – where? I could hardly take it home with me on the 17.31 from Euston. Nor could I leave it in the office. It would make mincemeat out of our electronic beam security system. I could just imagine my boss's face when I tried to explain to him. No, it was a bad time just at the moment. I still had to explain the fire in the wastepaper basket when I had been trying to destroy a sensitive document. It seems so easy on these old films – hold the paper up, light it at the bottom, turn it round and put the last pieces in the ashtray.

It was the lack of an ashtray really that was my undoing: I only noticed there wasn't one when I had the blaze raging in my hand. Of course, there are no ashtrays in offices any more. Anyway, I had this minor inferno reaching up to my fingers – and one lick of the flames satisfied me that I had to get rid of it – so into the jolly old wastepaper bin it went. I knew it would be safe because I had been on a fire safety course, so I knew how to use the right extinguisher. It all looked quite simple on the course. I got the ring pull out of the neck of the extinguisher, pointed it at the bin and let it have it.

What happened next was nobody's business. The force of the foam hit the bin, caught it like a whip and spun it across the floor, fire and all, into the coat cupboard. Amid screams from my colleagues, I extracted it with a bent coat hanger and put the fire out. Did I get congratulations for bravery? What do you think? A few coats were never the same again.

So, back to the bird. I wouldn't have to give it the chop if it was merely struggling about in shock but I would only know its condition if I caught it, so off I went in pursuit. Until now, the pigeon didn't look as if it would last ten yards. Now that I wanted to catch it, it decided to be resourceful.

It ran into the crowd. By now there were some people who had not seen the start of the farce, so one part of me was thinking that I ought to explain what I was doing, while the other was trying hard not to lose sight of the pigeon in the crowd. It wove in and out of the bus queue as if it knew what it was doing. It was on home ground and I was no match for it. Some people thought I was queue jumping and one old lady had a go at me with the business end of her umbrella. Another woman fancied I had designs on her – I guess my hands were in neck-clenching position at the time – and caught me sharply on the knee with her hard briefcase.

By this time I was in a bad way, providing free in-queue entertainment for thirty people or so. Several buses had come and gone and no one was getting on, preferring to see this thing through to the end. There was laughter from a group of teenagers.

"Hey," they shouted, "What's with you? Can't you eat pizza like the rest of us?"

Very funny. The bird was in poor shape, but uncatchable. I thought I had it for a second, but I couldn't get down to the pavement fast enough through the forest of legs. Then it veered onto the road and I ran upstream of it in the traffic to prevent the buses and the taxis in the nearside lane from careering down upon it. Although I was trying to save it, I now looked like some pigeon persecutor, inventor of a new lunchtime pastime. I thought up all sorts of stories as I was chasing it – I was a wealthy bird fancier and this bird was a valuable breeding bird worth thousands of pounds - but one glance at either of us blew that story.

I thought I would have one last attempt. I'd get it with the seed I'd bought. I tore open the packet and began to throw the seed around to lure my pigeon over. The people in the crowd must have thought I was a pretty prepared guy, happening to have seed on my person just for this kind of emergency. In my haste, I split the bottom of the seed bag and it began to trickle out. The laughter from the onlookers grew as they realised before I did what was going to happen.

Then they came, hundreds of pigeons and sparrows, all claiming a free lunch. Just then I saw my pigeon, obviously recovering from its stun, jump onto the roof of a car and launch itself into the air. Not so the others. With suicidal tendencies, they brought the street traffic to a halt as the breeze blew the seed around. Horns sounded. The laughter behind me grew raucous. The whole street around the Underground entrance was in uproar.

I'd had enough. I disappeared before the police came to sort out the mess. I think the pigeon survived it better than I did, but the budgie couldn't understand why dinner didn't show up that evening."

Brown was dozing, but Ronald was recovering his good humour. "That was quite good for you, Horace."

Pritchard nodded and gazed out over the hill. All the usual suburban noises, the traffic especially, failed to reach us up here. It was lovely. The cars on the main road ran along soundlessly, just like out of a science fiction film. Ronald lay back, looking up at the blue sky.

It was Pritchard though, I am sure, who started the next piece of action. He fervently denied it afterwards and blames Ronald who in turn thought Horace was the culprit. Brown blamed me but he was still dozing so how would he know? He says he wasn't and remembers my shout quite clearly. It's worrying that none of us remembers anything with any degree of certainty.

Someone said something like, "Look down there!" or, "Look at the smoke!" I do remember someone else asking, "Where is it coming from?" which would suggest more than one person had definitely seen the smoke, but of course with hindsight they could have just been asking to be shown because they couldn't see it.

Ronald was certainly off first. He always is. Man of action and all that. I know that someone else had said, "Why isn't anyone down there doing something about it?"

Next thing we were off, tumbling and rushing, presumably to get back to warn the village about the fire and help put it out. It was suddenly a primitive picture. One imagined red fire licking greedily at the dirty yellow roofs of medieval straw huts, and panic rising in the compressed lanes, children screaming, mothers running, black smoke rising.

It was all so plausible. A hot day, something had set something alight. In the heat haze maybe it looked like a pall of smoke. Brown was running before he was properly awake. Horace was off with a turn of speed I had never seen before. Pritchard loped effortlessly, until his foot slipped on something and he took a spectacular and very entertaining dive into a big bush. We stopped to get him out and praised his style but then the urgency was even greater. I especially did not want to appear to be cautious or to hold back. No one gets any prizes for being thoughtful in times of emergency, so I ran like the best of them, even finding myself out in front at one stage, feeling like one of those riderless horses in the Grand National.

Down the hill we ran and rolled, shouting encouragement. We did the route in a tenth of the time we took to get up the hill and our speed if anything was accelerating. As we approached the edge of the village some kids playing football abandoned their game and ran to join us.

"A fire," they whooped gleefully. "Let's go!"

Then some workmen doing repairs to a water main joined us, together with three girls who were out for a jog. Some people collecting for the blind put down their trays of paper flags and tripped after us. Through the streets we went, gathering people like magnets gather iron filings, the noise of the crowd giving warning even before it arrived. Women looked out of windows, men got their heads out from under car bonnets. A religious trio abandoned their door-to-door search for a welcome and tucked their briefcases under their arms to follow a new calling. Some ponies out for a run from the stables were spurred to trot after us. Dogs dodged between our legs.

We ran the full length of the High Street and came out of the village at the other end without finding the fire. Of course, everything looked different from down here. Maybe the fire was in another street. We backed up, causing great confusion. It was hard to get through the crowd, who were asking each other all sorts of questions about why they were running, where the fire was, who had been burned. I was breathless and could hardly explain, so we just ran again. This time we got to the Gentle Goat and stood outside. Someone from inside the pub put up a "No Coaches" sign. Where now? We didn't know. We could see groups of people now running in different directions, bumping into each other. We were coughing and wheezing.

Pritchard then gasped, "Who saw the smoke? Where did it come from exactly?"

"You did," I said. "I didn't see it."

"You must have, for God's sake," Brown choked. "You spoke with Pritchard about it, then ran. I just followed."

"You must have seen it, Ronald," Pritchard wheezed. "You ran off first."

"I only ran because you lot were taking all day to do something about it. I can't see that distance too clearly these days."

The crowd were milling around, looking for instruction, but there was none we could give, so we slipped round the back of the Goat and got out through a hole in the hedge. We then made our way along a lane to a quieter spot and sat on a bench, our chests still heaving from the sprint.

"Well that is strange," said Horace. "You know, although I didn't see the smoke at first, I was sure I saw something when it was pointed out to me."

"I can't believe it," said Brown, still looking a very dangerous colour of red. "Do you mean to say that none of us actually saw smoke, but we all ran like sheep down the hill without stopping to check?"

"You know what that was?" I said. It was an example of the …"

"The Chuck Berry Principle," Pritchard completed my sentence wrongly. "I see it all now. None of us wanted to hold the others back. Where was your common sense, Ronald?"

"Not the Chuck Berry Principle," I tried to correct him.

"Abe Lincoln," Horace said. "You lot have terrible memories. He probably used it in his Gettysburg address."

"Did he have more than one house, then?" Ronald asked. "These Americans. They're all filthy rich. Hey, listen. Maybe there really was some smoke and the fire was put out before we got there."

We'll never know. The insistent and piercing sound of an alarm preceded the arrival of a large red fire engine, bristling with men in yellow helmets.

We didn't wait to be introduced.

Pritchard's Tale

The Friends of the Old Folks throw an occasional event to raise money to buy a minibus or some other required object. I remember well the time they organised an Old Time Music Hall. The poster they put up all over the village that proclaimed, "Od Time Music Hall", should have alerted me. Sometimes you go along to these things partly out of a sense of duty but then find yourself having a thoroughly good time. Quite possibly one's prejudices prevent one from enjoying the full variety of life's opportunities. Maybe I could after all enjoy Opera, circus-on-ice, mud wrestling, sheep dog trials and orchid shows but a lot of pride would have to be swallowed first.

The Od Time Music Hall was packed out. I only just managed to get a ticket. People were having a good time. Brown was Master of Ceremonies. I hardly recognised him, he was doing so well, banging his hammer and using the longest words imaginable. I thought he was too withdrawn to be compère, but he attracted many bursts of surprised laughter from the audience.

Other locals made a pass at some well known songs,

accompanied by dances and sketches. Audience participation was high. People dressed up for the evening – not just the players. What was missing was an orchestra in a pit, but someone's aunt from another suburb did sterling work on the piano instead. Food was served early on by other willing helpers. All the members of the Old Folks Club were there to swell the audience.

They called the club the "Old Folks Club" because they couldn't agree on a different name. Some said "Senior Citizen" made them feel that they ought to call each other "Comrade". Since the club couldn't agree on a name, the Friends of the Old Folks had to keep their name too.

I was a "Friend" too. I looked after the books, which was a simple enough task. I'm not so good at doing the tasks other "Friends" are good at. The pensioners complained when I helped cook a lunch, that my potatoes were underdone. No one would allow me to cut grass for them. (No thanks, Love. We've seen your own lawn.) The last straw came when I had to be taken aside and asked not to visit them when they were sick because it made them even more miserable.

"What can I do?" I pleaded. "I do so want to help."

I was told that my skilled help with the accounts was enough, a great help. No one else can do it.

It was expressed nicely, but it didn't make me feel any better, especially when I was referred to in Committee as "Our book-keeper, the man who tells us why we can't afford to do things."

A dozen village children in old jackets, mufflers and caps sang a selection of First World War songs. Then a performer I didn't recognise at all wandered on stage with a dog and did some tricks.

What was especially good about the evening was that you could take yourself off to the bar for a fortifier if the good humour became too much for you. Horace was there.

"Thank goodness for some proper grumpiness," I welcomed him. "Moan at me, Horace. Tell me evil things about the world. I have had enough of jollity."

"And I thought you were coming out to congratulate me," Horace grumbled.

Then it clicked.

"You? The dog?"

"Absolutely. Got it in two."

"Well I never," I said. "That dog can't sit still, never mind do tricks."

"He can when he's sedated," Horace replied. "I believe he's a circus dog. He probably got a fright from the lions or cannon and it has made him excitable."

"How do you sedate him?" I asked.

"Mars Bar," said Horace.

"I didn't know they had that effect on animals," I muttered.

"They don't," he said. "It's the pill I put inside it. I think I'll give one to Brown. It sounds like he needs it."

Brown was over-dealing the adjectives, his white gloves waving everyone's worries away. Then he changed demeanour and the pianist did dramatic things with the keys.

"Quick," Horace whispered. "This'll be good."

"What is it?" I took my drink in my hand.

"Pritchard's doing a story. I've heard him rehearse it. It's worth hearing."

We returned to our respective seats. The lights were dimmed and the curtains were opened to reveal Pritchard, sitting in a pine chair at an old pine table. It was a simple but effective prop. Pritchard himself didn't look too different, although they had given him an old pair of trousers of coarse green material, an old colourless shirt and a sleeveless pullover. He looked

137

more at home like that than he does in his usual anorak and jeans or whatever it is that he wears.

When Horace said he was going to do a story, I took it that it would be a dramatic monologue of the Victorian kind, spoken in a cockney accent and containing awful poetry. I didn't know at that time that storytelling was one of Pritchard's skills, but from time to time he does go from being a quiet brooder into a conversation hog. When it happens, we have all come to accept it. Whether he's silent or monologuing, it's as if the rest of us don't exist. We can be there or not there. And that's the impression he gave on the small stage. The audience could be there if they wanted or not. It was all the same to him. Such self-sufficiency added to the effect.

"I want to tell you tonight the story of Brandon and Peggy Watt. They worked a small farm not far from here. The story took place at the end of the Eighteen Hundreds and very few people know it, because the tale became too strange to be absorbed into proper history. But I tell you, strange though it was, it happened all right and there's no use denying it."

I know that Pritchard is quite keen on local history and that one of his closely guarded secrets is that he is writing up some of his findings. What he will do then, I don't know. He's being occupied with it for years so maybe his journey is more important than his destination. Who knows?

Pritchard continued, "The Watts' farm was only large enough to sustain one family, but that wasn't unusual. They kept some animals, a cow, some sheep, ducks, a pig I shouldn't wonder and a large vegetable garden fenced off to keep the sheep out. It was a hard life and each year, like many before them, they depended on their animals surviving tough winters and the occasional drought."

This was something out of the usual. It wasn't in verse, for a start. Nor was Pritchard using notes. The audience was nicely settled down. No one was talking at the bar. All the seats were taken up and a few people were standing against the walls. Such a mixed audience: children old enough to like a good story and older people who were happy to sit and listen in the semi-lit hall. I hoped Pritchard had enough material to keep their attention and wasn't just improvising.

"Brandon Watt came from farming stock. His people had been tenant farmers for several generations. He was a large, quiet man, one who shouldered his responsibilities without complaint. His father had managed to farm quite a large holding and had gathered a little money but a succession of poor crops when he was in the twilight of his career reduced his savings and left him with little more than he had started out with.

Brandon's outlook on life was influenced by his father's fate. He seemed to know and expect that there was not much use in trying to escape from poverty, and not to rely on building up treasures on Earth. He kept animals and avoided crops. Crops were too uncertain. At least animals give you the basis of what you need in life. You can then buy a little corn for making bread. The vegetable field was large. It was worked intensively by hand. Brandon was able to use some of the produce as a cash crop and with the money he could buy cloth for his wife to sew into serviceable clothing. For a few years, with a little luck and a lot of industry, they more than got by.

Peggy was not of farming stock. She was the daughter of a trader in a market town; a younger daughter, it has to be said. She was not heir to a fortune.

They were an unlikely couple but both had dreams, like the rest of us. Brandon, despite his daily acceptance of toil and his fatalism, might have seen in his wife someone who was sympathetic, someone who represented a gentler kind of life, someone who might rear their children to have the hopes and the ideals to do better than him.

Peggy, for her part, harboured a romantic love of the countryside. She read the "nature" poets and saw wonder and the love of God in everything. The reality of the countryside came slowly to her and when it did, she was shocked and afraid.

The farm animals terrified her when they approached and nuzzled her. The weather too seemed to surround her entirely. Her husband, so exhausted by his labour in the fields, was no better company than the animals. She took a long time to learn that he was closer to the animals than she ever conceived possible. However, the facts of life were that she depended upon him for survival, for his labour and protection, more than for his companionship and conversation.

By the time she had a child, she realised she was committed to a life which, now she fully understood it, appalled her. She was unsure how she had got herself into such circumstances and began blaming herself, then others, especially Brandon. On the other hand, her pride prevented her from going back to her family. She knew she would have had to re-join local society with greatly diminished status, which was unbearable. So she faced up to her exile because there was nothing else she could do. But it didn't make her easy to live with.

The years passed, and although life was no bed of roses, hardships made them work together. Their son, their only son, linked them too. It makes you wonder how children acquire their characteristics, for in the midst of all this disappointment and dullness the little boy, Andrew, was a cheerful soul. Anything made him happy: attention from the animals, his breakfast, a touch from his mother, a look from his father. It didn't take much. And Brandon adored him. The thought of his son got him out to work on a bitter, cold morning."

Pritchard's audience was with him all the way. The story was so much in keeping with the evening and I have to say he told it well. The simple set, with him pretending to be cleaning some ancient piece of kitchenware, was sufficient and so there was nothing to distract from the story. I drifted off a little, thinking actually of Pritchard. I wondered what he would have been like in Victorian times. Would he have been much the same, quiet and moody, pining for a better age, or would he have been inspired by the Nineteenth Century's novelty, its energy, its tensions between the privileged classes and the reformers? What is it that inspires us? If Napoleon was born today, would he use nuclear power to conquer the world, or would he be a human rights protester, or a pop star? Maybe he would be an unknown, but wealthy Parisian plumber.

Pritchard got up from the table and walked slowly to the back of the stage, apparently to get something. When he returned, he didn't sit down.

"So there is the story so far and until now the folk memory would agree with me on all points. It was after this that events went sour, and the strangenesses crept in."

He made the word "strangenesses" evoke all sorts of sinister meanings. Sitting down again with an old cloth in his right hand and a heavy-looking, blunt instrument in the other, he began to polish the thing, which glimmered in the light from the table candle. No one moved.

"Until now," he resumed, "relationships between Brandon and Peggy might have been strained, but they always got by. They had to. And they did have moments of pleasure, mostly when playing with

Andrew.

The years passed and Andrew grew into a young boy, long-legged for his age, but always thin. It was not for the lack of food, because Brandon was then reasonably prosperous and although they never accumulated any wealth to talk of, they ate well. His mother traced it to her side of the family, saying that some people were more fit for using their heads than their hands. Brandon did not disagree, but it worried him.

His worries were justified. Andrew began to get thinner and weaker. They consulted a doctor, who said that Andrew was suffering from a type of wasting disease. In those days, there was little to be done except to make the sufferer as comfortable as possible. For two winter months, the boy sat in front of the kitchen fire, still trying to be cheerful but bewildered about what was happening to him. Four days before his twelfth birthday, he started to cough incessantly and within a week he was dead.

For those two months, Peggy and Brandon were as close as they had ever been, sharing the burden of watching over the boy but when he died, they began to act differently, oddly.

They argued. Brandon blamed his wife for the boy's death. He was inconsolable. He shouted at her, terrible things, accusations about how neglectful a mother she had been. Why had they not had more children? Why had he let himself be talked into marrying her? She was spirited enough herself and that was the problem. Maybe if she had let him rant on, it might eventually have passed as time mended the grief. But she stood her corner and gave as good as she got. Her temper, once aroused, was twice as fiery as his smouldering wrath. For them to inhabit the same house was almost impossible, except that neither of them had anywhere else to go.

One night after a gloomy silent supper, and it was not yet spring so the light had faded, a row started. It was the fiercest yet. They brought the worst possible out of each other. Brandon was beside himself with fury. So far he hadn't raised a hand but tonight he felt he was prepared to hang for her. He got to the point where he felt himself losing control, when he saw the cat crouching by the door. He screamed at it and the cat scrambled behind a heavy, Welsh Dresser. It was as if the scream had defused the situation. Brandon walked out of the house and came back later, stinking of beer.

At breakfast he was silent and chewed at his bread with sullen concentration. The water was frozen. The cat had recovered and was lying under the table.

"Would you ask your Mistress," Brandon said, slowly and thickly, "to heat some water so that I can eat this dry bread?"

Peggy thought that he had spoken to her until it dawned on her that he had addressed the cat. She acted as if nothing was wrong, but broke some ice and boiled it to make tea.

So it was that when they needed to communicate they did so through the cat. It was awkward because the cat was a farm animal and didn't always hang around the house. Peggy was resourceful.

"I'm going to ask that cat when she decides to come back," she said within earshot of Brandon, "if she will ask the wretch I used to call my husband for some money to go and buy food."

Brandon took some coins from his pocket and laid them on the table.

The arguments never ceased. When Brandon had been drinking, Peggy knew that he could be abusive. He was a strong fellow and fearsome when in a temper. Sometimes he cried at the loss of his son and then she felt safe because he fell asleep crying, but when he was in a mood to accuse her, she put up her defences.

They argued through the cat. They stopped facing each other when they shouted. The cat grew used to the noise. She seemed to sense her increased importance. The weather was still cold so she didn't mind curling up in the kitchen, ready to play her part.

The feud escalated. They seemed obsessed with one another, as if they needed each other to relieve the grief. Then Brandon began to suffer delusions that his wife was going to poison him, so he ate only when he was famished. She feared for her safety too and barred the bedroom door at night. Brandon slept drunk in the kitchen.

With the drink, the poor eating habit and the tension, Brandon's stomach and strength began to fail him. He worried all the more. He dreamed of being free from this witch who had killed his son and was plotting to kill him too. It was touch and go who would snap first. She was worn down, sharp-faced and sharp-tongued, alert for trouble, giving him no rest. Her teeth were falling out and it was as if she became old overnight. He made sure his back wasn't turned when she was near the kitchen knives; but even he wasn't ready for what happened next.

Coming home in the dark one night, he tripped over something in the doorway. His head muzzy with drink, he bent down and in the darkness felt something with an open mouth and sharp teeth. It didn't move. He sprang back with fright, but realised that although he had felt teeth, he wasn't bitten. Gathering his courage, he lit a lamp and found the cat lying dead. It was as if he had seen his own body, lying cold, a face distorted in agony. Although the ice was hard on the ground, he walked out and did not come back until near dawn. When he returned, he had no idea where he had been.

The cat was gone. His wife made no mention of it at breakfast. Had she removed it? He couldn't remember anything clearly.

He was sure the cat had been poisoned.

Now that there was no cat, there was no communication. She said nothing; she acted regularly and predictably to produce meals, to warm the house but like a shadow, like a ghost. Her movement was stiff and difficult. Her eyes looked nowhere. Brandon feared her. He feared this loss of human life in her. She knew it and was glad of it. She showed no more outward signs of fear herself. He knew he was deteriorating badly. His strength was sapped. He couldn't work half a day now without wanting a beer and the comfort of the local inn. He tried to reason things out but he knew she had the upper hand. Her mind was stronger. She had more stamina. If he was going to do anything, it would have to be soon but he would have to catch her by surprise. She was poisoning him. That was for certain. He felt so weak. Soon he would end up on the floor like the cat, his head twisted grotesquely as if jerked by a rope. He knew his mind was going, distorting things badly but he couldn't stop himself. The confusion of truth and distortion tortured him.

He told his story at the inn occasionally but people avoided him.

So it was that one day, he decided not to eat again until he rid himself of his problem. By midday he was weak, defeated. By evening however, he had drawn strength from his hatred and fear. It had to be done now.

He approached the house in failing light. A lamp was lit in the bedroom. Entering the kitchen, he could see very little except a thread of weak light under the bedroom door. Clumsily in the gloom, he grabbed some sort of kitchen tool, a blunt thing, and kicked at the door. It blasted open.

His wife was sitting on the edge of the bed. Her face was hard and forbidding, and in her hands she held a boy's shirt. He recognised it. What was she doing to it? Tears rolled from her eyes, but her mouth told another story. She was muttering. The sound was unusual, as if she wanted to speak, but there could be no talk. His fear returned and his body stumbled forward.

She half rose, her right hand holding long darning needles. He raised the metal and brought it down hard, half missing and knocking the lamp over. Everything went dark."

Just then the hall lights went out completely. The audience gasped. Someone screamed. Then all we could see was Pritchard, still at the table, left only with the flickering light of the one candle.

"They weren't discovered for about a week," he resumed, his voice tired and gruff, "but when they did, the scene was terrible. It must have been a horrific death struggle and both died with many and awful wounds. Blood ran over everything, so much that no one was prepared to wash the bedroom clean. Eventually the house became such a ruin that it was burned down, and you can still see the mounds of stone, covered with grass and weeds, if you care to walk that way."

Pritchard looked all round the room, and continued.

"You see why it was that conventional history didn't do justice to the story. It records only the facts, which were bare enough but if you piece together another, more complete tale from individual accounts of people who were around at the time, who would see what was going on, who heard Brandon's cry for help at the inn, who recalled things said by Peggy, then you'd realise that the facts concealed more truth than they revealed.

The cat's body was never found. Those of a

superstitious turn of mind claimed of course that Brandon was finished as soon as the cat was involved. His wife would have been in command of the cat. And how else could you explain it never being found?"

Pritchard slowly gathered his things into a cloth and wrapping it all together, picked it up, rose stiffly from the chair and walked off the stage, stooping like an old man. He was offstage before people began to applaud, slowly, individually at first, but gathering to a crescendo of noise. It was a success. Pritchard had pulled it off.

It was impossible for the organisers to follow that act so they announced an interval before holding the raffle.

Despite the merry show that continued afterwards, for me the evening ended with Pritchard. He made it sound like it could happen to any of us.

Chapter Seven

Midsummer Madness

Brown's Barbeque

A man has to abide by some principles. I mean, in this day and age of floating beliefs, Churches that don't agree on what's right and wrong, politicians who can quite easily express contrasting views in a single sentence, art which isn't, fantastic explosions of knowledge which we don't know what to do with – amidst all this, any self-respecting bloke has to make a stand somewhere.

So I've drawn the line. No skulking. No closet opinions. I have staked out the territory and declared it publicly. It may not be politically correct, but I DON'T BARBEQUE.

That may come over as hyper-assertive but on this issue I will not compromise.

Don't get me wrong. I like barbeques. I like other peoples' barbeques. I like the thought of going to a barbeque. But I won't do one myself.

I attribute this to consideration. Consideration for people who would have to, and certainly feel obliged to, eat the stuff I turned out. I haven't produced good meals *inside* the house yet, so I don't see that working with the inconvenience of live fire, breeze, fine ash and wasps will suddenly improve me. Hunger is the best sauce, but my guests would have to be rattling their skeletons before they'd welcome what I put in front of them.

And yet, I ask myself, how come so many men, and

I'm sorry to be so sexist but it does seem to be a male-dominated sport, how come so many men do actually succeed in making a go of it? At weekends they go striding about with their bags of anthrax or whatever it's called. I can't pay for my petrol because they clog up the filling stations. These guys can hardly burn toast but come the summer months there they are, standing with glossy red faces, sweaty foreheads, one hand grasping an offensive spear-thing and the other fist round a stubbie.

"Watcha mate," I shout at the roasting host.

"Hallo, old son," he cries jovially, squinting through the smoke, his bottle-end specs slipping half way down his nose.

"Devil's work," you say because you can't think of anything else.

"Yea, absolutely," he tries an evil grin as if your prompt was the funniest thing he's heard that afternoon. You wonder, with your fixed grin stiffening up the muscles in your face to twitching point, is he really enjoying this broiling, blinding, brain-busting experience? Apparently so.

"You all right?" He roars jovially over the loud sizzling of the hamburgers and his fingers.

He is very jovial. Saturnine would not do. I pick this out especially because I have noticed several things about barbeques and the way people behave.

The first and most important rule is that if you are standing at or near the barbeque you must be hearty. Maybe that's why I don't barbeque; being that hearty for that long would depress me. While the hamburgers are spitting, the sausages sleazing and the chickens sizzling, you are meant to be talking barbeques: barbeques I have built (give me a break); barbeques I have given; your new barbeque; what you've done responsibly with the old barbeque: barbeques on holiday. I'd want to talk about people I'd like to barbeque, but it's not on. It just doesn't seem in keeping. Wilful, nasty comments don't sound right around the barbeque.

The second principle I have noticed is that the bearer of the sharp implement is infinitely more important than you. If he needs to move, you get out of the way. He is the revered possessor of proud tribal knowledge, passed on from father to son via the barbeque instruction leaflet, which some men leave in the cardboard box that came with the barbeque and which they disposed of inadvertently. They never attain their full status as tribal elders.

You say nothing to antagonise this temporary king - and it's not because of the sharp implement. It's all to do with the fact that he is concentrating hard on seeing to such niceties as whether the end hamburger is getting evenly heated, each chicken leg equally covered in grit. You are there simply as an admirer as if you were in the studio of Picasso, witnessing the great artist at work.

"Pass me that pack of sausages," he commands.

And that's another thing. If we are going to barbeque, I want to see something real being roasted, like a game bird or a rabbit, or a bit hacked off a pig, or a gaping large fish. I might feel more excited, more primitive, although I'd have to be careful not to spill something on my light coloured chinos. But the usual round of burnt offerings, cooked from frozen, have come so far from their origins, that the concept of outdoor barbequing has become transmuted into a bloodless, synthetic pastime. Now if he were saying "Pass me that frozen mammoth rib," that would be different.

Thankfully the heartiness is confined to the men. Women treat it all differently. They come to inspect the gasping coals and the grizzling meats. They peer into the volcano's mouth and make encouraging loud noises to make the tribal elders feel good. But they don't stay. Whether it's because they don't want their hair to smell of smoke or because they quite simply want to have nothing to do with the cooking that day, I don't know, but they have the good sense to slope off to another group or on a cold day, back into the house.

And once all the food is gone, when we could happily stare for long enough into the dying embers, no one does. The area around the barbeque becomes deserted. If it were a campfire, the party would sit around, chatting peacefully, a quiet guitar thrumming. A small fire has that effect, but a dying barbeque is to be left to itself, outcast as a disused ironworks, the world having moved on.

You'll probably disagree. You'll probably say that the barbeques you give or attend are not like that, but I can rely only on my own experience.

What prompted me to reflect generally on barbeques was Brown's latest. He gives a barbeque lunch every year to members of his firm and to important clients. It's a well-organised affair. Brown doesn't actually cook himself. He's too busy schmoozing with his guests. No, he has a caterer bring in all the equipment, staff and food.

He holds it in his garden. Brown really has done well for himself with this firm. He seems to be good at what he does.

Divorced and therefore without spousely support, he asked a few of us over to help on the day in question.

I think there must have been about a hundred and fifty people present at the feast. He normally invites the largest shareholders, other members of the Board and a few of the senior managers. Some spouses attend, but the chat is so deadly boring and business-orientated that they seldom reappear next year.

Horace, Ronald and myself were asked to attend, just to see that things were all right and to run the free bar. We were not asked however to think about the preparation, otherwise we might have been able to prevent the chain of events which almost led to Brown losing his job.

The day began well enough. We went over to Brown's place, a lovely, old barn, converted to his specification, sitting on a large plot of land, surrounded on two sides by fields and the other two sides adjoining a neighbour's garden and the access road. The caterers were already there, setting up a tent but leaving its walls open to the fine summer weather. Brown holds it at the same time each year to make sure people can attend before they run off in August to their luxury holidays.

We were to place ourselves quite close to the caterers' stall, about twenty feet away, not so close as to get the two queues mixed up but close enough to let people get their food and drink easily on the one trip. We too had been given a small tent.

"If you'd like to set yourselves up in an orderly way," said Brown, "so that if you get a rush of people wanting drinks you'll be able to deal with them. I'm really not sure about you, Ronald. Perhaps you could let the others serve and you could pull pints in the background, as it were."

"What's wrong with me?" demanded Ronald.

"Well, I'd rather you didn't speak much with the guests. Jolly though you are, your line of talk won't be one they are familiar with. Best to leave it to the others."

"There's not enough beer," Ronald said.

"Of course there is," Brown said reassuringly. "The caterers are very good at assessing that sort of thing, you know." He walked off to talk to the head of the caterers.

"He's a cheeky beggar today," Ronald observed.

"Accurate though," Horace chipped in.

"How do you mean?" asked Ronald defensively, sensing a barb.

"Well, you are a bit rough and ready, Ronald. Not that I'd want you any other way but there's a time and place for everything, and this isn't yours. Now get back there and get the beer flowing without all that froth."

"I'll just take a saunter round," I said. "You two are doing so nicely and some early guests are arriving. I'll just check that they are being received properly."

"We should have been here earlier," Ronald was grumbling. "This beer is going to be hell to pull. It hasn't settled properly yet."

I strolled across the lawn to the reception point. Some people were carrying violin cases.

"Your body guards?" I teased Brown.

"String quartet," he replied. "Always have them. Adds a touch of class. I put them on the patio, switch them on and they saw away for hours on a few cans of Newcastle Brown. The guests behave themselves better too."

The players settled themselves down in a semicircle, tuned up, adjusted their specs and they were off.

"You should have them in livery next time," I suggested.

"I don't think so," Brown replied, distracted by the arrival of new guests. "You'll just find chicken, hamburgers, sausages, the usual stuff. Why don't you check the barbeque is all right? I'm doubtful that they are able to cook enough on that one. It doesn't seem large enough."

I did. It seemed to be ok. There were two crimson-faced chaps standing behind a large, hot trough. It wasn't quite time to cook yet, but they were beginning to separate the slabs of meat in readiness.

Then I ran into Sigmund. I was surprised.

"Unusual of you to forsake your shop," I said.

"Actually I asked Brown if I might attend because there's someone I would like to meet," he replied. "You see, one of Brown's shareholders owns the freehold shop premises in Sprighassle, and I'd like to expand a bit, you know, take the opportunity, as it were. Look, please don't let anyone else know that yet. I am only telling you because you have caught me and I can't lie very well."

I'm always suspicious when people tell me they don't lie well. It implies they don't lie at all: the truth can be otherwise. Anyway, why was he feeling so guilty about it?

Brown waved me over. I ran to his bidding. He was standing beside a gentleman who was, well, how shall I put it, fat. Seeing this gentleman, you realise that to be really fat is actually impressive. The man in question possessed authoritative bulk, which had equal measures of hostility and irritability. This guy carried weight, in every sense.

"This is Mr Brewer," Brown said, using a voice that was far too high for him. "Could you see that Mr Brewer is well looked after?"

Brown introduced me as a sort of accountant chappie who does odd jobs for companies. It's always interesting to know how your friends categorise you.

"Come over to the drinks tent and see what takes your fancy," I suggested to Mr Brewer. He came, but was surly.

"Do you come to Brown's barbeques every year?" I asked, trying to strike up a conversation. The do-you-come-here-often? opening with variation was all I could muster.

"Oh, yes," he managed. "I believe it cheers up the staff if I put in an appearance."

My eyebrows rose. Something told me that Brown had not fully disclosed who this was, but my instincts told me to tread warily. Pity the staff that needed his cheering up.

"Horace," I cried. "Let's have a drink for Mr Brewer."

"I thought he'd bring his own," Ronald quipped.

"I'll have a pint of bitter," Mr Brewer ordered, ignoring Ronald's joke.

"Quite right too, Chief," said Ronald. "Get in early, I say, because this lot's not going to go far. If I were you I'd take a couple. Old Brown's been quite mean."

"Ronald, just pour the beer. I'll do the talking," Horace pleaded.

"I like a man who speaks his mind," said Brewer to me as we waited for the drink. He said it in a way that made me believe him not one bit. Meanwhile Ronald was having trouble. The beer was hardly coming out of the nozzle.

"You've not got enough pressure," Brewer growled and leaning over, twisted the screw at the top of the canister.

Instead of increasing the flow gently, the tap spluttered violently and threw large bits of froth into the pint glass and straight out again. Ronald and Brewer stood the full force, Ronald in his face, Brewer all over the front of his shirt.

There was a moment's silence, still, tense; then Brewer took Horace's cloth, wiped Ronald's face with it and said, "I'll just have a whisky."

As I took him over to the food tent he explained. "People expect me to behave badly, but I don't. There's no point. I'll just quietly find out who the idiot was on Monday and have him sacked."

I was too cowardly to mention that Ronald was not an employee. Brown would have to cope with that one.

I next bumped into Sigmund again, who had succeeded in buttonholing his quarry, the other shareholder and owner of the shop premises. I couldn't get a word in edgeways. Sigmund attempted to introduce me but the other gave only the merest hint of acknowledgement and kept on talking.

"Fact is, I'm not cut out for this sort of thing at all. I'm not really a capitalist. I inherited the wealth from my grandmother, so I haven't even got the satisfaction of knowing that I earned it. Every year I lose a bit more. I don't know if I'd be jubilant or distraught if I lost it all."

"Do you feel that money has got in the way of your peace of mind?" Sigmund suggested, more as a line to keep himself awake than out of true interest.

"That's it exactly," the other said. "My goodness, you have a very clear vision of the world. Yes, I feel like I've been given security, but it's only a prison. And it's not so easy to escape, you know? Oh, no. People want to know why I don't just give the money away, or they probably would do if I asked them, but I can't because I'd be wasting what had been given to me. It's a dilemma."

"I really wanted to talk to you about taking the lease on your store in Sprighassle," Sigmund tried very hard to turn the conversation.

"Well I never," the shareholder stepped back. "I thought you were genuinely concerned. It's not often I open up but that'll teach me. Don't trust a soul. You get me to do all the talking just so you could screw that place out of me cheap. Not on your life."

And with that he stalked off to the barbeque tent.

"Sense of timing?" I said to Sigmund.

Brown's event was passing off rather well. I met

him in the middle of the lawn to check on his wishes. The quartet were taking a breather and a short queue was building up at the beer tent. Ronald waved to us, so we pottered over.

"The barrel ran out," he said. "I told you. Anyway, while you were swanning around, I got this load of canned beer from the off-license. You owe them quite a few bob, Brown. I put it on your account."

Brown went pale but took it bravely.

"And I handed out a few cans to willing helpers," Ronald added, indicating Horace and the two blokes behind the barbeque.

We strolled over to inspect the barbeque. While the quartet was resting up, someone was doing a juggling act, rather a good one.

As we arrived at the barbeque Brewer called out, "Look Brown. I bet you can't do this."

He took two of the cans that Ronald intended for the cooks and began to juggle. He was standing behind the barbeque trough and the effect was good, quite funny really. Then he took a third can and the effect was terrific. I stood back while Brown approached him, applauding.

Eventually all the cans fell to the ground, but Brewer was well pleased with himself and went to open one of the cans to quench his thirst. I couldn't see properly because of the hot air and smoke but I heard a cook shout out a warning to Brewer about beer shooting out.

"Nonsense," cried Brewer, still full of himself. "I know another trick. You just tap three times on the top of the can and that settles it. Look!"

He waved the can above his head, and then with theatrical style tapped the top of the can three times before pulling the ring. The beer shot out like cobra's venom, straight into Brown's eyes. He was thrown back and knocked against the barbeque trough. The whole thing rolled over and shed its load, leaving sausages and piles of hot coals all over the grass. Brown too fell.

Next thing, Ronald shot past me and made for Brown. I couldn't understand why Ronald had turned into this mini superman until I realised, with a tremor of apprehension, that from his angle of vision, Ronald had obviously believed that Brown had fallen into the fire. It was a perfectly easy mistake to make. Behind the smoke, Brown was certainly making a lot of noise but from where I was standing, I could see he was clear of the hot coals. Most people drew back but Ronald sped through fearlessly and rugby-tackled Brown, wrapping Brown's jacket tightly around him to smother the fire.

They rolled on the ground comically, coming perilously close to the real fire and then to Brewer who somehow re-appeared, as it happened, to his own peril. He did a silly-looking skip to avoid them, but being grossly overweight, he just made things worse and slowly, very slowly, toppled backwards and sat right down on a patch of fire. He howled and with astonishing propulsion for one so challenged, jerked up to his feet again, his bottom on fire, like something out of a boy's comic. At the same time terrible and funny, he jumped about and tried to slap the fire out but it only made it worse.

Such situations are meat and drink to people like Ronald, whose adrenalin works overtime. Realising his initial mistake and keen to make amends, he grabbed another of the fallen cans, held it aloft, tapped it three times, pulled the ring, aimed at Brewer's bottom and extinguished the flame.

First-aid people rushed Brewer off, away from the wreckage but Brown looked glum. Ronald was unrepentant. Horace could not stop laughing.

Horace was still laughing when I went up to the local that evening. Encouraged by a gathering audience, his account became more enriched each time he told it. Ronald tried to protest that he knew Brown hadn't actually fallen in the fire, but thought that the beer could have splashed into his eyes, which could have caused him to step into the burning fat. He sounded plausible, but it wasn't what we witnessed.

Anyway, for me at any rate, it just confirmed all my suspicions. It put another nail in the coffin of barbeques. I'm of a nervous disposition. My genuine belief is that Brewer, normally a man of unsmiling mood, was affected by being too close to the barbeque and was taken by a bout of heartiness and good humour. He had probably said something like, "Devil's work," to the cooks and, egged on by their completely undeserved laughter, got it into his head that he should frolic. I'd love to see his face when he returns to his normal hard-boiled self – and when he finds out he can't sack Ronald.

"Ronald?" they'll repeat, "No one called Ronald here."

And he might become obsessed with finding the fire imp who dogged his every step at Brown's barbeque.

No. While I am of sound mind and can still get to the pub without the aid of a golf-buggy, though I may experience peer pressure to the point of bursting, even if I see fifty percent off a barbeque in a sale, I shall firmly, and with absolutely no trace of joviality, insist that I DO NOT BARBEQUE.

The Signpost

Frequently we gather at the signpost, located at a disjointed crossroad near to the centre of the village. If

I were to be absolutely accurate, I would admit that I don't know where the centre of the village is. Two or three locations spring to mind but the signpost is, as you would expect, on the main road. Nearby, two small shops and the Gentle Goat snuggle together.

The signpost serves no useful purpose. People in cars can't read the place names because the white letters faded years ago and the locals don't need to. No, the signpost is now just a reminder of a bygone age, the age of the stagecoach, the horse and cart and the early graceful cars. It certainly does not tell you that we are twinned with Yvotte-sur-le-Plonk, nor does it pretend to convert miles to kilometres.

I get testy when this twinning business is mentioned. It hasn't come to pass in our village yet but I think it is an excuse, and a feeble one at that, for local councillors to go off to Yvotte-sur-le-Razzle to stock up their wineracks.

I tell you, any French village willing to be twinned with us must be desperate. There isn't much here, and nothing of interest to boast about. That's why I like it. You can tour it in five minutes and spend the rest of the time in the pub, not feeling guilty that you should be doing something else. So call me a wet blanket but twinning has gone bonkers if there is some place called Yvotte-pour-le-Weekend that has us earmarked on its Michelin Guide to England.

But don't get me wrong. This is a great place to live in. It is exactly what you would conjure up in your mind if you were asked to think of a typical English village. There would be stone cottages, an old church, a village hall, the odd thatched house, beautiful gardens and a rambling, spacious feel to the place, and of course the pub.

The fact that it is almost just a suburb now doesn't really spoil it. Maybe it will in the future but for the moment the village pretty well looks like what it has done for a hundred years.

I like it here. The people are real and they want you to be real. The ale is real and the stilton ploughman's salad is real.

Where were we? The signpost. Oh yes, I was telling you that we use it as a meeting place. Goodness knows why. It is one of the least attractive spots. Being on the main trunk road, you can't hear yourself speak when lorries go by for people coughing as they breathe in the exhaust fumes. The reason is lost in history. Maybe it signifies a primitive urge, the meaning of which is deep in the soul; the signpost showing us the way while we totally ignore it. What is certain is that we have to set out for the Goat before the exhaust fumes kill us off. What a healthy reason for getting to the pub more quickly.

Leaving all of that aside, what I was setting out to tell you about was the occasion when Horace's dog, Hardy, ran off with a sackful of newsletters.

Let me paint the scene for you. It's a lovely, summer morning, fresh, promising an afternoon of warmth and with a special brightness.

In winter, we dispense with gathering at the signpost and just meet at the pub, but in summer there is a whole outdoor ritual to be observed. I, for instance, finish my Saturday morning chores, potter about in the greenhouse, killing time and a few plants and fooling nobody. I have an understanding with the garden. I don't interfere with it and it doesn't come into the house.

As it happens, I do have a large garden but even if I had only a window box it would be a large garden for me. I don't get on well with it. I like to sit in the garden, serve drinks on my scarred lawn and watch the birds hack their way through over-branched trees. I stare in wonder at the beautiful flowerbeds tended by my wife, who knows weeds from flowers. For my part I do the digging and carrying, the physical jobs, somehow with less success.

Everyone tells me so. It's dispiriting. So this morning, when I judged that it was time to give the garden a break and let the blooms come out of hiding again, I closed the greenhouse door behind me, or rather, I lifted it back into place because the hinges were snapped in that storm we had some years ago, and skipped up the road to the signpost.

Pritchard and Horace were already there, hanging about like large schoolboys. Horace had his dog with him. I know Horace has his good points but Hardy isn't one of them. Some of the problem lies with Horace of course. In this case, Horace had tied the dog's leash to the signpost, which caused the animal to run around in ever decreasing circles as the leather wound round the post. When the leash became too tight, it whined and tugged without ever working out that its freedom would increase if it ran the other way again.

The damn dog wouldn't keep still. It was forever winding Pritchard and Horace into its web while they hopped from foot to foot, trying to release themselves.

Then Horace got his hand stuck in the leather thong as the dog circled and tightened the lead. His hand was pressed fast against the post. He got desperate and tried to kick out at the dog, but he hit Pritchard instead, making things worse.

"Give me a hand for God's sake," Horace yelled at me. "Pritchard's about as much use as a square tyre."

Pritchard had indeed made matters worse because he was concentrating his puny efforts on the strap binding Horace and not on the real problem, the dog. I don't blame him. It isn't the sort of dog you want to pet. It's a shame really. The dog has a patch eye, which makes it look untrustworthy. The dog can't help it, but that's life.

Then Pritchard's hand too became stuck fast to the post. He's a lugubrious old toad at the best of times and now looked completely out of his depth.

"I knew something like this would happen," he moaned. "Why don't you leave that mongrel at home?"

"He'd wreck the place."

"Give him a sedative."

"I'll give him a sedative up the backside," Horace promised, "if I could get my hand free."

"Is that how you give him a sedative?" Pritchard asked politely, trying to carry on the conversation as if they were in the village fete beer tent.

Horace stared at him unbelievingly then tried to kick the dog again. Because Hardy was on a short leash, he snapped back. Pritchard's voice rose in protest. "Do something."

I closed in on the dog with a degree of nervousness, grabbed him firmly by the collar, pushed his neck gently to the grass and unclipped the lead. The dog looked pleased. It was the first time I had made meaningful contact with it and I didn't feel too bad myself.

Horace was in no mood for congratulations. "Hold on to that devil while I get this strap off and I'll show him who's boss," he spluttered, red with anger and embarrassment.

"What's all this then?" came a voice approaching. It was Ronald. It has to be said that Ronald can have the effect of soothing a situation, but only if he hasn't caused it. He has the gift of cheering people up, even when they don't want to be.

Somehow Horace was restrained from dogslaughter. Pritchard also preferred to drop the subject and regain what was left of his dignity. I calmed the dog down more. He was looking at me as if I was an easy touch. Confronted by this conspiracy of silence, Ronald changed the subject.

"Here's the first batch of this month's village newsletter," he announced, indicating a large newsboy's sack hanging from his shoulder. "We need to think of the contents for the next edition because that will be the one to advertise the fund-raising week later in the year."

Ronald was right. Motivated by a rush of public-spiritedness to the brain, our little band had offered to organise the publicity for the week, probably in October, which was to be given over to raising funds to renovate the village hall. The hall is used a lot, and the Village Hall Committee, of which Ronald was a member, had ambitious plans to refurbish and extend it a little. The target figure we needed to raise was higher than anything achieved so far.

"Brown late as usual?" Ronald asked.

"He said not to wait for him," Pritchard replied. "He has some business to attend to, but he'll see us there."

We shambled off to the pub, content in the growing warmth of the day and anticipating that there were beers with our names on them, waiting for us at our usual seat. Our window seat is idyllic in summer, but awful in winter, when the cold draft from the window makes us shiver and snuffle. Somehow we never change, except if another group have taken the seat first, when we gratefully slink over to the inglenook to warm our backs.

But the days of winter were far away. It was hard to imagine anything other than the lovely cool which met us as we entered.

As you will have seen by now, The Gentle Goat commands a central position in the village in every way. The couple that run it, Andy and Zelda, are all you would want to find in an English pub, and that is their secret. Whatever you dream of in a pub, they provide it for you specially. You'd think that would lead to a collection of contradictions and incompatible features offered by the pub, but it doesn't. It all works fine. The collective wit of the village doesn't run to much however and they are inevitably referred to as the "Village A to Z".

"Four pints of Modest please," said Horace, "and a bowl of water for the dog."

"Is the dog under age?" Zelda asked.

"You look under age yourself, Zelda," Horace said gallantly.

"Four pints," said Zelda with a winning wink, "but we don't serve dogs."

"We'll have to have sandwiches instead then," said Ronald.

"With or without mustard?" Zelda offered.

"That depends on what's in them," Ronald said.

"Not really," Zelda replied. "There's only ham today."

Exhausted by the effort required of this high-level banter, we took our places at the window table. The dog hung around the bar and tried to melt Zelda's heart by looking cute, but when you look like a canine version of Long John Silver you need another strategy to win hearts. So it then tried to look pathetic and rolled on the floor, panting.

"Is that animal going to do that for long?" Zelda asked.

"It's ok," Andy said. "It'll make everyone thirsty."

"What's in this edition of the Newsletter?" Pritchard inquired. "Something interesting, I hope."

"Nope," said Ronald firmly. "The Editorial Committee chucked out anything remotely interesting, and instead printed the serial numbers of all the banknotes in our pockets, copied out a page of the Financial Times and told everyone what was on television in Hungary two weeks ago. We thought it would make a change."

"I think we do need a change," Pritchard persisted. "I can't read it usually. It is so smudged."

"That's not my fault," Ronald protested. "We can't afford expensive paper and print, you know. It's a tight budget. Anyway, it just so happens that the printers gave us best quality this month at no extra charge. We allowed them to advertise free in it. They have come out rather well."

We all had a look, and sure enough, it was much clearer. The print stood out from the page and you could actually see who was in the photographs. The usual articles were there: the diary of events; the Church section; the kiddies' bit; reports from the various social groups.

"Ok, so what about the next edition?" I said. "We need to do something bright and colourful to advertise the fund raising."

"Can your printer do a good quality edition again, now that he's got the hang of it?" Horace asked. "Let him advertise all he likes."

"Talking of advertising, look at this one," muttered Pritchard, leafing through the pages. "Séances organised. Get in touch with the dead."

"Who's advertising that?" I asked.

"There's just a telephone number," Pritchard replied. "I suppose they wouldn't want to be easily traced by the living."

"Everyone's easily traced here," I said. "It's impossible to remain anonymous."

"Here's another. Bubble Car needs repair. There won't be many who remember what a Bubble Car is."

"Makes you wonder what's hidden in barns and

garages all over the place," Horace mused. "Maybe one of us has gold plate buried in the garden, hidden by the Royalists to avoid the Roundheads getting hold of it. Do you know, I once thought I had found treasure?"

"You haven't told us this one before," I said.

"There's a lot you don't know about me. Yes, it was a long time ago. I had a summer job, working in the gardens of a large country house when I was still at school. I needed money to save up for something, I can't remember what. It was pleasant work, doing odd jobs in the sun. One day I was asked to clear a piece of ground so that the gardener could do something clever with it, like growing carrots. He gave me a spade and a pick because there were some very heavy stones on that patch of ground. I was giving it what-for with the pick when I touched on something that was very definitely not a stone. It rang when I hit it, as if it were a container with something in it."

"Gardener's lunchbox?" suggested Ronald. "Keeping cool underground."

"Keeping it safe from Horace more likely," I said.

Horace continued undaunted. "I thought it might only be an old piece of metal but then I began to think of all the possibilities. Maybe it would be of archaeological interest, like digging up Troy, or maybe I'd get a reward if it were a treasure chest. I imagined hacking off a rusty clasp and opening the lid to reveal gleaming coins, bright as the day they were put there. Anyway, the closer I got, the more impatient I got."

"Same old Horace," Pritchard commented.

"Instead of taking my time, I began to really drive the pick hard into the ground," Horace continued, "but I was stupid. I was on the brink of uncovering the container, when my pick went through the lid. There was immediately a funny smell."

"Rotting compost?" I suggested.

"Rotting gardener?" from Ronald.

"No," said Horace ruefully, "Just rotten luck. It was a drum of old engine oil, buried years ago, and I spiked it. I was exhausted with all this digging so I stopped to have a smoke and to think out what to do next. Then the smell changed. I couldn't think for the life of me what it was to begin with and then it dawned on me that what I was smelling was smoke, or fumes. Something was burning. It was quite possible that I had dropped my match down the hole by mistake. I couldn't find the spent match anywhere on the ground next to me, so I had to conclude it was possible."

"What did you do?" Pritchard asked, quite agitated by this lapse on Horace's part. "Was it the oil that was burning?"

"I think it must have been, but I didn't want anyone to know, so I shovelled all the soil back on top again. Looking back, I think I imagined it all. I'll never really know. But the story's not finished yet. I was scared to tell anyone. I imagined this oil burning underground. I'd heard that some fires burn for months underground, so even after I left the job I was worried sick."

"I think your fears were exaggerated," Pritchard reasoned dolefully, looking at his now empty glass.

"Well maybe not, you see," Horace eventually came to the point. "You were going on about Bubble Cars and it reminded me about Messerschmit. They used to make similar cars. But that also reminded me of old aircraft."

"And that reminds me of airhostesses serving drinks, which reminds me it's your round." Ronald said loudly, waving his tankard. He had long ago given up trying to follow Horace's memory trail.

Horace was tenacious in concluding, amidst growing unrest from the assembly. "The owner of the big country house kept a really old plane in an outbuilding and occasionally still brought it out under its own steam."

"A steam aeroplane?" Pritchard mused.

"Two weeks after I left," Horace said, "there was an explosion in the outbuilding and the plane was wrecked. The outbuilding was only about forty feet away from where I set the oil-drum alight. A painter got the blame. It was said that he had left his blow-torch on while he fetched something and the fumes from the aeroplane's fuel tanks had been ignited, but I fear it was my underground fire."

"Are you finished?" Ronald asked bluntly.

"Yes, but what do you think?"

"I think if you don't get this round in quick, the pub will be closed," said Ronald.

As Horace collected the glasses to take to the bar, Brown came in, looking very smug.

"I have just pulled off quite a success," he announced. In this mood, he is downright pompous, no other word for it. He gave us his deep voice and nothing-between-the-ears stare.

"Pray tell us what you have pulled off then," Ronald said, winking at Pritchard and giving him a nudge in the ribs sufficient to make him swallow a peanut down the wrong hole.

"I have been meeting with Mick Thompson, the Managing Director of Modest Breweries. Are you all right, Pritchard?" Brown interrupted himself.

Pritchard looked as if he had stopped breathing, but nodded. Maybe he just looked as if he nodded.

"And," Brown went on, "he will contribute twenty-five per cent of our target for the village hall if, if," he repeated grandly, "we allow him advertising and if, if, (every second "if" was said with well-practised emphasis) we permit him to mount a plaque on the Village Hall saying that Modest Beers helped with the modernisation."

Ronald consented first. "Fine by me. You've done all right, Browny."

"Seems great," whispered Pritchard, but he was unaccustomed to enthusiasm and had a relapse into silence while he contemplated the fretting Hardy.

"Will they cap it?" I asked, "or is it an open cheque? I mean, twenty-five per cent of what?"

"That's the beauty of it," cried Brown. "They will contribute twenty-five per cent of the cost, no matter what it is. Mind you, the limit is really dictated by how much we raise. That's the best way to think of it."

Our discussion of restoration finances was put on hold when Pritchard gave a dreadful wheeze and again began to look as if he had stopped breathing. We looked at him, and wondered if we should do something.

Then he took to coughing violently. In turn he wheezed horribly, and coughed horribly. Panic began to show. He stood up and in doing so, pushed against the table and knocked over his half-full beer mug.

Unfortunately for Horace's dog, the beer mug and contents dropped on top of it, sending it into an extremely bad mood. I think it was because the dog was thirsty and to see all this spilt liquid was an added torture. Whatever, it tried to lick some of it up, but it was not to its taste. It got even more bad-tempered and began to leap upon the coughing Pritchard to punish him for his clumsiness.

"It's the peanut," Ronald shouted, with sudden inspiration. "It must be lodged in his windpipe. It's ok. I know what to do."

He jumped up and attempted to get behind Pritchard. I knew what he was trying to do but it wasn't going to work. I'm told that if you get your arms around someone in these circumstances and with your hands clasped, pull firmly, then you will cause the air from the lungs to push out the obstruction.

The problem was that Pritchard is quite tall, and Ronald isn't, and Pritchard was definitely not co-operating. In his panic, he was revolving around with Ronald running around behind him, the dog barking aggressively and occasionally tripping Ronald up. The next thing was that all three became tied in a knot and tumbled to the floor.

Horace, Brown and I stood fascinated by this macabre dance. Inevitably it drew attention. Zelda shouted things like, "Stop them!" and "Do something!" but by the time they were on the floor it was too late.

The dog wasn't finished, not by a long chalk. Whether thirst was driving it mad or whether the beer it lapped up had gone to its head, I don't know. This pooch defies reason in every way. It's no use looking for a motive and as I said, it hadn't yet finished.

Freeing itself from the pile of bodies and dodging the pathetic attempts of Horace to capture it, it performed a lovely sidestep which any international rugby player would have been proud of, and grabbed the newspaper bag in its mouth. Before we could do anything to stop it, it ran out the door, pulling this great, heavy bag as if it were carrying feathers. Horace ran after it but too late. We got outside only to see it running hell-for leather down the road. We gave chase.

Worse was still to come. Excited by the chase, it picked up speed, shedding some of the papers as it went. Then it showed that it had fox blood in it, because it made directly for the brook to throw us off the scent. It cut through the water like it wasn't there, but the bag was left behind.

We gathered the papers and trudged back to the Goat. Zelda wouldn't let us in, especially with a bagful of soggy print, so we sat outside on the lawn and spread some of the pages out to dry.

"Can you still read them?" Brown enquired. He hadn't indulged in the pursuit and was feeling aggrieved at being denied a place in the pub.

"Actually," I said, "when they dry out they'll be no worse than usual. But we'll have to stay put while they dry."

So we lingered for some time. It was quite pleasant sitting dreamily on the grass, soaking up the sun and supping ale that Brown generously brought out to us. After an hour the dog came back, quite as if nothing had happened. Ronald got it a bowl of water and it settled down at his side. Even Horace was forgiving.

"I think we'll change the name of the village newsletter," said Pritchard, a little hoarse, but mostly recovered. "We should call it THE SIGNPOST."

"Why?" asked Horace.

"I don't know," said Pritchard quite honestly. "It just feels right."

And so we did.

Chapter Eight

A Summer Pantomime

The Committee

I market myself as a sort of problem-solver for smallish -sized firms having difficulties with their figures. I'm lucky; there's always work, but there's a sad side too. Often the firms are going out of business and it has nothing to do with careless accounting.

Frequently my work takes me to London. I can't say I enjoy the rail journey but now and again a lighter moment arises. One morning the carriage was fully occupied as usual, so I had to sit in the middle of a bank of three seats, which is quite a squeeze. I took papers out to study before lifting my briefcase onto the rack.

As I settled down I noticed with mild annoyance that the man opposite me was wearing iPod headphones. I didn't look forward to spending the next half-hour listening to the hissing and clicking sounds that you presume to be the percussion end of a mindlessly repetitive dance track.

However I couldn't hear anything at all. His eyes were closed so I thought he must have switched it off. My attention was brought back to my own situation when my neighbour yelped slightly as the car keys in my left pocket pierced into his flank like a spur. Apologising, I prepared to work.

We hadn't gone five minutes when the chap with the earphones gave a strange snort, then a cough. A minute or so later he did it again. Because I was still feeling disturbed by his first snort I was quicker to look up. Unmistakably his cough had been an attempt to hide the first strange noise. He was still keeping his eyes closed so for all I knew he could have been dreaming. Then a suppressed smile came to his lips. It might have been wind but no: an unmistakable grin spread across his whole face.

He was trying not to laugh and holding himself stiffly to prevent it, but you know what laughter's like. Never there when you want it and irrepressible when you don't. It lets you down. Most other feelings you can control or hide; sadness, envy, loathing, but laughter has no master.

I worked out that he was laughing at something on his iPod. Something infectious began to swell up in me also and I realised that if I wasn't careful I'd be the one laughing next. I got my head down purposefully into my papers and hoped it would go away.

I had it almost under control when he actually gave a laugh but still tried to cover it up by putting his hand to his mouth. I felt my own laughter bubbling up again. I couldn't explain it. Here I was, a sensible middle-aged man, feeling like a schoolboy in class, unable to control the desire to burst out laughing when I didn't even know what was funny.

He gave another shake, this time spreading his thumb and middle finger over his eyes. I gave a little snigger myself and felt terribly hot. His neighbour to the right, at the window, looked to be in some discomfort, fingering his tie knot and putting his hand to his face.

To my left, the flank into which I had dug my keys was shaking. The owner of the flank had folded his paper up in front of his face and seemed to be having breathing difficulties. This made the tension even greater. I felt my body going into a proper laugh, without my permission. I began to shake, as unobtrusively as I could but when you are sitting tight up against two others it's hard to be private.

The laughter by this time had communicated itself to all of us, facing each other in banks of three. One gentleman to my right, a very pin-striped sort, was acting most uncharacteristically, fidgeting about as if he were at Sunday School and the only lady involved in all this, facing me and next to the passage way, was already wiping silent tears from her eye makeup.

Just as the tension was becoming intolerable, the ticket collector reached us. As he shouted out a hearty "Tickets Please", the squirming, pinstriped gentleman to my right lost control completely and let go of what has become known in certain circles as a trouser cough. This was too much.

Five of us erupted into laughter - inexplicable, throaty, ruddy-faced laughter. The ticket collector was quite offended, thinking that the laughter was directed at him. I felt terrible. The poor chap was going about his business, entering an ordinary-looking carriage and asking six ordinary-looking people to prove that they have paid for their journey. A ticket collector has to take the task seriously. After all, his role is to catch offenders. That is his purpose in life. It is not funny. Yet here in the middle of carrying out his duties sensibly and responsibly, he is made fun of.

Retaining as much dignity as he could, he inspected five shaking tickets. The chap opposite me with the iPod, however, was still in his own world and hadn't so far experienced the chaos around him. The ticket inspector tapped him on the arm and amidst the painful laughter around him asked for his ticket. The man took out his earpieces, looked astonished and annoyed that such a small incident as the ticket collector having to ask him personally for his ticket could cause such amusement, showed his ticket and walked out of the carriage. He gave us filthy looks but that made us all the more helpless, the lady especially laughing cruelly to his face.

Well, our behaviour embarrassed us. The other passengers built a ring of disapproval around us and eventually we subsided, our chests sore and our eyes streaming. By the time we got to London, we were mystified ourselves as to how we got into that state and slunk off without looking at one another.

I happened to be telling this story in the pub to Horace, Brown, Pritchard and Ronald while we waited for other members of a committee to turn up. To be more truthful, we had arranged to meet half an hour earlier than the committee start-time so that we could get a couple of drinks in before the committee began. That way, it was all much more enjoyable. The beer made you more creative, less critical and gave you a good excuse to take frequent breaks to go to the toilet.

The committee? Ah. There seem to be so many. I've never known a place where people could form and reform into quite as many little groups of self-importance, some temporary, others as permanent as anything in this life. This particular committee was to organise the children's annual show.

Every year the school, along with some willing helpers in the village, organises an event, either a play, or a show, just to give a climax to the end of the school summer term. I'm told that originally the idea was to entertain the older people in the village. Some of the oldest inhabitants who couldn't get themselves about would even be transported to and from the show. As usual over the years the original purpose dissolved. The annual show took on a life of its own and now it gives the whole school a feeling of team spirit.

The committee included Mr. Robbens, the Head

Teacher, Mrs. Ribbons, (frequently mistaken for Mr. Robben's wife) who teaches the nine and ten year olds, Mrs Webster, the beautiful widow for whom Ronald pines still, and us.

I drifted out of my daydream to hear Ronald telling us how he believed he had managed to make himself appeal more to Mrs. Webster.

"I thought I was really in," he told us. Ronald can sometimes look so sad that the effect is comical. You could just see him as a little boy, using it to get out of scrapes with his teacher or his mother.

"I was fixing up a new clothes pole for her when I happened to mention that there was a football game on the box that I wanted to see. This was last night, you know, the England V France match. She was quite enthusiastic herself and said she had read about it in the newspapers. We really had quite a chat, and then - you could have pushed me over with a feather - she said why didn't I go round to her place to see it. Well you know my television's been on the blink for weeks now so I jumped at the chance. I even took her some chocolates to say thank you. Not only was I getting to see the game but it was an opportunity to talk about something *I* knew about for a change."

"Very romantic, and domestic," Horace commented. "I can just see the three of you, the Webster woman, you and the box of chocolates, all sitting on the sofa, illuminated only by the blue tint from the television."

"It didn't happen though," Ronald continued. "When I got there, she was just going out. She said I'd have the house all to myself and there was some beer in the fridge. She was off to see some friends. I had to think quickly, as if this was perfectly ok, but it was disappointing. I can sit alone with a beer at home, thank you very much. Anyway I sat and watched the match. As I left, I remembered the chocolates so I wrote a thank-you note and put them on the table."

We tried to make light of it but we all felt for Ronald.

It was almost time for the proceedings to begin. Mr. Robbens and Mrs. Ribbons sat together, organising some papers. Two minutes later Mrs. Webster hurried in, looking anxious about coming into a pub on her own but her face brightened up when she saw us.

"Sorry," she breathed. "Am I late? I was just finishing a book and I was so absorbed that I lost track of time."

We competed to tell her it was ok. She gave a general greeting to everyone and then, seeing Ronald, she mouthed a separate "hello" to him. He in turn gave an adoring look. I knew we wouldn't get his attention for the next ten minutes. I could see why. She really is a dazzler but with an untouchable, soft-focus quality, like an early screen goddess. I could feel my own attention wandering.

Brown called the meeting to order. He's very good at it, and we obediently took up pens, like a row of monks getting down to a shift of manuscript -copying.

"The first item on the agenda is Nominations. We have to elect a project leader, a treasurer and a dogsbody," Brown announced.

"I don't think that's a very attractive title," Mrs. Ribbons objected. I recalled that the kids called her "Rib". She liked the sound of her own voice. As she was always being taken for Mr. Robbin's wife, it is possible she had to assert her own identity more.

"I think the title is quite likely to be *Secretary*, but whoever takes it on ought to realise what it involves," Brown explained.

"Then I would happily accept the honour of undertaking that role," Mrs. Ribbons said. "It is a very worthy task."

Brown looked around the group, found no opposition and confirmed the appointment. "And I am certain," he nodded gravely, taking his cue from Mrs Ribbons' tone, "that you will bring all the charm and dignity to the role that it deserves."

Mrs. Ribbons beamed and looked to Mr. Robbins for approval. None was forthcoming. He was forming his own thoughts.

"I would like to put myself forward as project leader," he pronounced. This was hardly a surprise: every year he was project leader and she was secretary-dogsbody. But we observed the rituals loyally.

Brown again looked round and confirmed the appointment. "I'm sure you will as usual discharge your duties energetically and honourably."

What makes us speak like this when we get together in committees? The same bunch of people standing around the bar, some of us with one leg dangling over a barstool, will use words and sentences of half the length and make twice as much sense. But give us a square table with a guy at the top called "Chairman" and we begin to talk like people in a Noel Coward play.

Brown checked that I was minuting these points, asked if I would be treasurer, and moved to the main agenda topic.

"So what are we going to do this year?" he asked. "We have quite a lot to live up to."

We certainly had. Last year, the children concocted a kind of swimming gala, with races. They also bravely attempted synchronised ballet in the water, to music of course.

The gala had its moments. One event was a complicated relay with four teams, whereby two teams started at one end and the other two teams at the opposite end, using four lanes to do a relay race. Suddenly half way through the race, two of the children, starting at opposite ends, dived into the same lane and headed at speed for one another, doing the crawl. The audience noticed and tried to point it out to the organisers, who thought the audience was just getting excited about the race. Some mothers began to panic and to scream for the race to stop. There seemed to be so much time while the swimmers progressed blindly towards one another, like knights jousting, but with their visors jammed down over their eyes.

Suddenly Callum saw what was going to happen. He was a "helper" and was pacing the side of the pool. Callum, tall, aristocratic, a gentle-looking person, suddenly acted. Diving into the water, he swam right under the ropes dividing the lanes, came up perfectly in the right lane in time to get between the two swimmers and stand protectively between them. The place erupted. You would think he had just saved the earth from space invaders. Men cheered. Women wept. He looked such a hero.

But that wasn't all. At the end, the audience had to file out of the rows of seats and past the pool to get to the exit. Of course the side of the pool was extremely wet and the inevitable happened. One sweet old lady started it all with her walking stick. The rubber point on her stick slipped in the wet and got caught between the feet of an elderly gentleman, already experiencing sufficient difficulties of his own. This extra little problem caused *him* to slip into the back of a larger lady, who was fired mercilessly into the water without even having time to scream. The gentleman tottered on the edge for a bit and then, with all the condemned dignity of a felled fir toppling slowly to the forest floor, he lay on the water, on top of the first lady. It was shocking, but priceless.

We got them out somehow and they were good sports about it all. The one whose stick caused it all stopped being a sweet old lady and laughed like a drain. She was so stricken with laughter, I thought she would peg out on us.

"I wondered about putting on a series of events," suggested Mrs. Ribbons. "We could invite other clubs and societies to put something on, and make the whole thing a festival weekend."

Mr. Robbins got fired up with the idea. "Absolutely. We could even have a whole week and have neighbouring villages contribute pieces."

"We could have a theme of 'musicals' and put five different musicals on five different nights," said Horace, "and the kids could put on a rock show."

"I think something more cultural would be appropriate," Mrs. Webster offered. "A good choir, or a poetry reading. Much easier to stage."

The thought of a poetry reading subdued us but we didn't like to say anything. I thought the conversation was taking too elaborate a turn.

"How long do we have before opening night?" Pritchard asked. As usual, Pritchard had got straight to the point.

"Five weeks," Mrs. Ribbons replied, as automatic as a talking clock and the last to see the point. "The date is on the agenda in front of you."

There was a silence as we pondered the implications. There was very little time to organise a complicated series of events and it was probably also too late to book outside people to come.

"We should lower our sights and be realistic about what we can do," said Brown. "Keep things modest, where it's all in our control," he added, emphasising the last few words.

"How about a midsummer pantomime?" Pritchard suggested.

"What's that?" Mrs. Ribbons perked up.

"The same as a winter one but in summer. It'll be a novelty and you can get the audience to participate," Pritchard explained.

We warmed to the idea. Mrs. Webster was disappointed that we weren't taking up her idea of the poetry reading but she and Ronald (surprise, surprise) undertook to think how something of that sort could be included.

"How about Dick Whittington?" Brown put forward. "A good moral tale about someone making it in the world. Give them ambition, you know."

"You've probably just supplied the reason for not doing it," said Horace.

"I've got a script for 'Pied Piper of Hamlin," Mrs. Ribbons said. "It would give us a quick start and I remember it had some funny lines in it."

"Good," cried Brown, desperate to get one thing out of the way. "Do I get a common assent to that?"

He did. Such are the way decisions are made. Mrs. Ribbons felt good that she had made the suggestion. Mr. Robbins was happy that he had something to project-manage. Pritchard knew he had steered at the right point. Horace was happy because he could get to the bar. Mrs. Webster was content that she had had a warm reception for her idea of poetry reading, and it was obvious why Ronald was feeling good. Brown knew all of this and personally felt good because he had managed another productive meeting. All in all, the feel-good factor was high and we slipped off to the bar to speak like normal human beings again.

Why did I alone feel disquiet? Maybe I should have spoken up at the meeting, but ..... well, I don't know. It's just that the village school has had a bit of trouble with rats of late. Nothing much really. You have to expect it when you live in the country, and the brook flows nearby. I just felt, well ..... that it was all a bit close to the bone, really.

The Pied Piper

It is interesting to note the different responses of people when it comes to local productions of any sort. I personally am far too retiring to take a front-line part, acting or singing. I'm very happy to help or encourage and my attendance record at performances is exemplary, but standing up front? No way.

Some others can't be held back. Given the prospect of taking a lead in a show they change entirely, putting themselves forward with stunning generosity of spirit just so that they can tread the boards, I believe the expression is, for a few minutes of glory.

They wouldn't tread them so readily if they knew how flimsy the stage is in our village hall. We lash together somehow all sorts of woodenry to try to attain an even floor for the performers and we cover up the resulting mess with fancy paper and things so that it looks almost the real thing, but you can't get it exactly right all the time.

A grid of trestles supports the boards. There was one performance where a trestle somehow became loose, so that when a performer stood on a particular spot on the flooring, it brought the other end of the floor up like a seesaw and made the show look as if it were a circus. The actors most frequently on stage got to know it and avoided it. However a bit-part actor, running on to say his one line, trod perfectly on the loose end. The plank rose and smacked him on the face before he got his lines out. He then sank under a collapsing floor, pulling fragments of stage down with him, plus nearby actors. The scene stole the show, which until then had been deadly dull. Audiences improved thereafter, hoping that another entertaining calamity might take place.

If I am honest, I have also noticed that there is little correlation between the willingness to push for a lead part, and having the talent to carry it off. In fact, nature has perversely denied some of those creatures the ability to see themselves. So perhaps the first rule of casting ought to be to turn down those most keen. Make them do bar duties, sell tickets, run the raffle, anything except a lead role. I would in fact extend this principle to politics; those who are most desirous of power should be instantly disqualified.

The second rule should of course be that those providing most in the way of funds, facilities, costumes, musical instruments, transport or food should be asked to play the lead roles. This is already such a respected law of nature that it needs no further explanation.

The third rule is designed to avoid starting family feuds which will continue for centuries and therefore is extremely important. It is that the casting director should hail from elsewhere and after the casting should disappear again. You can even work an exchange scheme with another village or school. Casting is so unpopular that the selector should be saved from future abuse. Anyway the casting, apart from one important person, is so unimportant that it is best to get it done quickly and anonymously and then you can happily, throughout the whole project, blame the absent culprit for everything.

The one important person, by the way, is the curtains engineer. It is so obvious when you think about it but that person has the power, instantly on the night, to decide what the audience will or will not see, irrespective of what is in the script. A most merciful thing is the sight of a well-timed curtain close, just before the embarrassment rating rises too high.

My reasons for not wanting to perform under the

lights have no real bearing here but in a small community such as this, it is a feat to escape being roped in. I avoid it like the plague, but maybe I shouldn't use that expression. I'll explain later.

The Committee's decision to produce a modern version of the Pied Piper was taken enthusiastically into implementation mode by the teachers and children of the village school. They worked hard for the all-too-short period of a few weeks and before you knew it, the first night was here.

However, taking these things more literally than most, I was surprised, when I arrived and went backstage, to find one character walking around looking like Dick Whittington and another, a very beautiful young lady, looking like Cinderella at the ball. I was prompter, but I hadn't bothered to prepare, because I didn't expect surprises in the script.

During the run up to the Pantomime, I had gone to see the Headmaster, Mr Robbins. The school was for under-twelves and had always put on good shows but when I spoke with Mr Robbins he was quite glum about this year's. "It has not gone to plan," he said. "The kids have adapted it. Too ambitious, I think. Too way out."

I couldn't see how they could have injected much ambition into it. They only had a few weeks to rehearse. I was pondering his words when I came across Mrs Ribbons, secretary to the project leader.

"Ah," she cried above the hubbub of children changing, chirping and chewing all at the same time. "Here's your new copy of the script. It's moved on a bit since we spoke last."

When people use such words, my stomach churns. It can mean a whole range of things from, "It's a completely new project," to "It's gone terrifically wrong."

"The children thought it was boring to do the straight version of the Pied Piper, so they have introduced other stories into it. It gave them a few more lead parts to keep everybody happy. Quite a melting pot really."

She was called away to deliver a child from a shoestring, which was tied too tightly around its neck, and another small person was queuing up for treatment for slight concussion because he had walked into a piece of scenery. At least three of his friends were trying to tell Mrs Ribbons the story.

I looked at the revised script. It was unreadable. The changes to the original script covered whole pages, with lines and words crossed out and chunks of tiny print inserted that I could hardly read in a good light, never mind when I sat in the darkness at the side of the stage.

Well, it was too late to worry about that now. It was only ten minutes before the curtain rose, so I decided to check out who else was at their posts. Mrs Webster was gamely helping small children with their costumes. Digby, the local businessman who was sponsoring the show, was making sure that his advertisements were in all the best places. He had suggested that the whole cast wore T-shirts with his logo on them, until we pointed out that the audience would not have differentiated between the characters, causing utter confusion.

That set me dreaming. I mean, if all the cast of Hamlet came on wearing white T-shirts with the same red logo, you'd probably lose Hamlet in the melee, and the Ghost wouldn't stand a chance. Romeo and Juliet might be ok, I suppose, but if you had a situation where a girl was playing the part of a boy or vice versa, you'd have audience-drift within fifteen minutes. Great equalisers, though, T-shirts. If Marx and Engels had thought of them, they would have solved the whole problem of class inequality at a stroke. Fashion beats politics every time.

Looking up into the rigging or whatever it is called in a theatre, I spied the dusty soles of Callum clambering around and checking that all the wires, lights and other mysteries were in good order. I hoped he had a strap tied to his waist. It was a long way to fall, although I was sure Callum would never do anything so undignified.

Brown was doing sterling work in front of house, welcoming people, being generally gregarious and lending some spark to the proceedings.

Still, it was with an ill-defined sense of unease that I took up my position at the inner side of the curtain, where there was a dim pilot light. I could see most of the stage except the back, but usually when the actors are saying their lines, they are standing at the front of the stage. The right upper circle could see me if I stuck my head out but that didn't matter.

I felt more confident because Callum was up there, or wherever he was now. I recalled to myself one embarrassing occasion when I was sitting, ready for the curtain to go up, and minding my own business, when someone made the curtain which concealed me ride to the back of the stage. I was exposed. The audience didn't laugh at first: they thought it was the beginning of the play. We sat there for a minute, a very long minute, before I realised nothing was going to happen to get me out of the situation, so I stood up to effect a dignified exit stage right, when another curtain, tumbling out of control from above, caught me by surprise and felled me. Someone pulled me by the legs out of sight of the audience, half of whom were laughing, the rest still mystified.

"What the Hell are you doing?" the Director shouted at me. The play was a murder mystery and to this day some in the audience thought I was the person being murdered. Goodness knows what they made of the rest of the play.

Probably the same as me when I'm watching thrillers. If an exam paper came round while I was watching one, asking me what was going on, my answer paper would be blank. And yet I love watching them. There's a certain formula to be worked out, a ritual to be observed, and all the while I haven't a clue what's going on. So similar to life, don't you think?

Coming out of my daydream, I found the stage already occupied by small people in various items of dress. Looking at them, you wouldn't know where you were supposed to be. There were a few townsfolk from the Middle Ages. There was a witch, presumed wicked until proved otherwise. There was a Dick Whittington with a live cat on his shoulder. Very brave of Mrs Ribbons to have allowed that, I thought.

They sang a merry song and leaped about in an uncontrolled fashion. The song was a modern one, post-Berlin Wall probably, asserting that, "Girls just wanna have fun". I couldn't really see the point of this and didn't remember any previous version of the Pied Piper having such music. Another brave feature was that they had arranged for backing music to be recorded, so quite a good sound was coming across.

Next, the children all melted away to reveal a very Disney-like Snow White singing "Someday my Prince will come." I thought it was terribly sweet. The child was actually a nice little songster and you could hear a sigh of contentment settle over the audience.

I often feel that where most producers fail is that they misunderstand the reason why audiences show up. The producer thinks they come to see the show, to appreciate the artistry, the way the show is put together, and so on.

Not so. That's the last reason. They come because it's a night out, because they were told to, forced to, persuaded to, felt guilty about not coming, had nothing better to do, and for the beer. Humbling for a producer perhaps, but the smart producer accepts it. If some of the crowd are there for a good sleep, then lull them into sleeping. They will love you for it and go home feeling as refreshed as if they have just had a good massage.

Snow White finished massaging this particular audience when there was a God-awful squealing of guitars and drums and a disgusting little fellow began to bellow into a microphone, using words that couldn't, and probably shouldn't, be made out. The microphone caught the spirit of the thing and being turned up too loud, howled with feedback. The audience squirmed in their seats. Some called for travel sickness pills.

It was explained to me afterwards that there is some rock singer who calls himself Prince, and that the song was intended as a joke. This was lost on the audience. See what I mean? Don't try to be too clever.

Callum appeared at my side with a gadget.

"Could you take this over?" he asked. "I've a problem with the curtain wires and I'll have to move them manually up there in the gantry. Mr Brown is going to cover in the wings."

"No problem," I agreed, ever eager to please in a crisis, "but what is this?"

"Oh, it's easy," he said. "It switches on the tape. When the kids are ready for the next song you just press this button to start it. But don't press these buttons with the arrows. They are the fast forward and back buttons. You won't need them. All the songs have been recorded in order, ok?"

"How will I know when they need the music?" I asked.

"Easy again," Callum replied. "You have asterisks

marked on your page. Oh," he muttered, looking at my script, "the marks are a bit smudged, aren't they? Don't worry. It'll be obvious when the music is needed. You'll be all right."

"Look," he whispered. "They're just about to go into another number. Press the switch now."

I did so and as if by magic "Maybe it's because I'm a Londoner" came on.

Dick Whittington and his cat strolled on stage and sang with utter confidence, despite the fact he could reach only half the notes. The story was beginning to develop. Master Whittington, it would seem, had been voted in as Lord Mayor of London. Soon he was to have his procession and the Lord Mayor's Ball. As I skipped ahead in the script, the Pied Piper was being portrayed as the villain of the piece, threatening to bring all the London rats into the open if the mayor didn't pay him off with protection money. Our Dick however was made of sterner stuff, but I had to stop there because someone had forgotten his lines.

Ah, no. It was me. I was supposed to put the next song on. I pressed the button and the crackle from the P.A. reassured me that we were rolling. And very interesting too. The Pied Piper made his appearance, a tallish young man dressed in the usual motley, but sporting a gangster's fedora. I was beginning to feel that the kids had actually come up with some good ideas.

The music was "Mack the Knife," very appropriate and very threatening. The Pied Piper had a violin case and he opened it to reveal a large plastic toy saxophone, with which he mimed the saxophone solo in the song. The audience was nodding, a little amused, a little thrilled, some of them waking up.

And so it went on. Some things didn't really work. There was an episode where the two heroines,

Cinderella and Snow White, were competing for the Prince. The audience was confused. They wanted both to win, or rather to lose, because the Prince sounded and looked hideous. He sang a thrashing type of song which sounded like "Coughing in my Grave", but later I was told it was "Feeling in the Groove"; not that it explained the proceedings any better for me but I guess I'm past all that anyway.

While this four foot-six monster in a wig was strutting his stuff (you see, I can speak the lingo if I have to), it made me think back with a twinge of regret that I suppose I have never been "with it", even when I was young. It must be nice to be able to say, "Well, at one time I knew all the songs, knew the right thing to wear, the right parties to go to, the right words to use." If I'm honest with myself, I never did.

When I sat in a coffee bar, I stood out all right, but in the wrong way. One girl said to me she wished I'd go home because I made her feel as if her father was standing over her. I obviously got in with the wrong crowd, one which was more interested in steam railways, or hill walking, or astronomy. I'm sure we were happy enough, but never part of the mainstream generation.

"Stop the music," someone was calling.

In my dream state, I had allowed the recording to run on. The noisy rock song was supposed to finish and now I had let the tape go on to the next piece of music, which was cool, moody, atmospheric sort of stuff. The audience hadn't really noticed. I thought I'd run it back to the beginning to get the best effect when it was really needed, so I pushed the backward arrow, gauging from my own experience of hi-fi machines how long to give it before stopping. Right. That should have done it.

Now, on stage there was meant to be a big build-up of tension. The two main characters appeared. The Pied

Piper threatened. The Mayor told him where to get off. They circled each other menacingly, Dick with his cat extremely well balanced on his shoulder, and the Pied Piper ready with his saxophone to summon the rats to plague the Londoners. Would he do it? Now I was supposed to switch on the atmospheric music.

But I didn't.

I couldn't.

For onto the stage there had appeared a rat. A real rat. It was meandering from the back of the stage, unaware of where it was. The actors hadn't seen it yet. The audience had begun to see it and were transfixed. It was one of those situations where you just hope that someone is going to do something, but you can't possibly yourself.

The poor actors, not knowing of this development, were looking at me to start the tape. Maybe if we carried on, things would sort themselves out. I pressed the switch and a storm of noise came from the speakers. I must have run the tape back too much and caught the end of the screaming rock song.

The Village Hall was never quite the same again.

The rat was startled by the music and darted further out onto the stage and into the limelight. Whittington's cat spotted the movement and changed from a docile furry toy into a murderous tiger. With a piercing screech it leapt off Whittington's shoulder after the rat. They did one lap of honour round the stage before flying off into the audience. The crowd screamed in panic as people got onto chairs or began to run into one another.

From above there came a thundering, ripping sound and Callum, clutching at a falling curtain, fell to the stage. His weight caused him to go right through. The Pied Piper and Whittington were projected into the air and then disappeared into the collapsing shambles of stage and scenery.

People were now streaming out the door. In minutes, I was left alone with Brown, the Robbins/Ribbons duo and Mrs Webster.

"A poetry reading next time, Mrs Webster?" Brown said.

All was silent again as we surveyed the wreckage. It was an awesome reminder of how close our well-run society is to collapse.

The cat reappeared, looking as smug as a bouncer who has just seen off a few troublemakers. She settled down at Brown's feet to wash. Brown patted her.

Well, Callum was in hospital for only a week and then off work for a time, but he didn't mind. It got him out of the way of his obnoxious employer and we all spoiled him with lots of attention and goodies.

The village and school were famous for a few days while the local radio reported on the live rat scene and the newspapers enjoyed themselves with headlines such as, "You Dirty Rat" and "Rat brings House Down".

I suppose next year people will have forgotten enough to want to come back again, but I did remark to Brown that our fund raising for the village hall was more critical than before.

Chapter Nine

Pritchard and the Car Trade

"I was on a course last week," Brown announced.

"So that's where you were," said Pritchard. "You didn't mention it beforehand."

"No," Brown conceded. "I forgot I was going on the course until my secretary, Sadie, telephoned me last Sunday to remind me."

"That was above and beyond the call, was it not?" said Pritchard.

"She's very good," Brown allowed.

Ronald was impatient. "What sort of course?"

"A management course," Brown replied.

"You mean a course for managers?" Ronald asked.

"I mean a course about management," Brown explained.

"But you've been managing for years," Ronald said. "It's a bit late now isn't it?"

"Not at all," Brown retorted. "Things are changing all the time. You have to keep up with the latest ideas."

It was a Saturday lunchtime, a warm but windy and cloudy day. Meeting as usual by the signpost, we were now dawdling towards the Gentle Goat. I had carried out some desultory gardening, but the flowers were now breathing sighs of relief and getting on with their photosynthesis, or whatever they did when my back was turned. Pritchard was evasive when I asked him what he had been up to and I wasn't particularly interested, so I gave up. Ronald claimed he had been doing a newspaper round. Horace plus dog hadn't turned up.

"Sort of uncomfortable in this wind, isn't it?" I remarked. "It's hard to breath properly in it."

"Just like the Sirocco in the south of France," said Pritchard.

"That was the name of a make of car, years ago. I forget who made it," Brown mused.

"No," Ronald asserted with cheerful confidence. "It's the name of a good little 'orse I backed at Epsom last week. Came in a treat at eight to one, it did."

"Maybe it's a film," Brown went on, hardly paying attention to anyone else. "It's a good name for a film, in fact. *The Sadness of Sirocco*, or *The Steamy Side of Sirocco*, or it could be a comedy, *The Road to Sirocco*."

We danced around several topics, so that by the time we arrived at the Goat, we were thoroughly content with life. There is something about anticipating that first drink of the day that makes you feel at peace with the world. Already there were a few cars in the car park. We had to wait to be served but the Goat was pleasantly cool after the warm stifling atmosphere outside.

"So what did this course teach you?" Ronald returned to the earlier subject.

Brown hesitated. "Hard to say, really."

"Couldn't have been up to much then," Pritchard grunted.

"It was pretty good, actually," Brown tried to recover. "It made you think."

"What was your biggest thought then?" Ronald can be a real terrier sometimes.

"Well, I don't remember now," Brown snapped. "Some of it was about oneself."

"How do you mean, about oneself?" Ronald harried his prey.

"Well, about what kind of person you are and how you interact with other people," Brown began to

195

remember.

"So what kind of person are you?" Pritchard asked, intending to protect Brown from the inquisition. It had a bad effect on Brown, however, who clammed up.

"I did some personality tests once," I said. "I was applying for a job in a big European firm and they were very keen on using tests."

"Personality tests," Ronald repeated, rolling the words around in his mouth. He was having a field day. "Obviously there's more goes into management than just sitting around drinking tea. There's pers-on-ality tests. Do they do that with the tea leaves then? You know, an old woman in league with the occult comes along and reads your personality from the tea leaves."

Pritchard intervened. "Did they tell you anything interesting?"

I wasn't sure that I should tell them, but I knew I'd have to now I'd got this far. "They said I wasn't suited to the job I was going for. I should have been a circus trainer, a theatre manager or a car salesman.

"I don't see the connection," Brown returned to the conversation, "and they don't seem anything like you."

"It's interesting you should say that," I said, "because a few weeks later, I got a call saying I had been sent the wrong result. Pity, I was quite taken with the notion of cracking a whip at a few sedated lions."

"It's a pity," Pritchard commented," that you didn't take up selling cars." He said it almost under his breath. I knew he wanted to say something, but the hairs on the back of my neck told me not to provoke whatever it was, so I just kept the subject warm."

"Well, I think I could, you know," I said. "I have done accounting for a few car dealer chains. They didn't seem too hot at selling either. I saw some of their chaps at work. They had a gift for turning people away. I suggested to the manager that he should just line up the cars and let the punters choose for themselves."

"What did he say? Did he congratulate you on your breakthrough thinking?" Ronald asked.

"He said it was typical of the way an accountant would run a salesroom."

"Well, for my part, I think you may have had a point," Pritchard interrupted, "because this morning I have been experiencing the car trade at first hand."

We all looked sympathetic, except Ronald, who just looked thirsty. Once warmed up, Pritchard needed no prompting.

"I thought I'd treat myself to a different car," he began.

"Well you certainly couldn't get the same model again," Ronald sniped.

Before we go any further into this story, let me explain that Pritchard owns a 1965 Mini. He's very attached to it. It's a little racing-green number that was probably all the rage at one time. I've never known how long Pritchard has been the owner. I doubt if he is old enough to have owned it from new, but he may have bought it second hand, or his parents may have owned it. Anyway, there is a certain ridiculousness about Pritchard having this Mini because Pritchard is a big fellow. Seeing Pritchard getting himself out of the car is like watching a snake come out of a bin. First, he has to unwind himself slowly and then eventually, with a nifty backward jerk that lobs him out of the car, they are separated.

"So why do you want to change your wheels?" Brown asked.

"No reason," Pritchard said, "Except that I saw a particularly cheap E-Type Jaguar for sale."

"Wow!" Ronald exclaimed. "Cool. Now that was a car for all time, a car to make a man drool. Space age. How can you afford to own an E-Type?"

Pritchard's answer was simple. "It doesn't go and it looks awful."

We didn't know how to take this, so we signalled for another round of drinks and let Pritchard resume.

"There's a farmer called Jeb Nought - lives out in the country. He attends the evening lectures on local history. He has no interest in cars at all, so I'm told, but he has an E-Type. It appeared in his woods one night, many years ago and he put it into one of his barns for safekeeping. Apparently he meant to report it but it was harvesting time and his telephone was out of order, so he never did get round to informing the authorities until it was too late. He thought by then they would want to know why he hadn't reported it earlier."

"What do you think, Pritchard?" Brown spoke for all of us. "Is he genuine? How did the Jag get there? Weren't there any signs to tell him where it came from? It was obviously still able to be driven."

Pritchard slowly shook his dewlaps. "Apparently it didn't even have number plates."

"Chassis number?" from Ronald.

"Rusted over," Pritchard sighed. "At least it is now."

I thought the story had more holes than a golf course, but decided to let it unfold.

"So if this thing won't go, how will you get around?" Ronald asked.

Pritchard's reply was not very coherent. He said he'd work that out in due course but the Mini would have to go because there is only parking room for one car. He would use Jenny's car while he did the Jaguar up.

"You don't know a thing about cars," Ronald reminded him.

Pritchard slowed down. It was as if this very telling fact had only just occurred to him. But soon his irrational desire for the car broke through.

"Where there's a will," he said sagely, "there's a way."

"So what is our farmer friend going to charge you for this dubious car, then?" Brown asked, watching a man at the far end of the bar dipping his cardigan sleeves into his beer."

"He hasn't said yet," Pritchard replied, "but he suggested that we find out how much it will cost to restore it, and we'll take it from there."

"Well, it's not the way I'd do business," Brown declared, his voice assuming its pompous edge, "but why have you got it in for the car trade? What were you doing this morning?"

"I was trying to sell the Mini," Pritchard's voice tailed off as he too saw the chap sitting at the far end of the bar, trailing his sleeve in his beer."

Conversation lapsed while we watched this. The sleeve seemed to be absorbing the beer. A dark stain was creeping along the edge of his sleeve and up. It was like blotting paper. I couldn't understand how it was happening. I wondered if it would reach his elbow. Was the sleeve of his shirt also soaking it up? We watched, never for a minute considering saying anything. My imagination wandered. The sleeve became a sinister mouth, drinking the beer. When the poor guy looked down eventually, he would find an empty glass.

What actually happened was that he must have felt something wet and horrible crawling up his arm (or so he said afterwards). His arm shot out involuntarily, flicking his pint neatly into the air. It fell onto the lap of a rather county-looking lady sitting up on a barstool, who promptly tossed something somewhere in fright.

The first consideration was to clean up the beer, from the bar counter, from the floor, behind and in front of the bar, from this poor lady's lap. You wouldn't think a pint could go so far. It never seems to last very long with Ronald.

Suddenly, the husband of this woman, and they were both fairly angry with the cardigan chap, remembered that she had been eating. Apparently the thing she threw away had been a piece of pork pie. Where is it? He asks. I don't know, she says. Well you should, he says. How should I? I'm being assaulted by a yob throwing a glass at me and you just stand there. What do you expect me to do, he says, do you expect me to catch it in the air like a bloody cricket ball? I wouldn't, she says, because you've never shown that kind of quick-wittedness in your natural. I agree, he says, otherwise I'd never have landed up with you and your father. Leave my father out of this. It would be the first time, the chap replies, because it feels like I've married your whole family.

With a jolt, they both remember the pie again. "There it is." She points to the cat, sleeping peacefully on the linoleum under the fruit machine. Sure enough, just next to its curled tail is the pie.

Stung by the charge of not being a man of action, the chap, instead of just going and picking the pie up, did a sort of violent long stride which went wrong. He obviously wanted to be seen to be as good as any stuntman, but his movement made him slide out of control across the floor, as if he was going to smother a grenade that had just been tossed through the window. But some people are forever destined to remain waiting outside the Halls of Valour. His eagerness to impress caused him to cover the ground so quickly that he couldn't get his brakes on in time. The cat, sensing an attack, raised her head and met the oncoming hand expertly with a mouthful of sharp teeth. With a yelp he tried to get away and smacked his head on the fruit machine, which promptly paid out noisily and handsomely. Peter the barman came out, picked up the pie, took it away and brought a new one on a clean plate for the lady, with a serviette.

"I don't like dealing with the car trade either," Brown declared. "That's why I get the firm to buy my cars."

"Well, I'm going to sell the Mini privately," said Pritchard, "because the best offer I got this morning was £200. One fellow thought he was doing me a favour by offering to take it away if I paid him £100."

"How much do you think you can get for it?" I enquired. The £200 seemed ok to me.

"About a thousand at the very least," Pritchard cried. "It's a vintage car, you know. But these garages are in the wrong market. I need to sell it to a collector, someone who will see its potential."

Ronald and I couldn't see the potential at all and thought Pritchard was raving, but Brown got a new lease of enthusiasm. The businessman, the wheeler-dealer, emerged. You could sense his eyes were seeing £ signs and his brain went into gear.

"You are absolutely right," he spoke firmly, clutching Pritchard's arm. "We'll make good use of the course I've been on. We did a bit of work on knowing how you come across to other people, and another part was about the techniques of selling. I'll help you, Old Man."

"Quite right," Ronald chipped in. "You could put the Mini in the back of your BMW, Brown, and sell it in a car boot sale."

Brown had taken receipt of yet another new car. It seemed like he got a new one every time he wanted to change radio channels. This time it was an even bigger BMW. Goodness knows why. He only has himself to carry around in it.

"Let's see what our selling proposition is," Brown began. "Essentially, what is it we are selling? Is there something unique about it?"

"Yes," Ronald offered but not really getting the hang of Brown's procedure. "It's the only car Pritchard has had for years."

Brown appeared irritated. "I can't see what I can make of that. You're not catering for a buyer's needs with that one. It's too....literal.

"It's the best I can do," said Ronald. "I've got to go and see about the evening round of newspapers. Have to meet with my supplier, you know. I'll check out how I come across to him. Too literal, I expect."

I asked Ronald what the newspaper round was all about.

"It maybe only looks like a newspaper round to you," he replied, "but it's the start of something big for me. I'm going to build up a business empire. I'll become a press baron, a magnet."

"You mean a magnate," I corrected him.

"I don't care as long as it attracts the women," he said and winked.

"Any woman in particular?" Pritchard said, barely concealed mischief in his voice.

Ronald reddened and went out. I think it was just as well. Pritchard and Brown were beginning to annoy him. Anyway, if they were going to plan out their sales campaign, it was better that Ronald wasn't present in that mood. I didn't stay much longer myself and left Brown and Pritchard to hatch up a sales line for the car. Maybe it was my lack of imagination, but I couldn't see that the car was worth all that bother. I was wrong – in a way.

During the next week I was able to do most of my work at home. It's all very convenient really. In my house I have my office just the way I want it. Firstly,

I've managed to correct the aberrations of the heating system, which has a sense of humour you would associate with the Spanish Inquisition. I also got myself up to speed with enough technology to connect my computer with my clients'.

But working on your own can be claustrophobic, so on the Wednesday I thought I'd treat myself to the lunchtime roast at the Goat. The oppressive warmth of the weekend was giving way to something more bracing, which fanned my hunger as I stepped out towards the pub. The trees alongside the road swished happily as their topmost branches swayed and birds found their landing strips moving away from under them.

I was delighted to find company, in the shapes of Brown, Pritchard and Alf. Brown and Pritchard looked as if they hadn't moved since the weekend. I gave my order and sat down with them.

"Good Man," said Brown, cheerfully taking the pint I handed to him. "Sound fellow. We have much to tell you."

"You've found a buyer for your car, Pritchard?" I guessed.

"More interesting than that," Pritchard said, and nodded conspiratorially toward Alf, who kept his silence for the moment. "After you left us on Saturday Alf rolled in. He said he knew people who supplied the film industry with props. To cut a long story short, they are interested in using the Mini in a film about London of the Sixties."

This was good news. "So you've sold it?"

"No," said Pritchard, "I have leased it, for £200."

"That's not going to find the thousand pounds you were looking for?" I commented.

"Short-sighted as usual," Brown pounced on me. "Think of the value of the car when the film is released.

We'll clean up, or keep it and lease it another time."

I didn't like to be the wet blanket. Lots of films flop. This would leave the car as obscure as ever. Still, people don't always want to hear my pessimisms so I kept mum.

"And do you know?" Pritchard continued. "They are interested in the E-Type too. If I did it up they might hire it from me. It could be a nice little earner."

What with Ronald going to be a press baron and Pritchard supplying the film industry, I was going to be in exalted company.

"But won't you have to invest a lot of money to get the E-Type into shape?" I asked, trying not to sound like a killjoy.

"Not in this case," Alf spoke for the first time. "These film laddies are always working to a tight budget. All they need is a static model for a set they're doing. If they can get Pritchard's cheap, they'll save a lot of money. They don't really need a runner. Pritchard has the advantage there. All other hire companies would want an arm and a leg for their E-Types."

"I see; so you have bought it from your friend then?" I asked.

"No," Pritchard immediately looked guilty. "I haven't quite tied it all up yet."

Alf obviously was unaware that Pritchard did not own an E-Type and it had equally obviously been convenient for Pritchard not to clarify the minor details of ownership. He said he was working on that one.

"Well don't hang around," Alf advised as he got up to go. "The film chappies are at the point where they need that car so don't let the chance pass you by."

Pritchard sank into silence. I sat back and enjoyed the thought of the roast I was about to eat. Maybe it was hunger but I imagined the smell of the roast all about me. There was a convivial hush in the bar today.

I noticed a new picture on the wall over by another table. It was not the customary eighteenth century hunting scene but an impressionist piece – an old man sitting at a pavement café, with his solitary drink on a round, wooden table. The man is expressionless but the implausible light around him seems more important than anything else in the painting. The more you look at it, the more you realise the man has lost something, nothing so obvious as money, or love or a loved one – but a lost opportunity. As I stared at it, two ladies came and sat at the table beneath it, and the picture became bland.

Pritchard moved, disturbing our pleasant reveries.

"Are the two of you engaged this evening?" he asked." Later on in the evening, that is?"

Both Brown and I failed to think quickly enough to find alternatives and had to admit we were free.

"Good," said Pritchard with an air of mystery. "I'll pick you both up around ten."

With that, he got up and left. By the time my lunch arrived, I had to eat it alone.

Shortly after ten, Pritchard arrived. Brown was in the car already, shivering in the back seat.

"Fell asleep," he muttered. "Feel a bit chilled coming out just like this. Didn't know how to dress. I don't remember these cars being so tight fitting."

We drove off. I don't know if car headlights have improved a lot, but Pritchard seemed to be driving on next to no light at all. The mystery deepened when we headed out into the country. I had hoped Pritchard was taking us to some new and dubious pub he had found.

No such luck. Before long, he turned down a farm track and we were treated to a rutted path in a car invented before suspension. The track opened out into a farmyard, surrounded on three sides by farm buildings with few windows. Stiffly we got out.

"Why are we here, Pritchard?" Brown moaned. "I could be getting to bed now."

"Look," Pritchard rounded on him. "I'm giving you a little bit of adventure. You wouldn't have heard Robin Hood whimpering about getting his head down on his pillow when there were heroic deeds to be done."

Pritchard's speech had the opposite effect to that which he intended. Brown immediately looked startled and wanted to know what heroism was demanded of him.

Pritchard explained. "This is where the Jaguar is: to be precise, just behind that door. Now, the farmer is away in Spain on holiday this week so I can't finish the negotiations. A bloke comes in during the day to look after the place and keep it ticking over. But he hasn't been involved so he'll think I'm stealing the car. He doesn't know me from Jack the Ripper."

"Jack the Ripper is dead," Brown mumbled.

Pritchard growled at Brown, "Don't be so sure."

"So what do you want us to do?" I asked, slow as ever to appreciate what was going on.

"Well, it's obvious," Pritchard hissed. "I want to get the Jaguar away without being spotted. The chap who comes during the day won't even have noticed the car, and when the farmer comes back, I'll be able to hand him his half of the hire fee, minus whatever expenses I will have incurred. I'm doing him a favour."

"Do yourself a favour," Brown advised. "Let's go home. You could be had up for theft."

Pritchard was dismissive. "Don't be daft. Now come on, let's have a scout around. We need to know what's in there besides the car. We don't want to let anything out that will be difficult to get back in."

We took torches and walked around the building. Windows were non-existent. You couldn't see into the barn unless you opened a door. There was a light breeze and now and then, unfamiliar noises in the trees behind us caused a strange sensation in the stomach. Rustles and scrapes from inside the buildings suggested livestock. I felt reluctant to disturb anything possessing horns, hooves or teeth.

"We'll have to take a chance," Pritchard said. "If we open the door slowly, we'll see if anything is trying to get out. Bring your torches over here."

Brown and I were reluctant adventurers, but we shone our torches obediently on the door. Pritchard was amazing. He was so optimistic. He really believed that this heavy wooden door would open up nicely, that nothing would disturb us, the car would be there and we'd make off with it peacefully. One of his assumptions soon proved unfounded.

Pritchard tugged at the door. It moved easily, almost as if it was on oiled rollers.

"Easy, easy," urged Brown. "There's probably a gaggle of geese in there waiting to get out."

Pritchard for once did as he was bidden and eased the door open as gently as he could. We didn't see it at first, because of the poor light. The gap widened further. Still our torches didn't pick it out until the very last moment. Then with a snort of breath and a stamp of a heavy, hairy foot, there appeared in the weak torchlight a part of a bull. Unfortunately it was the business end, horns and all, hostility in its large, dark eyes.

"Oh, my God," cried Brown, dropping his torch and stepping back onto my toes. Somehow, I had slunk behind him and now paid the price. "Close the door, Pritchard."

"Can't, Old Man," said Pritchard. "It's stuck."

For what seemed like an eternity, we all stayed frozen in our positions. The bull, understandably, was least impressed and gave another threatening snort.

"Let's go," I said in as controlled a manner as I could possibly attempt in those circumstances, but my voice came out in a strangled squeak.

"I would," Brown whispered, "If my legs could move. I don't suppose you have a red cape or suchlike. You could run in a different direction and distract it."

"I always knew you were a coward," I told Brown, "but I didn't realise how treacherous you were too."

The spell was broken when the bull, with a shake of his massive head, began to move forward. It was too big to get through the gap, but the door was distinctly threatened. Just then, Pritchard stepped forward, clapped the bull roughly on the neck, gripped its ear and directed it backwards into the barn. Far from protesting, the beast seemed to like Pritchard's handling. It was not the first time we had seen Pritchard's skill with animals. He led it back into a stall and secured it with a stout rope, which looked right for the purpose, and called us to come in.

We took some time to become accustomed to the darkness inside the barn, not to mention the smell and the overpowering thickness of the air. Eventually we began to see where we were. It was an untidy hole of a place but sure enough, there was the Jaguar.

"So what do we do now? Brown whispered, in between coughs. "I'm not all that happy about this, Pritchard. You are implicating us in a robbery, a break-in and goodness knows what else. I only have your word for it that the owner wants to sell."

Pritchard ignored the morality play and started to examine the Jaguar, tugging at bits, kicking the tyres, pushing and rocking it. Eventually he said, "Right, Brown, you go and get the tow rope from the boot of the Mini and then reverse the Mini in here."

He told me to get the foot-pump from the Mini and

blow up the Jag's tyres. He himself got the bonnet up, did a few things then got into the driver's seat.

Brown was inexpertly reversing the Mini into the barn, and adding petrol fumes to the already suffocating air. The bull kicked at his stall and Pritchard had to go and calm him down.

"You are not going to tow the Jaguar with this car, are you?" Brown said.

"Well I can't pull it myself." Pritchard retorted. "It'll be fine."

I was taking too long to blow up the tyres. I'm sure they were deflating as quickly as I pumped air into them. Pritchard fastened the towrope to the Jaguar. As soon as I finished, he directed Brown to take the wheel.

"My fingerprints will be all over the wheel," Brown complained.

Soon, we were out of the barn and the barn door was closed, as if we had never been. Pritchard even swept our tracks behind us. The rutted track was a nightmare. I expected never to reach home, but somehow Pritchard coaxed everything and everyone along and by one o' clock, the Jaguar was in the back of his garden, camouflaged under a tarpaulin, and I went home to a whisky and water.

Nothing happened for about two weeks. I had a work contract that took me out of the country and had arranged to meet the family out there for a few days holiday. It was good to be out of the village for a while. It can become limiting and I feel the need to talk to different people. Still, I was just as glad when we turned back into our driveway a few days later. I spent the afternoon in the office, returning calls that had queued up on the voicemail and seeing to my emails.

After dinner, I sauntered along to the Goat to catch up on the local gossip. Brown was already there. He seemed relieved to see me.

"Pritchard's in some sort of trouble," he said immediately.

It is a feature of friendship I guess, that people will go straight to what's bothering them without all the preliminary politeness. There was none of the, "How was the Continent, then?" or, "How much wine did you manage to cram into the car?" No. He went straight to the point, as if I had just come back from the Men's Room. Sometimes I feel taken for granted.

"I just hope he's not incriminating me," Brown went on, clearly rattled by events.

"How do you know?" I asked, trying to get him to disclose some facts.

Brown looked annoyed at being stopped in his tracks. He was making the most of being indignant. "I'm a man of some position and to be involved in this would sully one's reputation. It is not good at all. At all," he repeated. "My company will not like it."

"I thought you became the owner of the company," I said.

"I own a portion of it, twenty-five percent of the shares to be precise, but ownership of the majority of the shares has passed into the hands of a consortium, headed up by a chap with whom I do not get on. He knows nothing about the work and is a very unpleasant person into the bargain. We have a humdinger of a business: it throws off cash like there's no tomorrow and so I really have to hang on in there, but it has its downsides."

"So Mr Brewer isn't there any more?" I said, surprised and remembering the tyrant who came to Brown's barbeque.

"Oh no. Everything changes very frequently in this world." Brown shook his head.

"So how do you know about Pritchard?" I tried again.

Brown nodded towards the door. "He'll tell you himself."

Sure enough, Pritchard was bending his large, bloodhound's head to get through the door. He came straight to us, calling for three pints on the way."

"I don't need one yet, Old Man," Brown said.

"You will when you hear what's happened," Pritchard replied, his voice betraying a nervous quiver. I've noticed it in people coming to tell me there's a flaw in their accounts and instead of a £5m profit, they are actually in the red by £9m, and can I do anything?

Pritchard also dispensed with any pretence of being interested in my holiday. It's a pity, because one of the enjoyments of going on holiday is to hog the conversation in the pub on the first night you get back and here I was, being denied my statutory privileges. I thought momentarily of going off in the huff but I'm far too inquisitive to do that, so I stayed, curiosity emasculating temperament yet again.

"We're in trouble," Pritchard started, immediately confirming Brown's worst fears, not just that Pritchard was in trouble, but that Pritchard was using the word, "we".

The pints came. The pub continued its usual hum of conversation broken by periodic laughter from some young lads at the bar. The pub cat wove its way around the low tables, nosing the odd beer mat off and occasionally dipping the curved tip of its tail into a glass of beer, then flicking the drops onto someone's clean jacket. Pritchard raked round in his baggy trousers while the barman eyebrowed all there was to say about the fact that he had other customers to serve, and didn't have all day and could someone else help out? I'm easily pressurised by this, so I got a note out and loaned it to Pritchard. I would have been better off buying the round myself because he never remembers to pay back his borrowings.

"The film company used the Jaguar," he began. "I had it done up in two days and they used it on the third."

"That's terrific," I tried.

"No, it's not," Pritchard almost shouted, and banged his half-empty pint down, causing our full pints to spill copiously onto the table, which now looked like the Nile in flood. The cat fetched her tail along and I moved my light-coloured, newly cleaned trousers further away.

"It is not terrific and I will explain right now. Why you two normally sensible people allowed me to accept your advice to lift the Jaguar I shall never know. You're boring enough at the best of times. Why did you act out of character on the one time I needed you most to be firm and stable?"

"Are you going to explain everything to us or not," I said firmly, annoyed at Pritchard's tone. If there was to be a falling out of thieves, I was going to start early.

"I telephoned farmer Jeb to give him the glad tidings. He hadn't noticed the car's absence at all but it forced out of him the strangest confession."

Pritchard took a final pull at his beer, almost sucking the glass in as well, struck it empty down on the table, with similar results. The pub dog now came to lick up the spilt beer. Peter came over to clean the table, obviously disgusted by the sight, and rightly so. Pritchard wanted another drink. Peter asked if he wanted it in a bigger glass this time.

"This Jeb Naught fellow has the cheek to tell me that he doesn't want the Jaguar displayed for all to see because it might not actually be his."

Brown shivered. "What do you mean, *might not*? Surely he owns it or not."

"Not so," Pritchard continued. "The old fool seems

to have five of them."

"Five E-Types?" I exclaimed.

"Five," Pritchard confirmed, "and not all of them arrived as clean as the driven white stuff."

Brown was fidgeting something awful by now and spilled more beer over the table. We shooed the animals away because they betrayed us and I didn't want Peter and his mobile mouth over again. The mess on the floor made it look as it Brown was incontinent. At that moment, for all I knew, perhaps he was.

"It seems that his first one really was found in the woods, although I don't know if I can believe anything he says. He developed a weakness for them and came by one or two legally, although he never checked ownership at any time so they could have been nicked somewhere down the line before he got them. Two of them he whisked out of old scrap yards when no one was looking, just for kicks. With one of the latter, he masqueraded as an insurance official. The car was apparently more glamorous because it had been a well-known getaway car, in a job where the thieves were never traced."

"So which one have you got?" I asked, knowing the answer already.

"He doesn't know for sure," Pritchard stalled.

"OK, so which one does he *think* you've got," Brown pushed.

"Which one do you think?" Pritchard moaned. "Just my luck."

"Not the getaway job?" Brown put his head in his hands. The dog rose from where it was lying and tried to lick Brown's face. Brown batted the dog away. It growled and Pritchard's nervous knees shot up, sending the whole table flying. We gave up and ran out.

Suddenly we felt hunted. We didn't want to stay out in the open so we hid in Brown's car.

I tried to summarise our position: "*our*" position? Pritchard had even got me admitting it was *our* problem.

"So it looks likely that you have taken a valuable, classic car, without permission from the owner – which is a theft – and gained financially by hiring to a bona fide customer. You also altered the appearance of the car. The car itself was in all probability not honestly come by. However, being in a film will expose it, if the film is at all successful, to the gaze of thousands, including some who may recognise it because of its notoriety."

"How do we get out of this?" Pritchard bleated.

Brown proposed that we look at the situation from all angles. "How will they identify your particular E-Type? Apart from the colour, they all look alike."

Pritchard wobbled his huge head. "Not to an enthusiast."

"What if the film isn't successful?" I ventured, always the pessimist.

"From what I've seen it looks to have every chance of success," Pritchard said.

"Could we ask them nicely to get another car and re-shoot the scenes containing your car?" Brown offered.

We both looked at Brown. He's not usually so naive. The strain was telling on him. We decided to go back to his place and see whether a coffee and a pampering from his large sofas would calm us down.

It did not. We got worse. We began to imagine terrible consequences. Pritchard got gloomier than I have ever seen him.

"You know what will happen? Farmer Jim will deny all knowledge of the car and leave me to explain how I got it. What can I say? And what if those people whose car it was in the first place see it? Those scrap yard people can be rough, you know. And what if they stole it from the real owners? I bet they were big chiefs in the underworld. I mean, what if this thing blows up and it turns out that the car connected them to some robbery where they murdered a security guard and the car was the missing piece of evidence wanted by the police? I mean, they're not going to think much of me if their past suddenly shows up in every cinema in the country. The film could become famous for the wrong reason."

"Hang on. You are getting yourself all wound up. Let's not exaggerate. Put the whole thing in perspective," Brown said, trying to cool down Pritchard's raging imagination. "All you have done is supplied an old car to a film maker. The farmer, if there is any danger surrounding the history of the car, will keep quiet. So what we need to do is play up the threat in order to make him back off. The chances of the car being recognised are slim. Of course," he continued, "it would be even better if we could manage to get rid of the thing."

"I wouldn't like to do that, really," Pritchard objected. "It's a piece of history, and anyway, it's not really mine to get rid off, is it?"

Brown sighed. "You can't have your cake and eat it. If you feel that bad, why don't you give it back to your farmer friend?"

"He's not likely to want it," I objected, "not if he remembers the dubious provenance of the goods."

Pritchard snapped his fingers and assumed a harder look. "That's it," he said, narrowing his eyes until he looked like a bloodhound trying to bring up a bone stuck in his throat. "We'll take it back to where it came from."

Brown asked how.

Have you noticed, the shorter the question, the harder the answer.

"Something will turn up," Pritchard declared, with a

renewed resolve.

A few more days passed. The tranquillity of the village tends to lull you into thinking that nothing has happened, is happening or ever will happen. But the feeling of disquiet refused to leave me. Sigmund was alive to my mood when I went in for the weekly sherry and some tins of soup.

"You're not your usual self," he observed. "That'll be eight pounds and forty pence, please. No, you are looking as if something's on your mind."

"Just some work problems," I lied.

"No. I know your work problem look. This is different. Well, better out than in, as they say."

Sigmund was busy, otherwise I might have told him the story, just to see if he could think of a solution. As I left his shop, feeling that I really should have consulted with him, I passed a stranger coming in. He was thick set, dressed in a dark suit and wore spectacles with a very heavy, dark tint. His hair was cut very short into the scalp. As he looked at me through the opaque lenses, I felt hunted and guilty again. When lunchtime came, I scurried up to the pub, hoping to see some of the gang. Brown was there.

"I've seen him too," he said, when I described the stranger. "He could be a detective of some sort, trying to find Pritchard's car."

"He gives me the creeps," I admitted.

Pritchard came in. Peter looked sour but I don't think Pritchard noticed.

"Look, it's getting too hot for comfort," were his first words as he brought his glass to the table. "I have just seen someone who could easily pass for a hit man. He's so obvious, I'm surprised the police haven't picked him up straight away."

"You mean the bloke in the dark suit?" Brown asked.

"You've seen him too?"

"So have I but we thought he might be a detective," I said.

"No, no," Pritchard snapped at us. "You two are so blind. Don't you ever go to the cinema? It's obvious. He's been sent here to put an end to me if he can connect me with the car."

"We've got to get rid of it," Brown said.

"Not so easy," Pritchard interrupted, "when it's one of the most eye-catching cars ever, and it can't go back under its own steam, and needs to be towed. You don't just put it into a large black plastic bag and take it along to the tip, you know. It would be less trouble if it were a bright yellow Chieftain tank."

We lapsed into subdued contemplation. The sinister stranger put a new complexion on the affair. We didn't stop to think that he was just someone visiting his aunt or a sightseeing stamp collector who had wandered off the beaten track.

The pub cat and then the dog came across to see what they could pick up in the way of spillage but we drank with care, hoping not to attract any notice whatsoever. I tried to shove the cat away but a friendly flick of the tail transferred some of my beer onto the front of my clean, white shirt.

Pritchard gave us a determined, tough look. "Well, I'm not making myself a sitting target." He stood up. "Let's meet here tonight to work out a plan."

And so we did.

But the plan didn't come. By nine-thirty we still had zero ideas and sat brain-dead around the table. The bar was quite full. We asked why. Peter signalled that it was because there were a few things happening in the village tonight. An old village family were celebrating a twenty-first. It gave me a warm feeling to know that. Although we are at the edge of suburban development, the place still truly thinks of itself as a village, and families will still think of themselves as village families.

There was also a joint meeting of the WI and the Village History Group so that a certain speaker could address them both. Whatever the reasons, there was a busy ebb and flow of people.

"We could repaint the car entirely," Brown suggested. "I could put it in my garage for a while until the heat dies down."

"I could also torch it," Pritchard said, "but I'm not such a Philistine. What do you feel when some art treasure has been damaged?"

"Nothing much," I confessed. "There's so much of it anyway."

"I usually wonder if it has been insured," Brown said.

"You can't bring it back with insurance," Pritchard stated with passion. "Nor will the money let you buy another. Once it has gone, it's gone."

"Well, I don't see that you are going to find a solution that is going to let both you and your car off the hook," Brown sighed.

We were still sitting clueless when some overflow from the history lecture came in the door. There would be about eight of them. Pritchard stiffened.

"There he is," he whispered.

I looked. So it was. The man in the dark suit.

"I'd rather he didn't see me," Pritchard whispered.

I thought Pritchard was treating the situation with admirable understatement. Here he was, facing an adversary who could have been anybody, from a special agent to an armed killer, with courage I could only admire.

"I should have known he would be here tonight. He attends most of the meetings," Pritchard spoke low.

"I thought you'd never seen him before," I asked, puzzled.

Pritchard gave me a withering look. "Sometimes, you can give the impression of being slow," he said with biting directness.

"You said only today," I replied frostily, "That you had never seen him before."

Brown, thank goodness, intervened in one of his rare moments of insight. "You, Pritchard, are talking about your farmer friend: you, on the other hand, are talking of the stranger in the dark habit."

"I have an idea," Pritchard hissed, too dramatically by far. "It is as simple as it is brilliant. We are going to return the car to the barn without that lying toad knowing anything about it."

"And how," Brown demanded in his deep, well-pronounced manner, "do you propose to do that? Anyway, that won't solve all the problems. The film people will still know that it was you who hired the vehicle to them."

But Pritchard was too far gone by this time to be reasonable. An action plan had presented itself, and action was better than doing nothing.

"It's a cert," he went on. "One of us will contrive to keep Jeb here and fill him so full of ale that he won't be home for hours. Meanwhile, we shall replace the car where we found it."

"What about the bull?" Brown and I had the same thought.

Pritchard misunderstood. "We'll leave it where it is."

"All right," I said. "And what about the following? How do we keep him here against his will? How do we get the car back in the barn, which is presumably locked, and are we not once again breaking the law by effecting illegal entry?"

"You are such a wet blanket," Pritchard accused me. I felt I had won the argument though, as he offered no counter arguments and had just rubbished his opponent. "Anyway, the answer to your first question has just walked in. Good evening, Ronald, what will you have?"

Ronald looked pleased and suspicious about this welcome, and rightly so. He was seated with dignity and deference by Pritchard and had a large lager in front of him before he knew where he was.

"I've just been doing a repair to Sigmund's premises," he announced. "His burglar alarm wasn't doing what it was supposed to, so I've mended it."

"Good for you, Ronald." Pritchard was all smarm and oil. It was sickly. I could hardly watch. Only raw curiosity kept me there. Personally, I was using the time to think of a way out of this escapade without Pritchard adding "wimp" to his list of names for me. It's all very well for him, but I shall lose business if I become known to the police. You can't have a convicted break-and-enter man doing your accounts, can you? I get enough references to creative accounting, cooking the books and massaging the figures as it is. Anyway, if it goes wrong, Pritchard will blame Brown and me again for letting him go ahead with his mad plan.

"So do you think you can detain him while we sort this little matter out? But we need time, Ronald, a lot of it." Pritchard concluded. He must have been persuading Ronald while I was thinking of something else.

"Right, no problem," Ronald was saying enthusiastically. "You're a brick, Pritchard. Do what you have to do."

Brown came back. I hadn't noticed he had gone. He gave a spare mobile phone to Ronald.

"I know you don't bring your mobile to the pub.

This one works just like yours. Let us know when your quarry has escaped," he winked. Ronald put the mobile into his old leather jacket pocket.

Then we were out, leaving Ronald to his job, and before the farmer had the opportunity to notice Pritchard. Brown checked his mobile was on. Suddenly the operation looked possible, just because of the mobiles. It made it seem professional. It also intensified the feeling that it was a crime.

"What did Ronald mean, you know, when he said you were a real brick, Pritchard?" I enquired. "What have you told Ronald?"

"Well, I didn't want to incriminate him, so I told him we were off to spoil a badger-baiting ring taking place on Farmer Jim's land, and with Farmer Jim's consent."

"That's terrible, Pritchard," Brown reprimanded. "You are being drawn deeper and deeper." Then with a chuckle he added, "But there is a certain excitement. Can we pull it off? That's the question."

Off we went to Pritchard's to collect the Jaguar. The night was mild. It possessed light without there being moonlight, and very still. I seemed to be the only one with butterflies in my stomach. With Brown at its wheel, we towed the Jaguar along miles of road, hoping we would not meet anyone. Noises seemed to travel loudly for miles, echoing and reverberating back to us. The farm came into view and then suddenly we were parked in front of the door of the barn where we had first come across the Jaguar.

Brown wondered where all the other E-Types were kept. Were they hidden, or just tucked away, forgotten?

I said I wasn't interested. I just wanted to get this done and be out of here as soon as we could.

We got out of the Mini and stretched. Pritchard stopped the engine. The silence was awesome.

"Do you think there are any farm labourers sleeping on the premises?" I asked. "We ought to be really quiet."

"I don't think so," Pritchard whispered, thereby betraying his own doubts, "but you never know. We are going to have to make some noise. Let's get this door open and see what we are going to have to deal with. I wonder how Ronald is doing."

We slid the old door open a crack. It wasn't locked. I remembered the previous time, when there was a large bull on the other side.

"I think the livestock will be tied up properly, but you never know," Pritchard anticipated my concerns.

We could tell that there were living creatures inside. You could hear the muffled rustles and rattles of their restraints. Occasionally a snort or a grunt was heard, but by and large it was peaceful. I began to think that maybe we would get away with it after all.

"Should we contact Ronald?" Brown suggested. "Just to make sure he is still sober enough to use the mobile."

"Not yet," Pritchard said. "Anyway, we might interrupt him at the wrong time."

We were concentrating so much on our own task that we didn't notice another car glide up next to ours virtually until it pulled on its brakes. My heart leapt into my mouth. How could Farmer Jim, as Pritchard calls him, have known to come straight to his barn? And yet even in the dark the car was familiar.

Instinctively, Pritchard, Brown and I had drawn back into the dark of the barn to gain cover. The Mini gave us away. Pritchard found an eyehole in the barn door and could see the newcomer. I could hear someone getting out of the car and then the car door was shut. There was a muffled bark from a dog. Pritchard's breathing was heavy and erratic; then he let out a long hiss.

"It's Horace and his dog," he whispered. "How did he get here?"

The story was soon told. Horace was in the pub, had met up with Ronald and been told about the badger baiting so here he was, to lend whatever help he could.

Brown enlightened Horace about why we were really here. I don't know why, but Horace accepted the reason quickly and without fuss.

His dog however did not. It was obviously disappointed to miss a good fight and tried to make up for it by barking and kicking up a din.

"Shut up, you clown," Horace snapped at him and tried to land a thump on his head with a stick. The dog disdainfully caught the stick in its teeth, disarmed Horace and ran off with it into the barn.

"Get that disaster of a dog under control, Horace," Brown cried. "There's a bull the size of the Sphinx in there somewhere, and God knows what other farmyard things."

Then from the far end of the barn came a storm of flapping, honking and hissing, not necessarily in that order. Horace's dog re-appeared, whining. He tucked himself in behind Horace. Following it came several bad-tempered geese. Are there ever good-tempered ones?

I don't know if you have encountered geese. They are fairly unapproachable at the best of times, prone to making fierce attacks on one's legs and hands. When aroused, there's no negotiating with them. Their long necks come honking and pecking, and there's only one thing to do. Run.

We were about to do precisely that when Pritchard shouted, "No!"

"Don't run out of the barn," he yelled. "They'll escape and we'll never catch them. Run back into the inside of the barn."

He might as well have said, "Jump into the mouth of that volcano."

"Come on," he drove us back. "I'll shut the door."

With the door of the barn shut, peace descended. The dog dropped to the floor and panted. Miraculously, the geese shuffled off, from what I could see in the semi-light. We tried to take a breather.

"The phone. I can hear the phone," Brown shouted, his ears picking up the sound of his mobile. "It's in the car. It'll be Ronald."

"No, it's not, it's in here," I said. "You brought it with you."

"I can't see it in this light," Brown complained.

"Well, follow the sound," Horace suggested.

We did, but the sound was everywhere. Eventually we tracked it down and Brown whispered into it.

"Where the Hell have you been?" Ronald cried. "I've been ringing for ages, then I got put onto voicemail and I had to start again. He's left. I couldn't keep him any longer. You've probably only got five or ten minutes."

Pritchard took command. "Horace, put your dog into your car. Brown, keep those geese back with a stick or something."

I was ordered to open the door so that Pritchard could back the Mini into the barn, pushing the Jaguar into its original spot. Uncoupling the Jag was the work of a minute and with Brown keeping up a staunch rearguard action against the honking enemy, we closed the barn door and ran to the cars.

"Too late," Horace shouted, pointing to a light in the distance. "The only way out is along the same road. It's single track. He'll wonder why two cars are coming from the direction of his farm. He could block us if he wanted."

"Ok," I said. "Start the cars up but keep your lights off. I'll go first on foot. Follow me round to the back of the building. When he passes us by and parks up at the house, I'll be able to see when he's gone indoors. Then we can slip round the field and onto the road without being seen."

We did just that. I led them between ditches and boulders to the rear of the buildings, where we killed the engines and waited. Jeb Nought's car whined and stuttered as he drove along in the wrong gears. He had obviously put away a few drinks with Ronald. There was a crash of a sort, then silence. A minute later there was the sound of a car door opening and steps crunching unevenly. I could just make out in the gloom that he was in a heavy contest with his front door lock. Eventually there was an impatient tinkling of glass and he disappeared inside. I could see his car door, wide open, and maybe his front door too. Apart from a light appearing in an upstairs window, there was no more sign of intelligent life.

By the same tactics we left the field. I guided the cars through various hazards, round the far end of the barn and onto the track. Only then did we feel safe to put the headlights on again.

"We ought to phone Ronald and let him know," Pritchard suggested.

Brown tried. There was no reply. "If he's in the same state as Jeb Naught, he won't be answering." Brown smiled at the thought.

Well, it was a more relieved party that met the next day at lunchtime in the Goat. Of course, there was no reason to be, logically. If there really was an enquiry of some sort, Pritchard could easily be implicated. But somehow it all blew over. People had other things to think of, other priorities to pursue. What seems important, or terrific, or terrible one day is hardly remembered the next. Moving on takes up most of our time and energy. The film was a box office flop. Farmer Jeb didn't even notice that his car had come and gone, or rather, had gone and come.

The incident seemed to give Pritchard's Mini a reprieve and he quit his verbal abuse of the car trade.

"Well now, Brown," Ronald teased. "You were supposed to learn quite a few things on that course of yours. What would you say the lessons are here?"

"Funny you should say that, Ronald. I was just thinking the same thing"

Brown had resumed his slightly pompous note, tempered only a little by the risks he had taken over the last few days. "I was thinking of a business venture, actually. That farm is worth more as a stockpile of old E-Types than it is as an operating farm. We should raise money to buy it, and strip out the assets before selling it on as a working farm again. What do you think? There are five of us: that means we each buy 20% of the shares, raise the rest by bank loan and we are ready to do business. What do you say?"

There were no takers.

Chapter Ten

Ronald's Run of Luck

Brown phoned me at eight o' clock, Monday morning. He was lucky to find me up. I had been woken at 2 am by a client, who was presenting a set of figures to City people at ten o' clock that morning, but had forgotten what some of the figures meant. He was a marketing person, poor soul, and his familiarity with numbers was less than it might be. Still, that's what I'm paid for and when I heard the phone ring at eight, I thought it might be him again.

To be fair to Brown he was very civil, asking me if I had had a good night's sleep and sympathising in that deep voice of his when I told him about my interruption.

"Mute it more often," he advised. "That's what I do."

The telephone is in the hall and I could smell toast from the kitchen. Dulled by the lack of sleep, I forgot he was on the phone and gazed through the open kitchen door where a cat was sitting on a windowsill, looking out at the birds in the trees.

"You still there?" Brown cried. "Look, I'm sorry about the early call but I have a long day today, over to Barcelona and back. But we have a crisis. Did you read the Sunday papers?"

I confessed I hadn't.

"No?" He was disappointed. "Well, Modest Beers are being taken over by Corpulent International. Nothing will be left of Modest."

"So no donation for the Village Hall," I deduced.

"Right first time. We need to get the fund raising committee together pronto to decide how to proceed," said Brown. "I'm phoning around to organise an extraordinary meeting for Wednesday evening. Now, could you possibly find us a ballpark figure for the restoration fund? Then we'll know our target. We need to get a move on. The original timescales are too long now."

Later, over toast and orange juice, I reflected that Brown had been justifiably proud of getting the management of Modest to match whatever figure the village raised itself, as long as they were allowed to mount a prominent plaque with the Modest logo in the Hall.

As usual, finding credible figures for the Committee was more difficult than you'd think. It all depends upon what you want to do. The final total could be double, or half, depending upon even quite trivial, or apparently trivial, decisions.

Brown asked for ballpark figures, and that's what he got.

The Committee met on the Wednesday, a splendid turnout for a meeting convened at such short notice. I suspect Brown had used the word "crisis" quite liberally and people would respond cheerfully, using phrases like, "the old wartime spirit."

Callum attended, his leg still not fully healed from his curtain fall. He was there to make sure sufficient funds were spent on the village hall, in particular on the technical stuff up on the heights, a jungle canopy with a whole world of different life forms, where the rest of us fear to tread.

Digby was of course present. By some manoeuvring, either on his part or that of his friends, he was now Committee Chairman, where his gifts for partisanship and rubbing people up the wrong way could be exploited to the full.

Paula Parkinson was present. I believe she would make a good chairperson. She follows the issue and keeps personality out of it. I like that.

Brown, Horace and Ronald were of course there. Digby looked suspiciously at them, as well he might, given the trouble Horace and Pritchard had caused on a previous evening. The Ribbons-Robbins duo attended, and Mrs Webster, who actually took her seat next to Ronald. It was a big committee and included some people I didn't yet know. I voiced my concern to Brown, who said that he preferred to get a good representation, and the urgency might pull people together.

Conversation subsided as Digby took his seat and placed papers carefully before him. Brown was talking easily and a little loudly with Paula and Mrs Ribbons and had to be hushed and pointed towards his seat. He didn't seem to mind that he was on the backbenches today.

"Right," Digby opened up the meeting, a little more aggressively than I would have preferred. "Here we are again, you could say. Never mind how we got here, but we are in trouble getting the Village Hall renovated if we want it done this year. Mr Brown, would you take us through the situation as you see it?"

With somewhat more polish, Brown outlined our ambitions with regard to the hall, gave my figures, and set out the necessary targets to achieve the goals.

"Why I believe we have to act fast is that, in my experience, a project of this sort can drift on and on. And the building meanwhile deteriorates faster than you can imagine. Momentum must be maintained. I'm not proposing a solution at this stage, merely setting out the problem."

I dreamed that Brown was Chairman of our local

Council, or of a large corporation, or of a Government Review body, or indeed chairing the Cabinet itself. Whatever the situation, that is how someone like Brown will run a meeting, using the old clichés, communicating the obvious to us, telling us what we know already, and offering next to nothing.

Digby thanked Brown and turned to Paula for an update of recent decisions taken by the Committee, especially relating to the Rock Concert. I got a strong impression that Digby liked the Rock Concert idea. Horace glowered, but said nothing. Mrs Webster shrank back in her chair at the very thought of it.

Paula was brief. "In the cold light of day, everyone realised what a huge and risky project it would be. It's tremendously exciting, of course, but we have very little experience of anything larger than garden tea parties, and the disruption would, it was generally felt (she emphasised "generally"), dissuade people from supporting it. But what," she concluded, noticing Digby's impatience with the conservative village toads, "what really delivered the hammer blow was the insurance cost. The premium required to put on even a small show such as this is larger than the total budget we have and," (pausing for effect), "is more than the takings of any previous event."

"Did you get competitive quotes?" Digby asked, clinging to the wreckage of his dreams.

"Three," said Paula, "but one insurer wouldn't even quote, given our inexperience. So our conclusion was that we would have to start small, gain experience and work up to a bigger event. If we got it wrong, we would lose a lot of money, which the village frankly does not have."

"So I guess," said Brown, forgetting he was not in the chair, "that it's time for more suggestions. We want to do something which will involve lots of people, which we can get up and running quickly and will give us our target, unaided by brewery sponsorship."

"In a nutshell, yes," Paula agreed.

"Right," said Digby. I think it was his habitual bullying tone of address that annoyed me. "Let's see if we can get some ideas down on paper." He took his pen in his right hand and looked around at the rest of us, implying that he personally had none.

Brown interrupted respectfully and gently. "I should say, if I may be so bold as to give a steer, (I immediately imagined a large, American longhorn cow being offered to the group: it's the effect which Brown's phrases have on me). "I should say that we are not talking of raffles and cake sales. Worthy though they are at the right times, they produce well below what we are looking for here. We need bigger ideas, I'm afraid."

"Did you happen to have any yourself?" the Chairman asked.

"Well, now you mention it," Brown smiled unctuously. "I did wonder whether some people might be prepared to pitch in with serious sums of money to buy shares in the new hall. It would be quite nice to own a bit of the communal real estate of the village."

"Quite innovative, Old Man," said Horace, "but it could cause a division between the owners and the rest. Would they expect privileges over booking times, for example?"

"Why don't we mortgage the Village Hall?" Paula proposed.

We kicked that proposal around for some time, but apparently there was some question about who owned it in the first place. Also how could repayments be guaranteed? Those large ideas that Brown wanted were not so easy to come by.

"All right," said Brown. "If we had time we could

arrange a competition for the best ideas, but we don't. That would take an extra two weeks."

"What's the rush," I asked. "I understand that you don't want to lose momentum but does a few weeks make any difference?"

"Well," said Ronald, "it would mean that the refurbishment could take place at a time when the hall traditionally is not so busy. If you do it during the season when clubs want to use the hall the most, they might not come back if they find good substitutes.

"Do we need to do all the improvements at the one time? Couldn't we stagger them?" Mrs Webster asked.

"We could," said Digby, "although the most expensive works will come at the beginning. But I see your point. We could do the rest next year."

"It's just that we could put on a Village Festival, with a lot of small things, like poetry readings," she turned and flashed a smile at Ronald, who almost dissolved.

"We would be successful if we attracted interest groups of that sort," someone agreed.

"What about a vintage car display?" Callum suggested. "They could do a tour round the nearby villages. Pritchard's Mini could qualify."

I wondered at that point why Pritchard wasn't here. Maybe he was busy. I hadn't noticed he wasn't present until his Mini was mentioned.

"That's a good idea," Brown said. "It's colourful and visual. It's got movement and it's nostalgic."

"What about a sponsored run?" Ronald offered. "If the cars go slowly enough, the run could follow them round the same course."

Mr Robbins spoke up for the first time. "We could add our bicycles to the run. In the middle of the day, we could have a procession, followed by a tour round the villages. The cars go first, the bikes next and then the runners. That would be an interesting spectacle, and if it is even moderately successful, we could do a bigger one next year."

"Horses too," added Mrs Ribbons.

By the end of the meeting, a skeleton plan was in place: not too ambitious, but it would provide an attractive spectacle, and there would be something for everyone to do. We all had tasks to perform. However, Brown rushed towards me as we broke up.

"I've dropped a clanger," he said. "I've forgotten to ask Pritchard to the meeting."

"Ah," I replied, immediately foreseeing the consequences. Pritchard would be hurt: he would play on it for weeks.

"Could you speak to him for me?" Brown pleaded.

"Me?" I backed off. "I didn't do the forgetting."

"Nor did you remind me. I can't attend to everything. Anyway, I've another day in Barcelona tomorrow. I won't have time. I have to leave at seven."

I agreed to speak to Pritchard, but didn't look forward to it.

Next morning I caught up with him. Predictably, he was miffed at being forgotten.

"Par for the course," he said, lowering his chin to good effect. "I'm used to it, especially from Brown. His world is so far removed from mine that I can't expect him to remember me in my lowly status."

He persisted in this tone for some time quite unselfconsciously, without needing any prompting from me. I began to think of other things, such as how I was going to get through my string of phone calls. Then I heard Pritchard asking, obviously for the second, maybe the third time, what the meeting had been about. I told him, and reported the conclusions as faithfully as I could. He was silent, but the suggestion of a mirthful smile came to his lips.

"You are all wasting your time," he wheezed. "Instead of feeling self-important in this meeting of yours, you could have found out the facts."

"What do you mean?" I demanded.

"Modest Beers are indeed being taken over, but the effect upon our lives will be bigger than just losing a gift for the Village Hall."

He was being irritatingly coy so I jogged him a bit.

"The company taking them over, Corpulent International, are going to close the Goat and knock it down to make way for a motel. We'll lose our watering hole because this motel will be full of day-trippers from town.

"How do you know all this?" I was aghast. The Village Hall is one thing: the pub is a different kettle of fish.

"Because, instead of sitting smug in a committee, I came up last night to find out how Andy and Zelda were taking the news. They told me about the motel. They were devastated. The pub sank into misery like it was the end of the world. But it's the end of the line for them. The new owners had done all their research before they pounced. Corpulent reckon they have found a company to buy, where there is a lot more value to be squeezed out than Modest could ever do. That's the system. We can't complain. But the Goat is on their list for demolition.

I was utterly shocked. The consequences became clear to me. "Do they realise what they are doing?" I asked Pritchard. "It's not just a matter of us having a convenient watering hole. It's the fact that a motel will change the nature of the village forever. We'll become plastic. People will come to depend upon the motel for employment, but there will be no loyalty to the staff. I think house prices will come down."

On reflection, I have no idea how I arrived at that

conclusion, but it made Pritchard sit up. "You're right," he said. "I hadn't thought of that." All his grievances over last night's meeting disappeared. "We need to mobilise the village to resist this latter day evil," he said, in true committee-speak.

I emailed Pritchard's news to everyone on the Committee, suggesting that we keep to the format of our plans, but to change the cause to "Saving the Village Spirit". Word travelled fast and replies came swiftly.

A sub-committee met that evening in the Goat, the members being of course Brown, Ronald, Horace, Pritchard and myself. We were joined by Alf, who was livid to hear that the peaceful haven he wrote in, quite anonymously, was in danger of becoming an out-of-town target for bus parties. I privately believed we were overcooking the effect of the change, but you know what we are all like when something central to our existence is threatened. Indignation runs high.

"We have to be resourceful," Brown boomed. It seemed a very wise thought and we all looked meaningfully at one another and nodded. "We need to think how we can tackle this thing head-on."

"Maybe it is best that we don't tackle it head-on," I suggested. "It may be more effective to take it from behind."

The mood was against such a less hostile approach, but Pritchard gave me another chance. "Example?" he prompted.

I blew it. I always do. I couldn't on the spur of the moment come up with any good illustration.

Horace tried to help. "Maybe you mean we ought to nobble one or two of their insiders. Get them thinking our way."

Brown was adamant. "I have thought this thing through and I cannot see any other way except to battle this one out publicly. We'll get some of the politicos on our side, educate them into being rurally-correct. There's going to be an election soon and they will be sensitive to things such as this. Big business is ok in between elections. They pay the taxes after all, but the politicians will need our votes in the very near future.

I noticed Zelda standing behind the bar. Usually she is all action, but tonight she stared into the middle distance, imagining that all she had worked for was to be destroyed by someone who had probably never been near the pub, an impersonal pen-pusher, or rather a keyboard-tapper these days. At least, that's what I imagined her to be thinking and anyone seeing her in that pose would have vowed to work his socks off to help save her dream.

I turned over some thoughts in my mind about how so many impersonal decisions, whether in business or public office, and driven by finance or ambition, are too single dimension. Decisions have many outcomes, knock-on effects that sometimes are greater than the original outcome itself. People making such decisions fail us, they fail the community of the world, they fail to envisage the whole effect and even if they do, their rewards are so determined only by the immediate results that they would inevitably *still* take those limited-vision decisions.

The next week saw instant progress. The village, in Pritchard's phrase, mobilised itself into full frontal resistance. We asked Paula Parkinson to head up PR, which she was delighted to do. She immediately enlisted the wordsmith himself, Alf. "Why have a dog and bark yourself," she quoted, and Alf barked obligingly. A Newsletter Number One for "Save the Village Spirit" was issued, warning residents what was in store if the invaders got their way. One had to be impressed with Alf's tone. What he missed, or failed to find out in the way of facts, he made up for in red-blooded prose. Paula egged us on to talk to people we knew; politicians, sports personalities, industrialists, civil servants, former residents of the village who now held positions of influence, and anyone else who might listen. She took on the Press herself, setting up a temporary home in the offices of the Evening Tide, a newspaper publisher in the nearest suburb. It was owned by a larger media and news-publishing group, located more centrally in the city and she hoped to get the plight of the village onto the agenda of this bigger voice.

Her instincts were well rewarded, as were Brown's. The editor saw the media opportunities offered by the spectre of big business destroying the culture of the countryside and commissioned Paula to provide him with something interesting to write.

She reported back to the Committee, which was now working on a virtual basis, with anyone who felt that they had something to say or contribute joining in with the chat and emails. Her text read:

"Will Walters of the Evening Tide is on-board but he needs interesting copy for his readers, and preferably a story which he can play out over the next two weeks. Public interest will wane after that and things will move on, so we have just this window of time.

I propose we move fast. The banner is, "Save the Village Spirit". We'll recruit the villages around us. They must be worried too. And we'll lean on our MP on a rural-correctness issue. It won't be divisive, like some other rural issues, and parties will queue up to be seen to be on our side. It helps that the company acquiring Modest Beers is an international conglomerate. Nobody loves those. And apparently it is run by an aggressive American Management that hopes to flood our market with American beers, so there are several lobbies we can enrol to the cause.

I can't do all this myself, so volunteers please!

The procession we planned the other evening will be ideal. We will portray village life in its real setting, from past to present. The Evening Tide will cover it in the last of its articles, so it needs to be a climax – a how-can-you-allow-this-to-be-destroyed platform.

OK? Got it?"

You have never seen such action. Everyone, it seemed, was doing something. Like ants, we all seemed to know what we were doing and no one was late with anything; no one let anyone else down. The community feeling was amazing. I had never been part of anything like this and was exhilarated by it. We got to know people whom we usually passed in the street with only a token greeting. Someone asked why it couldn't always be like this.

We held an evening meeting in the school hall for all who wanted to attend. It was full to bursting point. Brown replaced Digby. It was too critical an issue for us to be polite. Brown was the man and showed his mettle as soon as the meeting started. More than most of us, he appreciated that there were too many people present to be able to discuss items properly, so he went at it like an auctioneer, his hammer banging agreement on the table to every single item, so that he took very little time with the formal proceedings and left plenty of time for tea and cakes and the roar of conversation which took place afterwards.

"Impeccably judged," Horace said to Brown.

"I thought I was going to have trouble with that small chap over there, the one with the red nose," Brown indicated an older gentleman holding forth to two elderly ladies.

"Oh, he was nuked by Pritchard," said Horace. "I crowded Pritchard right up to him."

"Oh," Brown grinned, "I didn't realise Pritchard was prepared to get physical."

Horace shook his head. "He wasn't but his anorak is very abrasive and stinks, so I shoved him right in front of the old geezer. We were so crowded and close that Pritchard's anorak sandpapered his nose. That's why it's red."

One of the highlights for me was going with Brown to meet with our MP. Brown had unfortunately at some time in the past run into him over some trade matter and although Brown assured me that neither of them was likely to bear a grudge, I sensed that the MP was less warm than we would have liked. It developed into a barely-concealed arm wrestling match.

The MP, Crowther Backwoods, or Bendover Backwards, as Brown re-labelled him, seemed ok to me. He had a deep, loud, slightly mocking voice that I attributed to his being on the backbenches for so long. I felt you had to give weight to a man who had been in Parliament for twenty-three years, yet was entirely unknown. That must have taken a certain type of skill and resourcefulness, which our younger career politicians of today would do well to study.

But he was slippery.

"I can't see what I can do, positive-wise," he frowned, after Brown's summing up of the situation. "There's no law being broken here, is there?"

"If it were a matter of law, we would have gone to the courts. No, it's a social issue," Brown countered. "It's about people and their environment, and preserving a way of life."

"We can't stand in the way of progress," Backwoods said automatically. It sounded like a customary response to justify inertia. "But I could have a word with a few people, I suppose." He drawled this out, supposedly to impress us that he knew the big players. He looked out the window, his voice turning into an irritating nasal purr. He wasn't with us at all.

"It's a matter of people feeling that they have been listened to, that they are not just being ignored because they are rural, away from the centres of power," Brown elaborated. "They are deeply committed to resisting this intrusion– all the villages are. It's about political representation. It's really about votes, Crowther."

Backwoods eyes showed slight interest, but this lever had been pulled on him many times before. "You think people would actually switch votes on this, positive-wise, if we supported you in some way? This isn't just people getting worked up about nothing?"

"Absolutely not," I said, sensing that Brown almost had his opponent's arm down on the table.

"Because," Backwoods countered, "this rural-correctness stuff can backfire, you know. Most of my constituency is urban, population-wise, and they might like the idea of a motel to drive to, take the kids, let them jump around a bouncing castle in the car park, let them see what the countryside is like."

The arm wrestling was suddenly going Backwoods' way. He was showing his years of experience. He could have sat on a fence comfortably one mile above the Niagara Falls. "You'll have to do better than that," he was really saying.

"You do know," Brown said, lowering his already basso profundo voice, "that Corpulent has been involved in a financial scandal in the States. Nothing big discovered yet, but they all start small, don't they. We could find, I'm not saying we will, but we just could be faced with a situation whereby the Gentle Goat is gone forever, and because of financial difficulties, nothing is put in its place. Now, that's lose-lose as far as most people are concerned, and it will look like once again the British Government backed down in the face of US muscle. Now how would you, Crowther, explain that one?"

Backwoods narrowed his eyes. Brown had got him. In material terms it didn't matter how small the Gentle Goat was, but Backwoods knew that papers like the Evening Tide could magnify it, and once the TV channels got into it, he would be made to look ineffectual. Better to do something now, no matter how slight a gesture.

"What a pillock," Brown said, getting back into his car. "He must spend more energy in trying to do nothing than he would if he got off his butt for once."

"I think you got the measure of him." I gave Brown some consolation.

"Well, even if he only shows his face on the day it will be enough," Brown replied. "As long as it looks like he's on our side."

In a few days, Paula was able to show us what the Evening Tide's campaign looked like. Firstly, there was to be a profile of the Gentle Goat with Andy and Zelda, and the Village. Next week's would portray the sinister side of Corpulent International. The final week would cover the Day of the Villages, with a full page of photographs. It was good, the best we could hope for. Pritchard and his History Society people would dredge up some interesting historical colour to beef up the Evening Tide's efforts.

Paula was almost certain she could get regional television to show the Day of the Villages but she needed to be sure that there would be celebrities there to justify it. It was a chicken-and-egg situation: if celebrities were present, then television would come, and if television were there, the celebrities would show up. So basically, she told them all that everyone would be there, and hoped that luck would fall her way.

Robbins and Ribbons were organising a million and one projects: kids making things, kids doing things, kids being sponsored for things, kids being trained to run, cycle, serve drinks and doughnuts, and clean up; kids persuading their parents to do things, parents being trained to run, cycle, clean things, serve things, mend things, put on sticking plaster; parents ready to do car park duty, parents making contingency plans in case it rained, mothers baking, fathers cutting playing field grass.

Digby had all the shops displaying "NO CHEAP MOTELS" signs in their windows, some hanging them from their TV aerials.

Everyone was having a whale of a time. Mrs Webster was organising a literature and music programme, calling upon her many old contacts.

Pritchard and Callum got into the car project. They were well aware that the official car clubs required more notice, so they got as many local old cars as possible and formed a temporary vintage car club. Word of mouth got them members. Conveniently, no one defined "vintage", so anything of has-been nature was included.

The village hall was opened up again. It had been closed since the rat episode. The stage area was roped out of bounds, but it served as a useful information and control centre. Someone put in a computer and an Internet link.

V Day, or Day of the Villages, was being put together with astonishing speed and teamwork, but there were some hitches. The strangest of these was when the Police contacted us to say that they had heard of our intent and were concerned that we hadn't contacted them. It was true. We hadn't even considered it.

Off Brown, Ronald and I went to be interviewed by the local chief police boss. I have no idea what rank he was. He was dressed in a suit and obsessed with detail. We made lots of apologetic noises, but he waved those away. He didn't want the motel any more than we did and claimed to be on our side.

"But what we are most concerned about," he said gruffly, "are protesters."

We looked round at each other. Ronald pointed out that we are the protesters. Why would people turn up in droves to protest about our protesting?

"Some people will protest about anything," the policeman said. "Believe me."

"They will protest against us?" Ronald checked his understanding.

"Yes, and they can be violent. I think we better put a few plain clothes people in to be certain," the police boss said.

Brown looked worried. "How will we recognise them?"

"They have beards and other distinguishing features," the policeman said, entirely without humour.

"Green jackets?" Brown threw in.

"That too," agreed the boss.

"Well," Ronald said, quite deadpan, "We'll recognise them easily."

The policeman looked pleased that he had made a favourable impact and said we'd be ok. We wouldn't need any licenses. Just keep him informed.

The countdown began

V Day minus 14

The Evening Tide's first campaign article came out. Sigmund ordered lots of extra copies but they were sold out within half an hour of delivery. It was like wartime rations. Paula personally brought copies to the

Committee and we sat or stood in the Village Hall, flapping the pages like vultures their wings, searching for the expected piece. At first sight, it looked disappointingly small, tucked into a lower corner on page fourteen, but there was a good picture of Zelda, looking tearful.

Closing Time for Popular Pub

Once again, we are expected to witness the destruction of our own homegrown cultures and customs by a foreign invasion. Not content with stuffing our High Streets full of fast-food outlets, making fatties of our kids, and not content with jamming our roads with cheap foreign cars, they are going to kill off that most British custom of all, the local.

Zelda is the manageress of the beautiful old pub, The Gentle Goat, in the village of Crumbly. Lots of readers regularly visit and admire the village and its pub, not to mention the 13th Century church. But Zelda will be out of a job. Corpulent International is taking over that grand old English brewer, Modest Beers. The Gentle Goat will be demolished and in its place will stand a garish, American-style motel, serving tasteless American beer.

"It's a shame," says Zelda. "Village life just won't be the same. There will be no real community centre any more, and no welcoming log fire in the winter. The older villagers won't be seen dead in a motel."

So here's the moral, dear readers: if you are Modest and Gentle, two admired British qualities, then you will have no defence against more aggressive cultures.
What's your opinion? Send emails to
theeditor@eveningtide.co.uk

Paula asked us what we thought of it. Mr Robbins

thought it was nice that our cause was being supported, but did not think that the article was a model piece of writing for the children to copy.

Most of us thought it was all right, but were unsure about being associated with anti-foreign feelings. "Using prejudice to fight your cause is not very laudable," Pritchard said.

"Get real, People," Brown snarled. "That's what newspapers do. They plug into prejudice. They don't believe that peoples' good intentions will get things done. If we can't live with that, we are going to be sunk. As it says, we are too gentle and modest. Well, you have to fight any way you can when you're up against a bigger force. And anyway, we need to go with the Evening Tide's agenda, otherwise they won't lift a finger for us. Time and Tide wait for no man," he concluded.

V Day minus 12

Pritchard and Callum reported good progress with the vintage cars. More than thirty cars had been volunteered and probably more would turn up. So even if some of these old bangers didn't start, it was beginning to look like there would be a good display on the day.

Pritchard blanched when Ronald suggested that a few E-Types would lend glamour, and did Pritchard know where there might be a few he could get his hands on.

"We have taken advice from more experienced organisers," said Callum. "One particularly useful piece is that the route must be wide enough to allow moving cars to overtake stalled cars. Otherwise you get a logjam and no one can get through. We should put the horses and riders in front of them. Then it wouldn't matter if the old bangers stalled."

"You'll have horse's muck in the road and the

runners won't like that. They should go first," someone suggested.

"Let's keep to the original plan," Brown interrupted. "Cars and motor cycles, horses, pushbikes and runners. It's a better spectacle that way."

V Day minus 10

We were having trouble getting sufficient runners. Paula asked Alf to write a newsletter with a "Your Village Needs You" message. Ronald said he would run. We questioned the wisdom of this, given his age, shape and anything else you need to take into account when thinking of Ronald and running in the same sentence.

V Day minus 7

The second Evening Tide article came out.

Resounding Vote Against Corpulent International

Last week we asked you to let us know your feelings about the closure of the Gentle Goat and its replacement with a cheap motel. As we thought, it's a no-brainer. You have pretty well unanimously voted for the Gentle Goat to be saved. Only one reader voted "for", but obviously had misread the choices, and wants cheap models to become available. Sorry Sir, but your pipedream has gone up in smoke.

Our team of researchers and analysts have come up with some interesting information on Corpulent International. Firstly, it is a re-branded company, attempting to distance itself from an unsavoury past as a snacks and crisps producer. It built a string of motels in the US, partly to get more outlets for its snack foods. The motels and snacks were obviously too cheap because they got into trouble with food standards agencies. Holiday and accommodation firms boycotted them to safeguard their customers. They sold up their properties and made a lot of money from real estate dealings.

They know nothing about beers or beer drinkers. They will sell American beer because they are in hock to the beer producers.

Finally, no one would talk to us from Corpulent International. No spokesperson was available to tell us why they want to come across here and rip our old pubs from our lovely villages where they have been serving people with good ale for centuries.

Come on, you Politicians, you know the way we feel. Do something!

Once again we read the edition immediately, all together in the Village Hall, copies supplied by Paula.

"Not bad," Horace was first to speak. "I thought it was too flippant at the beginning, but it toned up quite firmly at the end."

"If they had something stronger to go on, they would run an editorial on it, but for the moment this is as good as it can be," Paula said.

She looked a little downcast.

"What's the matter," we asked.

She was almost tearful. "I'm just disappointed when I actually see the article. It's good for what it is, but it's small. The page opposite has a full-page advert for electrical goods from one store. That puts it into perspective – and we worked so hard to get people to vote."

Brown patted her shoulder. "You've been terrific, Paula." he said. "No one here has done more, but column inches in newspapers are expensive. We have to face up to it: this thing is in our hands, and our hands only. And they have put a particularly nasty smell around Corpulent International. Maybe we should make sure the investors in Modest Beers realise they might not get their money if Corpulent do the dirty on them. Modest Beers is a nice old family firm. They wouldn't want to be ripped off, or their tenants, for that matter.

V Day minus 5

Preparations continued in a frenzied fashion. Now the emphasis was on making sure the events of the day were well recorded, reported, filmed, broadcast. Local television would be there for a short time, as would local radio. There was a hint that national television, if time permitted, would take a thirty-second clip of the story for the evening news.

All local photography enthusiasts were enlisted, both to take photographs, but also to use their contacts for wider publicity.

Only three people have been injured in training so far.

V Day minus 1

The evening before V Day, I sauntered up to the pub, relieved that at last that time had come and we were going to do our best. Many of the Committee were there. In fact, the place was quite full, maybe a sign that people felt they needed to enjoy the Goat while it was still there.

Brown was buying. Modest beers all round, flavourful, traditional, cool but not frozen. A lump suddenly came to my throat. It's not just the pub or the beer. Where would we meet? Where would we gather to enjoy the chat and the chaff? Locals of all descriptions had been sitting here, sometimes lit only by candlelight, for years beyond living memory. And it can all be made to disappear.

Pritchard was telling them about cleaning his car up

for the morrow. "It's as good as new," he said proudly. "Only a couple of dents in the front where I ran into two hitch-hikers."

We were shocked. "You knocked two hitch-hikers over?"

"No," Pritchard scorned. "They were two pretty young ladies being given a lift on the back of a hay-wagon. I was distracted and ran into the hay-wagon. They squealed a lot."

That's one of the most famous English paintings, you know," Horace mused. "Constable's *Haywain* "

I could see that Ronald had lost track of this conversational change. He's not well up on painters, except those who paint and decorate, and Horace could have said something about John Wayne, by Jove, for all Ronald could make of it. It was like watching an old, slow computer working.

"Constable who?" he asked eventually.

Now it was Horace's turn to be mystified. He didn't know how to enlighten Ronald, so Pritchard tried.

"He's not a policeman," he explained to Ronald. "He's a painter."

"What?" Ronald sought clarification. "Of the wagon you hit?"

"What a cretin," Pritchard slumped back in his chair. Ronald, knowing he was best not to pursue it, sighed and folded his arms.

There was a funny atmosphere in the pub. People were subdued. I think they weren't fully confident that tomorrow would make any difference to the outcome. We are so used to big things doing things to little things, that there is a pervading, uncomplaining resignation, an acceptance that this is how it will be.

I went up for the next round, but they had run out of Modest Beer. It seemed symbolic. We had to make do with lagers.

"Are you fit for tomorrow, Ronald?" Brown enquired.

Ronald assured us he was. Despite our concerns, Ronald persisted in going through with his run. I wondered if partly it was to impress Mrs Webster. One didn't like to say to Ronald that it probably would make no difference to her opinion of him, but one cannot possibly interfere in such matters.

I didn't enjoy the lager. Maybe it was too much a foretaste of the future. I wandered down the road, thinking back to the early months when we came here to live. If there had never been a Gentle Goat, I wouldn't have missed it, not being used to that kind of local pub where we lived before, but now the future looked pretty bleak. Without the Goat acting as centre for many things, people would naturally go back to being more isolated, more alone in their own houses, and at its worst that can mean more distrust, less co-operation, less neighbourliness.

The next morning started grey enough. I walked round the field where the main events would be held and where the processions would begin and end. The village looked a little sad, as if it were awaiting the postman to bring bad news. There was no wind. Someone had started an early garden fire; the smoke travelled straight up into the low sky and hung about before dispersing. I went back to work at my desk but I wasn't as productive as I should have been. Just before lunchtime, I ventured out again.

This time it was much better. The sun was beginning to show through the cloud, which was thinning out and even disappearing in places. The leaves on the trees looked brighter and reflected the sun enthusiastically. Lots of canvas was erected for stalls or events: the striped colours set against the green made one think of Medieval times, chivalry, knights in chain mail sitting astride warhorses.

I made for the Control Centre, the only plain white tent in the field. Mr Robbins was ticking things on a clipboard and looking very happy with himself.

"This is the plan," he chirped. "Everything is in place so all we need now are the people."

And they came. Some brought lunches with them. Others came looking for lunch and were not disappointed. Two or three large marquees competed for their trade. You could buy food and eat it on trestle tables in the marquee, or you could bring it out into the sunlight and browse the other stalls.

To be honest, we didn't really know where half the tents and stalls had come from, but their owners seem to sense and converge upon an event. Were they travellers? Were they gipsies? Were they folk from two miles up the road who happen to have pottery skills or archery equipment? Whoever they all were, we were grateful, for we could not have staged anything as interesting on our own.

Maybe this is what it was like in the Middle Ages when fairs were organised, and traders travelled for days to get to them. People didn't have television or computer games and were hungry for excitement, some colour in their lives. The fairs must have been huge draws for all that was bizarre, exotic, funny, cruel, lawless and greedy.

Until about two in the afternoon, we felt that people would want to stroll, gawp at the stalls, and each other, eat, and generally drench themselves in the atmosphere. Then we would begin the parade around the perimeter of the park and then through the centre. The cars, horses and bikes would go on their way on their pre-determined route round the nearby villages and return in triumph to the field. The runners meanwhile – and about fifty of those had miraculously materialised –

would do an initial lap of the field before following the cars, horses and riders.

Brown arrived, his blazer preceding him by at least ten paces. It was loud, punk rock loud, and stripes? A tiger would have been consumed with jealousy. Red and yellow, it fuzzed ahead of him until, getting closer to my protesting eyes, they merged with Brown. It was magnificent, but it was not wardrobe. It was theatre. Brown wore also a huge smile. "One must make the effort," he shouted.

I felt pale in comparison. Why couldn't I do these things? Why could I not even *think* of doing something like that?

Horace, Belinda and the dog Hardy rolled up in Victorian garb. Well, the dog didn't, of course, but it wore presumably what Victorian dogs wore. Belinda looked the part, as if she was just going to supervise the cook to rustle up a big steak and vegetable pudding with thick gravy.

I went across to the cars. Pritchard was visible from a long way off. He was wearing a white rally suit, helmet and goggles - the lot. I couldn't understand how he could get everything into the Mini.

"Nonsense," he cried, obviously in extrovert mood today, "I just put the helmet on the passenger seat when I'm driving, and wear it when I'm not."

To me this was an unusual reversal of helmet routine, but it was an unusual day. Behind Pritchard was a line of gorgeously gleaming pieces of metal, wood and leather. The other car owners and drivers polished, revved, posed, smoked like wartime heroes and generally entertained those who were looking on. The cars were bright, greens and blues, yellows and reds, with flashing chrome and little flags flapping listlessly in the becalmed afternoon.

Paula strode around purposefully, not only making

sure all was as it should be, but also that someone was capturing it onto something permanent. More villagers strode around in old costume, although they were wearing just anything they could find. As a result, Robin Hood's merry men in green stood shoulder to shoulder with a Regency beaux and 19th Century industrialist.

A painter sat at her easel, quietly and with very little movement making an impressionist-style painting of the scene. People were fascinated, especially the children, and stood respectfully behind her, as silent as she was. She mixed and applied, mixed and applied, potentially building up a treasure.

Now there was a lot of noise coming from the control tent. It was the Tannoy system, but instead of a clear sound, there was a rapid-fire stutter of indistinct words.

It turned out to be only Brown, welcoming the crowd and telling them what to expect this afternoon. However, at the far end of the field, Pritchard took this to mean that Brown was announcing the start of the procession. In another corner, Digby thought that Brown had said something about the horses and riders, took it to mean that there was a change of plan and sent the troop of horse across the field to the starting point. They were very grand; all the horses beautifully be-ribboned, some pulling glossy traps, with lanterns and leather all over the place.

Coming from different angles however, the cars and riders met in a cluster at the starting point.

"What are you doing, you Great Fool?" Brown shouted at Digby, astride a monstrous hunter. "You're not due here yet."

"Sorry, Old Man," Digby brayed. "Thought you were calling us."

The horses and the line of cars now tried to back off

simultaneously, to give each other room, but this considerate action on both their parts caused them to become intermingled. Because the horses were more agile than cars, they moved further out of the circle, causing it to look like a war party of Red Indians surrounding a line of gaudy covered wagons.

Brown tried again to issue instructions over the Tannoy, but it just blurted and snorted, frightening the horses and angering some dogs that, like Hardy, had come to see the fun. They got more than they bargained for. One horse reared up when a snapping collie on a leash barked at it. The horse reversed on its hind legs into the control tent, which promptly collapsed with Brown in it. You could see a struggling figure twist himself further and further into the canvas, his striped jacket making him look like a stick of rock, before we managed to get him out.

Temporarily there was chaos. As anyone who has organised an event like this will tell you, it is easier to get people *into* a space than out of it. There was all the confusion of an ancient battle, no one knowing exactly what was happening, making their own decisions, reversing decisions, the noise, and most of all, every single person thinking that everyone else is behaving like an absolute fool.

Without the Tannoy or announcer, there were no directions, but eventually Digby got his Red Indians back to a safe distance and let Pritchard and his wagons form a more-or-less orderly file. This however involved much backing and forwarding, much shrieking from the bystanders and howling from the dogs.

We extricated the Tannoy microphone from the collapsed control tent. I toggled its switch a few times and it began to work perfectly, content that it had caused mayhem, if only for a short time. Brown was still coughing up something he swallowed from the

254

canvas, but still held ambitions of directing events. His coughing into the now perfect sound system angered the dogs further, and they showed their discontent by setting up a side show of bare-fang fighting, long prohibited by law, but try telling that to them while they are having the time of their furry lives.

Eventually order was restored, although I gather from what was said later in the Goat, that many people had just accepted it all as part of the scheduled programme of events, and much appreciated it. It could be difficult to replicate next year.

Off the cars went, once around the perimeter of the field, hooting their horns cheerfully and belching only a few black clouds of smoke. They stood up well to the run, considering their age and lack of real preparation time. We expected some of them not to return for some time. The second last car, a Singer Gazelle, stalled on a bend. The last car ran into it, and they both sat there, as if they had fallen off a toy railway. As it ran into the Singer, the last car gave one final honk of defiance on its horn.

It was becoming warm, the sun rising high in the sky. Unless you were in the shade of a tent, you could get quite hot. People took their jackets off, or slunk into the beer tent to quench their thirst. Andy and Zelda, supported by Peter, were on top form, dressed in medieval gear and pouring the beer – Modest was on again – in bendy plastic glasses that spill when you grab them in one hand. Peter served his customers with all the insolence of a court jester. People sat on bales of hay in the increasingly close atmosphere of the beer tent. The warmer it got, the more you smelled the hay, and more besides.

The horses trotted off with much ritual and ceremony. I'm not sure why, but the stirrup cup came out. All was colour and celebration of life, just as we wanted it to be for the Press.

The Press. Where were the Press? I buttonholed Paula.

"Oh, the TV cameras have gone. They had to. They don't stay for long you know."

"So what have they filmed?" I asked, already anticipating the worst.

"The cock-up with the cars and horses," Paula said casually.

"That's terrible. We'll be made to look like fools," I complained.

Paula laughed. "Not at all. I told them it was all part of the entertainment. They hadn't seen anything so funny in years, especially Brown wrapped up like a Mexican pancake."

"They won't show that, will they?" I was horrified. Brown would be suicidal.

"Cast-iron certainty," she said, grabbing a newspaper journalist in passing. "It was the best bit."

In looking for Paula, I missed the start of the runners, but I could see them disappearing, after their trot around the park, into the distance. They looked from here like a string of dancing sweet papers, all colours and many shapes. They were doing a shorter route than the cars and horses, so that they could be back at roughly the same time.

Right, it would be some time before everyone was back so I high-tailed it to the beer tent and had a very pleasant half hour, chatting to villagers I don't usually see, and one or two minor celebrities that Paula had succeeded in getting to stay for the afternoon. I greeted Crowther Backwoods, who had put in an appearance to hedge his bets, but he couldn't remember me.

Sure enough, after a while, the car procession returned. I don't know if they had magnetic properties, but they seemed to have attracted more cars behind them. I guess a few must have fallen by the wayside, but the procession was certainly longer than when it left. Horns tooted, cameras clicked, the onlookers cheered.

Then came the riders and horses, trotting now, looking less gleaming, more steamy. All the smells mingled into a heady mixture of horse, leather and petrol. Riders dismounted, clearly pleased with their ride, the attention they were deservedly getting, and the prospect of a nice drink.

Where were the runners? A large crowd waited to cheer them in. Yes, here they were, more straggled than the cars and horse, but pretty well all there, if a bit more stretched out. Where was Ronald? Then I saw him. He was last. Boy, would he take some ribbing if he came last.

They ran all the way round the field, keeping to their course. It was hot, not a breath of wind to relieve us. The first runners were now coming up to the line. They were young chaps, and laughing. They made a great show of racing each other to the tape, but they didn't mean it, and continued right on to the beer tent without slowing down.

The crowd cheered each group of runners crossing the line. It was all done with great humour and mobile cameras caught the action. Some people had serious cine-cameras.

Last and alone ran Ronald. He was not looking good. His movement was a torment. His neck rolled and he looked very red. With only fifty yards to go, he faltered, but managed to keep going. The crowd had only Ronald to cheer now, so they gave it all they had, willing him along.

I could see his face now. It was red, a horrible red. He was exhausted and dehydrated. I doubt if he knew what he was doing. I looked around for the first aid people but they were already on the case.

Towards the din of the cheers and applause, Ronald tottered, his eyes not seeing properly.

"For God's sake, help him," a woman cried.

Ronald put up an arm to ward off help. His pride wouldn't take it. He had to see it through himself, but with ten yards to go he was losing control of his legs. With five to go, he began to lurch forward, and one yard after the line he was gone.

They turned him over. Cameras were still clicking. Ronald was unrecognisable, his face contorted with pain. He was unconscious now. The onlookers whispered "Heart attack," and backed off to give the medics a chance. They appeared to be forcing something into his mouth, but I couldn't see properly. Quickly they lifted him onto a stretcher and gently carried him into the gaping back door of an ambulance. It drove off quietly, but with lights flashing. We followed it with our eyes until it disappeared, then eerily we heard its siren wail when it reached the main road. Ronald was taken away from us.

Released from the obligation to be quiet, the shocked group of people gabbled loudly, some even giggling nervously. The other runners crowded round, some with beers in their hands, to assure each other that *they* were all right.

I joined Brown, Pritchard, Horace and Belinda, but there was nothing to say, so we split up. I passed Mrs Webster. I wondered if she might want a friendly word, but she merely nodded, her face expressionless, very pale, if anything slightly angry. She didn't stop.

Before leaving, I caught up with Paula to congratulate her on the afternoon. She was tearful, sobbing quietly now and again into a large, man's handkerchief.

"He's a gonner, isn't he?" she whispered. "He used

to give me sweets out of his pocket when I was a kid. Always telling me stories."

Maybe that was the bad news the village had been waiting for this morning. We had put on a public triumph, the best we could do, but right at this moment, I couldn't quite remember what it was for.

Around midnight I was still up. My wife had gone to bed. I played around with the pages of a book. I rang the hospital once, but didn't want to bother them again. Ronald had suffered a stroke, but that was all we were being told. Before turning in, I went for a stroll: I needed fresh air after the heat of the day. My steps took me to the field where it had all taken place. Marks on the grass from car tyre tread and hooves were everywhere, but it was as if nothing had taken place. A light breeze was wafting through the tops of trees, making them wave slightly, but making me shiver. It was needless, I told myself. Why don't we speak up and prevent such things happening? Maybe because we respect each person's right to behave stupidly: maybe because we would never achieve anything if we were sensible all the time.

Twenty past twelve and my mobile gave a muffled ring. It was a text from Paula at the hospital.

"Ronald sort of ok after stroke. Will take time. Doctor positive. Luv, Paula."

I woke my wife to tell her.

V Day plus 1

The Evening Tide was true to its word. We got a whole page of photographs and a covering article. The piece took the form of a letter to the British Government, in a typically aggressive tone.

Here's What You're Helping to Bury

Dear Sirs,

We beg to put our case to you concerning the village of Crumbly Down and more specifically the village pub, The Gentle Goat. Keep Crumbly standing, is our advice. It is a rural community in danger of losing its spirit when its village pub is closed by faceless profit-mongers from abroad. Our rural communities find it hard enough to survive without having to sustain a broadside from an international company with a larger GNP than some Third World countries.

Yesterday, the village of Crumbly did all it could to show us that our countryside, and the culture which goes along with it, is more than worth preserving. Without it we lose our history – and once broken, you can't mend it.

But the day was marked, not marred but marked, by an example of selfless endeavour in the cause of his village. The oldest runner in the race may have run his heart out (see picture, bottom left) when he collapsed at the winning post.

We urge you; for once take action to do something that we, the electors, want. Forget all about your foreign trips and trade agreements. Come down to earth and help real people conserve the lifestyles and culture they prefer. They haven't given up. Nor should you.

It was a good piece, better than we ever expected. Maybe Ronald's determination touched them. Still, it remained to be seen whether it would have any effect.

V Day plus 2

The Village Day Committee met formally to monitor progress. Digby was in the Chair again. Brown apologised for calling him names in the heat of the

260

moment during the Day of the Villages, when Digby had misunderstood Brown's intentions and advanced his cavalry prematurely.

"Not a problem, Old Man," Digby assured him magnanimously. "Water off a duck's back."

He started the meeting. He was looking rather pleased with himself, as was Brown. We soon found out why. Digby could hardly wait to tell us.

"Corpulent International are backing off," he grinned.

There was an immediate surge of noise. Question upon question. Lots of congratulations. Paula weeping again. We all felt choked, great lumps in our throats. Someone even kissed me.

It took some time before the noise subsided and Digby could continue.

"To be precise, they are reviewing their bid, but that means they are really having second thoughts about buying Modest Beers. They thought that it would be a good way to test the UK market. They didn't realise it would cause such a stir, and Brown found out they were already in some PR difficulties over accounting irregularities back home in the States."

"What about Modest Beers?" Pritchard asked. "Are they strong enough to survive, or will some other company make a bid?"

Digby explained developments. "Modest have been forced to have a serious re-think about their business and feel that if they don't change direction, that is what will happen to them sooner or later."

"But what about the Goat?" Mrs Webster asked impatiently.

"Well," Digby continued, "Modest are going to allow certain of their tenants to bid for their pub premises, but with a clause tying them to Modest products for a considerable time. Basically, Andy and

Zelda are going to get a loan from the bank to buy the Goat. The village pub is ours for the keeping, as long as we use it, of course."

"No problems on that score," said Horace, looking as cheerful as I have ever seen him.

"So was it our campaign that clinched it?" Mr Robbins asked.

Digby became political. "It contributed of course, and I think it were best that people believe it was. The Evening Tide will certainly report it like that, but as usual the truth is more complicated. In fact, we have to thank Brown here for pressing some of the right buttons. He used some of his contacts to get the message to Corpulent that basically they would find it very difficult to get planning permissions for a motel, and no local Council is going to let an old pub like the Goat disappear."

"Corpulent have significant internal troubles," Brown added, "and deep divisions within their management. We had only to swing a couple of their directors against it, which they readily did for personal reasons, and the balance of opinion on their Board changed."

Paula typically brought us back to our original task. "What about the village hall? That still needs cash."

"We won't get money from Modest now. We may in a year or so, but they have too many immediate worries," Brown said. "We have to be realistic. Did we make any money from the Village Day?"

"Nothing to talk of," I said. "It was to raise awareness, not funds."

Digby summed up. "Right. That's probably all we can do today. We need to meet in a week's time to start the Village Hall Fundraising Campaign all over again. Well done, everyone. Paula, can you see to the newsletter?"

So that was it. The village community saved, the Goat reprieved, Andy and Zelda become owners and the other villages feeling more secure from the ravages of the modern commercial world. Just to reward ourselves, we went off to have a drink in the Goat.

I didn't stay too long because I was going to visit Ronald. "Give him our best wishes," said Brown warmly. "I'll go in tomorrow to see him."

Arriving at the hospital gave me a low, bleak feeling; a starker realisation of how near Ronald had been to snuffing it. The outside of the building is depressingly functional, with concrete walls and closed, forbidding windows.

I had the usual long walk via various long corridors. After two bends and a corner, I was lost in the criss-crossing of paths.

People wander the corridors in various states of undress, some in dressing gowns, shuffling slowly in slippers, others seeming to wear tops over pyjamas. They do so because that's all they can do, or because it uses up a little time, and time is what they have lots of.

I followed signs to the appropriate ward, at the front of which is a reception desk. I passed the exam there and went to look for Ronald. It's not easy. Everyone looks the same in a ward, all white and greys, and horizontal. Ronald was lying down but raised himself gamely when he saw me, to sit up propped with his cushions.

"Hello, Old Boy," he said. "It's good of you to come."

His voice was coarse and his face older and more tired than I have ever seen him. "I won't be long in here you know. They like you to get up as soon as you can."

"Will you go back to your house?" I asked.

"Not yet," he admitted. "I have family in Humblebridge. They'll look after me for a couple of weeks, then I'll go back."

"That's good," I said.

"Yes," he said.

"That's ok, then," I said.

"It is," he said.

He wanted to say something but you just have to wait with Ronald. Eventually it came out.

"I need you to do something for me," he asked. "I've been lucky, sort of."

I couldn't see any signs of his luck, but of course I said I would help if I could.

"Oh yes, you definitely can," he said. "That's why I'm glad you came first. We can talk privately. The thing is; I've won a lottery."

The fact took some seconds for me to realise quite what he was saying. Then I laughed out loud and only just stopped myself from clapping him on the back. A passing nurse looked across at us and with a raised eyebrow said, "Steady now. No excitement."

That made us laugh all the more but Ronald quickly became serious again. "I want to donate money to the village hall fund, enough to complete everything it needs."

"Wow," I said. "That would be great, but don't you want a little time to think it over?"

"No," he said simply. "What if I suffer a stroke or something while I'm in here? The village would lose out. So I need to make it legal fast. Can you get me a solicitor to come in here?

"Of course," I replied. "Wait till the others hear you are going to fund the Village Hall."

He shook his head. "That's not what I want," he said. "I need it to be anonymous."

I was dumbstruck. "Why don't you want people to know? You have just told me."

"Yes," he said. "You are discreet. It's not just your

job. It's your nature. Please do this for me."

"Of course, Ronald," I agreed. "I'll see to it."

It was just as well we sorted that out because Pritchard arrived.

"Hello, you old coffin-cheater," he barked. I think only those at the far end of the ward couldn't quite hear him. "Last time we'll allow you to enter races. How are you feeling? You look awful."

"Most of all I feel stupid," Ronald said, surprising me again. "In my heart of hearts I probably ran the race in order to look young and cool and make an impression."

Pritchard and I knew what Ronald was saying.

"And I made an impression, all right," he went on. "I made an impression in front of a crowd of people. I looked like an old man who doesn't know when to stop. But you know, these feelings, of not wanting to give in, of getting to the line, they don't leave you just because you're old."

"You're not old, Ronald," Pritchard consoled him.

"Well maybe," Ronald concurred, "but the fact was that I made a fool of myself – a self-inflicted wound, you might say. Anyway, I'm going to give her up. That's what this has taught me. I've been foolish all along. I've let my feelings get the better of me. I'll never win her over. I can see that now. And that's why I feel so stupid. So I'll stop trying to see her, and get back to my old life again."

"Quite right," agreed Pritchard. "It has just been a temporary madness – and the spell will now be lifted." They both laughed.

I watched, half-disbelieving Ronald. He reminded me of the promise we make to ourselves in the midst of a huge hangover, never to touch another drop, but by the evening we are ready for a small one again. What a turn of events: Ronald nearly kills himself and wins a lottery in the same day, wants to be an anonymous benefactor, and gives up the love of his life. What would Miranda Webster think of it if she knew everything?

Pritchard and I were about to leave when the lady in question materialised by Ronald's bedside.

"Good evening, Gentlemen," she said briskly. "Glad to see you have company, Ronald. I just thought I'd make a passing visit. How are you?"

"Absolutely fine," Ronald stated, almost convincingly except for the unnatural quality in his voice. "And sorry about making all the fuss. It really was nothing."

"That's not exactly what I have heard," she said. I could see she was uneasy, but covering up well enough. Maybe she was remembering her late husband, or hospitals made her nervous. Or did she somehow know that Ronald ran the race to impress her? She especially would know just how ridiculous that was.

"Well, what I wanted to say was," she came to the point, "Your house is, by your own admission, not very suitable for you while are temporarily infirm so if you like, you could take up a spare room in my house. I can supply good food while you build up your strength again."

Ronald's mouth was too far open for him to make any sensible reply. Her offer was awkwardly made, but very kind. Pritchard and I left them to work out how this would be managed.

"I can't stand it," Pritchard moaned on the way out. "Did you see his eyes? They've gone all dewy again. Where is the man's resolution?"